A
SECRET
IN THE
FAMILY

BOOKS BY LEAH MERCER

A
SECRET
IN THE
FAMILY

Leah Mercer

bookouture

Published by Bookouture in 2022

An imprint of Storyfire Ltd.
Carmelite House
50 Victoria Embankment
London EC4Y 0DZ

www.bookouture.com

ISBN: 978-1-803140-713-0
eBook ISBN: 978-1-80314-712-3

ONE

RACHEL

'Ouch!' Rachel Varma jerked her hand away from the hot oven, trying not to drop the tray of cupcakes. She sucked in her breath, wincing as the skin on her wrist turned a deep cherry red from where she'd touched the elements. She should have worn oven gloves, but who had time to find them? Actually, she didn't have time to bake these monstrosities either – the hard brown discs were more like frisbees than cupcakes – but she couldn't resist her nine-year-old daughter Matilda's last-minute plea to bring 'something nice for Friday' for her class. These were more likely to give the kids food poisoning for the weekend, but with some buttercream frosting, maybe they wouldn't look so bad.

Sighing, Rachel sat back down at the laptop, desperate to finish a client report due in tomorrow. The latest Taylor Swift song – or whatever tune her eldest daughter Tabitha had programmed into her mobile to alert her to a call – rang out, and Rachel glanced around the train wreck of a room. Where on earth was that phone? She'd need to clean up before Mo got in from work. Not that he cared, but she did. She'd watched her mum fly around the house every evening tidying before

Rachel's father came home, and it was second nature that she do the same... not that she was anywhere near the level of devoted wife her mother had been.

'Tabitha! Can you help me find my phone?' she called out, before realising that her twelve-year-old had headphones clamped on her ears and was staring at her tablet as if it held the secret to the universe. Rachel put the laptop down and got to her feet, rushing into the kitchen where the ringing was loudest. What *was* this song?

The mobile stopped ringing just as Rachel pushed aside a plate of half-eaten toast to find it underneath. She squinted at the screen, surprise filtering through her when she saw her sister's name. Victoria was only sixteen months younger, and with their dark hair and pale skin, they could have almost been twins. They'd been close as kids, with only each other to play with on the huge tract of land their parents had owned. They'd grown apart in their teens, though, and had stayed that way. They were very different – Rachel had always been happiest with her nose in a book, while Victoria was more like their mother: brisk, efficient, with no time for daydreaming.

That wasn't the real reason for their distance, though. It was because Victoria had what Rachel wanted: a closeness with their mother, an easy love and affection that Rachel craved. Love and affection Rachel had once had, too, before everything changed... before her father died in a motorcycle accident when she was ten.

An accident that had been her fault.

She swallowed, trying to push aside the childish notion that had haunted her for years. It hadn't been her fault. It *hadn't*. Her phone call urging her father to hurry home that stormy night hadn't been the car that slammed into him, but she'd never been able to shake the notion that if she hadn't rung, he might have gone slower. He might have seen that car. He might have made it home that night, saving her mother from a lifetime of pain... saving Rachel from a lifetime of longing.

Because even though she'd never said it, the belief that her mother blamed her for the accident had haunted Rachel for years too. Her mum had collapsed into bed for days after her husband had died. And when she finally got up, she was like a ghost of the woman – the mother – she'd once been, floating through the house as if it was a foreign land. At first, Rachel tried to break through to her, saying over and over how sorry she was. Her mother would hold her limply, gazing at her daughter through lifeless eyes that made Rachel shudder and back away, afraid if she looked too deeply, she might find her mother hollow and empty.

Hollow and empty because of her.

So Rachel had done the only thing she'd thought might make it better: she'd retreated from her mother, where she wouldn't be a constant reminder of the damage she'd caused. She'd spent hours in her room, tears streaking down her cheeks, loneliness and guilt pressing down on her as she listened to her mother and sister downstairs. The rise and fall of their voices cut through her, the pain twisting her insides until she was almost sick. She didn't deserve her mother's love the way Victoria did, she'd remind herself. Victoria hadn't done anything wrong. Not like she had. She'd curl into a ball and try to make herself as small as possible, almost as if she could disappear from this family.

And in a way, she had, Rachel thought now, thinking of the years that had passed and how little she'd seen her mum or sister. It had been easier to keep herself apart rather than watch them together – watch her sister soak up the love Rachel so desperately wanted. Her mother had accepted Rachel's distance with a grim resignation, becoming as taciturn and cool as Rachel herself, pouring all her remaining affection into Victoria. Over time, the two of them had become an impenetrable unit. They had each other, and that was all they needed.

But Rachel had needed her mother too. She still did, despite having a family of her own. As an adult and a parent now herself, she realised it had probably never crossed her mother's mind to blame her – that her own pain and grief had been overwhelming, rendering her unable to comfort her children. But even so, the tangle of guilt and blame stayed knotted inside, entwined with the nagging fear that her mother *did* believe it was her fault. That knot had lodged deep inside of her, a core of darkness buried under so many layers it was almost impossible to reach. And despite the longing that remained, the ties bound tight, paralysing her from trying to rebuild any relationship with her mum.

She hit Victoria's contact number, holding the mobile in one hand while she tidied up with the other, pausing to bat away Matilda as she tried to grab a cupcake. God, she still had to do that buttercream frosting... from scratch, of course, since Matilda hated shop-bought. She'd be up until one tonight trying to get everything done. That was all right, though. She liked the chaos of her world; liked being at the heart of her family. Its warmth and love flowed through her, buffering her from that hardened knot and the ache when she thought of her mum.

'Hey, Vic. Victoria, sorry,' she hastily corrected herself, remembering too late that her sister preferred her full name, saying 'Vic' was hardly appropriate for a woman who ran her own 'highly successful' accountancy firm.

'Hi. Haven't got long.' Victoria's voice was brisk, but there was an odd edge to it. 'I'm about to go into a meeting, but I wanted to touch base with you while I have a quick second. I'm just back from taking Mum to a hospital appointment. Rach...' Victoria paused, and Rachel raised an eyebrow. What was going on? Normally, Victoria talked a mile a minute, personifying her favourite expression 'time is money'.

'It's not good news. Not at all. God, I can barely believe it.' Rachel bit her lip as her sister's voice broke. Not good news? What did she mean? She couldn't mean their mother was ill, could she? Rachel tilted her head, raking her memories for when she'd last seen her mum. Maybe before Christmas? That was almost six months ago now. She'd been fit as a fiddle then, spending most of the visit pruning the bushes in the back garden. Had something happened? Mo waved as he came through the front gate, but she barely saw him.

'Mum has...' Victoria drew in a shuddery breath. 'Mum has pancreatic cancer. The consultant said it's at an advanced stage and that it's spread to other parts of her body. She only has a few months left.'

'A few *months*?' Rachel's voice rose, and Tabitha shushed her, but Rachel didn't notice.

'Three at most, but it could be a matter of weeks.' Victoria sounded like the words were choking her, gasping for air, and an image from years ago flashed through Rachel's mind. Vic had tripped and skinned her knee, gasping and choking like she was now. They'd been miles from the house and all on their own, and Rachel had dried her sister's tears, then fashioned a bandage from leaves and weeds. Vic had hugged her tightly, saying she was the best sister in the world. Rachel swallowed, pushing away the memory. Victoria wasn't that little girl anymore, and she wasn't the best sister. They were practically strangers now.

'What about chemo?' Rachel asked. 'Or other treatments? There must be something we can do.' Cancer. Oh, God.

'Chemo might give us a little extra time,' Victoria said, her voice back to its usual business-like tone. 'But that's all. And it will reduce Mum's quality of life. With so little time, she doesn't want to go through that.'

Rachel nodded, trying to absorb everything her sister was saying. Their mother was dying. Their mother was *dying*. Mo raised his eyebrows and snaked his arms around her waist, but even his warmth couldn't comfort her. All she could hear were Victoria's words in her head.

'I'm hiring a nurse to be there for her around the clock,' Victoria continued. 'She'll prepare meals, help around the house, do whatever Mum needs right now. She tires quickly, although she doesn't like to admit it. And the nurse will help with palliative care, too, when the time comes.' Victoria's voice broke again, and Rachel breathed in. *A matter of weeks.*

'I'd take care of her myself,' Victoria said. 'But between the business and Felicity, I can't be there as much as she needs. I'll visit every day, though,' she added, as if she was trying to placate her guilt. 'Once I get back from this work trip I'm on for the next couple of weeks. I've already tried to move it, but it's impossible. Anyway, Mum begged me not to change anything.'

Rachel sighed, thinking that her sister didn't even know what busy was. She and her husband lived in a pristine house on the outskirts of High Wycombe, with a cleaner coming every day and kits of fresh food ready to be cooked piled high on their doorstep. Their five-year-old daughter Felicity was so scarily self-contained and quiet that you'd barely even know she was in the room. It was a far cry from Rachel's wild brood of three, who were often more feral than human, and the cramped three-bed flat she and Mo owned in Ravenscourt Park, West London, which was bursting at the seams.

'How is Mum now?' Rachel asked, sinking into a chair as that old familiar longing ballooned inside. She needed her mother. She needed her mother, but soon... She swallowed, unable to complete the thought.

'Mum's okay,' Victoria responded. 'She's tired, of course, and this news is a lot to take in. But she seems all right. In some ways, I think she knew it was coming. She told me she'd felt quite ill for ages. Thank goodness I persuaded her to get some tests done.'

Rachel nodded, finding it hard to speak.

'Right, I'll let you go,' Victoria said. 'And look, don't worry about anything. I'll take care of it all, just like always. Anyway, you have your own life to worry about.' Her tone implied it was more than Rachel could handle. Rachel sighed, thinking of the burnt cupcakes and the stack of work still waiting. Her sister was probably right, but Rachel wanted it that way. She'd needed it that way, to try to keep this terrible yearning pushed down.

She croaked out goodbye and hung up, her mind spinning as the noise of the family whirled around her. In a short time, her mother would be gone. She'd be gone, and Rachel would never have a chance to say she loved her. She'd never have the chance to feel her love again – the love she'd held herself apart from because of the age-old fear and guilt deep inside her.

She shifted on the chair, feeling that knot tugging inside, the tangled ropes of emotion still trying to restrain her. This time, though, the ache to see her mother was too strong to keep in check. She didn't *want* to keep it in check, because if she didn't try to mend things with her mum now, she never would. She needed to escape these ties before it was too late.

She needed to do all she could to show her mum how much she loved her.

But *what*? Her heart sank as she thought of the years of distance between them. How could she ever make up for it? It wouldn't be enough to turn up for a quick visit here and there and then leave again – not even close. Maybe she could drive up during the days after the school run and go home again in time to get the kids? She shook her head, thinking that would only give her a few hurried hours. The weekends? No, by the time she roused the kids and delivered them to their many activities, there'd be no time left. Anyway, this wasn't something she wanted to fit in around other things. Her mum needed to see that she was the most important thing now, in the time she had left.

Rachel bit her lip as a thought floated in. Perhaps she could move in with her mother? She'd be there 24/7, in a way she never had been, taking care of her mother; doing all she could. Victoria wouldn't have to hire a nurse. Rachel couldn't imagine her mother wanting a stranger in the house anyway – she was a stickler for keeping everything in its place. Her home was her sanctuary, remaining unchanged for years.

Rachel turned the idea over in her head, her gaze sliding to where Mo and her youngest child Ryan were laughing as they watched a YouTube video together. Her heart wrenched when she thought of leaving behind her family for weeks at a time. She'd always been here for them, and the kids were so attached to her. They adored Mo, but it was Rachel who kept everything running, and Rachel they called when they wanted a cuddle. Mo barely even knew when the school holidays were, let alone organising the complicated weekly schedule for three kids. For the past twelve years, this family had been her whole world, and Mo before that. She needed them as much – or more – as they needed her.

But she needed her mother too, and her mum needed her. The kids might find it difficult without her and she'd miss them like hell, but they'd still be here. Her mother wouldn't, and Rachel had to do this... now, while time still remained.

She needed to try with all she had, or she'd regret it forever.

TWO

RACHEL

'Okay. I'm all set.' Rachel slammed the car boot closed, then turned to face her family. Her childhood home was only about an hour away in the Chilterns, but gazing at her children's downcast faces, it felt like she was off on a mission to Mars. In some ways, leaving her family and moving in with her mother did feel as implausible as rocketing into space. She'd had the night to absorb the news her sister had told her, but she still couldn't believe her mum was dying. Sadness filtered in as she pictured the coming months, but she pushed it aside. It would be awful watching her mother fade, but she would be there every second. They would be together in a way they'd never been before, hopefully banishing the distance between them... finally able to be mother and daughter once more.

Her mum had protested Rachel coming, of course. She'd said over and over that she was fine and that she didn't need anyone; that Victoria was only down the road and that was enough. But Rachel hadn't given an inch, and eventually, after a stern talking-to from Victoria, their mother had quieted. Rachel might have been more offended that she didn't want her there, but she understood her mother's discomfort. Rachel was practically a stranger, and now they'd be living on top of each other. It would be awkward at first, but it would be worth it in the end. She swallowed at the words.

Rachel gazed at her three children, her gut twisting at the thought of not seeing them every night. Tabitha, the eldest at twelve with her dark hair and light eyes so like her mother. Matilda, with her wild mop of curls, splatter of freckles and eyes that were blacker than coal. And then her youngest, Ryan – the happy surprise, conceived only a few months after Matilda had been born. In the middle of colic and sleepless nights, Mo hadn't been so sure they could handle a third – not to mention their tiny place was already full to the brim, and a larger home was out of the question. But Rachel had been delighted. She'd always wanted a big family, children piled onto her lap and into her arms, and this had seemed like a gift. It had been a very busy few years and she'd almost lost her mind – not to mention ageing ten years in half that time – but she wouldn't change a thing.

The kids aren't babies now, she told herself to placate the guilt at leaving. It would do them good to be away from her for a bit. Mo always said she did too much for them, and this was their chance to gain more independence. Anyway, it wasn't like Rachel would be far. She'd come home and see them as often as she could, and Mo could always drive them all up and stay for the weekend. Her mother would get the chance to know her grandkids apart from Rachel's hurried missives every few months or so. And as for work, well, she could handle everything from her mum's house. She had a busy few weeks ahead 'finessing' the report for her client before final approval, but she could work when her mother was sleeping.

Although it meant extra work for him, Mo had been 100 per cent supportive of Rachel going. Mo's mother was happy to help out, too, offering to get the kids from school each day and feed them supper. Being so close to his own mum, Mo had

never understood the distance between Rachel and hers –
distance Rachel had always explained with a simple 'we're just
very different' before hurriedly changing the subject. She'd
never been able to bear dredging up all that pain and fear into
her present, fearing that the darkness might leach into the light.
Thankfully, Mo never delved into it. His large family, with a
plethora of aunts, uncles and cousins, was more than enough,
keeping both him and the kids too occupied to really notice her
mother's absence. Rachel had been happy to keep everything
buried inside... until now.

God, if only she'd tried harder sooner, she thought, swallowing back regret. If she'd only *tried*. She could have had more
time with her mother. The thought made her even more determined to do all she could now. She'd let light and warmth into
her mother's last days – into the cold dark space between them
– if it was the last thing she did.

'I'll FaceTime tonight,' she said to the kids. 'And you'll see
me soon – Dad will drive you up or I'll come down. It won't be
for long.' Pain shot through her once more as she said those
words. She had to change things.

Mo's mum Shireen reached out and squeezed her hand.
'Don't worry. Everything will be taken care of here. You're
doing the right thing, going to your mother when she needs you.
You're a good daughter. I'm proud of you.'

Rachel met Shireen's eyes, her heart flooding with a mixture
of guilt and warmth. Mo's mother was the pinnacle of what a
maternal figure should be, and praise from her meant everything. But Rachel *hadn't* been a good daughter – far from. She
would be now, though. Finally, she would.

Mo folded her into his arms. 'I'll miss you. But I'm proud of
you too.' He pulled back, pushing aside a strand of hair that had
fallen over her eyes. 'Mum's right. We have everything under
control here.' Ryan chose that moment to let rip a very loud fart,
and they all burst out laughing. 'Well, sort of.'

Rachel leaned into her husband for a second, almost as if she could store up his love for later. He'd been her rock ever since they'd met at the mixer for new students her first week at Imperial College in London. She'd been so timid, unsure of who she was or her place in this new world after growing up in such a small village, where a big day out meant taking the bus to High Wycombe. She'd still been reeling at how much there was to do in such a big city and the endless possibilities of people from everywhere that you could meet. Everyone seemed so cultured, so knowledgeable, talking about bands and films she'd never even heard of, let alone had an opinion on. And she was so used to holding herself apart that she wasn't really sure she knew how to strike up a friendship anymore.

She'd been wandering around the student union reading notices on the wall to try to look occupied rather than the no-friends loser she really was when she'd bumped straight into Mo.

'Sorry!' she'd said, scurrying out of his way and over to the next poster.

But he'd followed her, peering at it alongside her. 'Want to go?'

She'd swung towards him in surprise. 'Go where?'

'To the meeting.' He'd pointed towards the poster and her cheeks had flamed. She hadn't really been reading it – she'd been way too distracted by the heat of his body and the smell of his aftershave.

'Oh.' She scanned the sheet in front of her, advertising a talk on renewable energy by a professor she was probably supposed to have known about but never heard of. 'Yes, sure. I'd like that.'

He'd grinned as if he knew she'd had no idea what it said, but he'd given her his number, and a couple of days later they'd sat through the interminable talk. She'd tried to listen, but all she could think about was his presence beside her and how much she liked sitting with him. They went out for drinks afterwards, and his open warmth and confidence made her slowly unfurl, like she was a flower under the sun... like she belonged here too. The instant ease between them was a balm to the unfamiliar surroundings and the loneliness that had followed from home – and a reminder that she could connect with someone, after all.

They'd had some bumps along the way. Shireen had been far from keen about their relationship at first, unsure Rachel was the right fit for her son, but things had smoothed over when she saw that Rachel was here to stay. Rachel was every inch a member of their family now, as if she was one of their own daughters. And Mo loved her with absolute devotion, in a way she'd never felt since pushing away her mother. Sometimes, in her quieter moments – when she'd still had time to have them – she'd wonder what it was about her that made him love her. He was so full of life; so complete. Beside him, she felt like a half-person, one part of her still trapped in darkness despite the light he'd given her.

'Right. Okay.' Rachel cleared her raspy throat. 'Give me one more cuddle, then, guys.'

She squeezed each of the children tightly, trying not to let the tears fall from her eyes as she got into the car. As she pulled away, forcing herself to give a jaunty wave and cheery smile, the tears dripped down her cheeks. She swiped at them with the back of her hand. She was doing the right thing, she reminded herself... the only thing she *could* do. And this would be good for her family too. Once she and her mother reconnected, Mo and the children could be a part of the time that remained. At long last, the two worlds Rachel had kept apart for most of her life could come together.

And maybe, she could finally feel whole too.

· · ·

An hour later, Rachel pulled into Presdon, the village where her mother lived. She followed the twisting road through the centre, marvelling at the changes. The only entertainment here used to be a high street with a smattering of shops and two pubs, but now there was a huge supermarket, outlet shops, a cinema and restaurant chains sprouting glossy and fresh from the centre like new growth on a very old tree.

She turned down a track towards the family home where she'd grown up. When her mum and dad had moved in, there had only been two houses on the lane. Now countless others had been built and a massive development was going up a few hundred yards away. It was certainly different than when she'd lived here, where you could feel like the only person in the world at night-time.

But even if things around the house had changed, the land and the building were exactly the same as they always had been. Rachel pulled into the drive and parked, eyeing the sprawling, ivy-covered stone structure in front of her. The large bay window in the lounge gaped out at her, the two dormer windows above it like eyes. The gravel path curved towards the front step, with her mother's prized rose bushes on one side and some kind of flowers – Rachel could never remember what they were called, despite her mother telling her several times – on the other.

She got out of the car and breathed in the fresh country air, so different from the soft, cloying air of the city. She should feel like she was home, she knew. She'd heard many times from her friends at uni how they couldn't wait to be home again. Even Mo – who was from London and had only moved out once they'd married – relaxed in a way she'd never seen when he entered the door of his mother's home. Rachel had never felt that way returning here, though. Ever since her father had died, she'd always felt cold, like she needed an extra blanket, even though she knew nothing could warm her... nothing except her mother's love.

Her heart pounded as she crunched up the gravel steps and over to the door, knocking loudly before yanking it open. It would be different this time. This time, she wouldn't hold herself apart in fear and blame. She was ready now to reach out to her mother; to be here for her with all she had.

'Mum?' She walked through the kitchen and into the lounge. Like the exterior, the inside of the house had remained the same, exactly like when her father had been alive. Her mother had refused to change a thing, and the house was practically a memorial to him. Victoria had tried to get her to move into a smaller place, but her mother hadn't even given the property brochures she'd brought a cursory glance. The reminder of how her mother clung to her husband's memory made the guilt swell inside Rachel and her heart beat faster. *It wasn't my fault,* she reminded herself. *Mum doesn't blame me.*

She took a breath and stood in the middle of the kitchen, thinking of her father. It was funny, but he'd never seemed like he belonged in this house. Although he hadn't been around much, Rachel reminded herself, always coming in late from work and leaving early the next morning. It was her mother who'd been the steady presence in her life, always there to care for her and Victoria. She'd been the one to make their meals, put them to bed and soothe their childhood fears.

A smile curved Rachel's lips as she remembered one summer when she'd been convinced a ghost was haunting their home. Her mother had sat steadfastly beside her bed for nights, reassuring her over and over again with a sombre face that ghosts did not exist, holding her hand until Rachel relaxed enough to drop off. Even now she could recall that feeling of safety and comfort; the knowledge that whatever terror Rachel conjured up, her mother would protect her. And now it was

Rachel's turn to give her mother safety and comfort; that protection and love.

She glanced out the back door to see her mum on her knees in the garden, pruning a leafy green bush that looked fine to Rachel. She peered closely at her mother, trying to spot any sign of illness. Did she look paler, maybe? Thinner?

'For goodness' sake, stop staring.' Her mother's tone cut into her thoughts, and Rachel jerked.

'Sorry,' she said, coming out into the garden. She forced her lips into a smile, every bit of her vibrating with tension once more. Relax, she told herself. There was no reason to be nervous. It was just... this was a new start; a new beginning, even if her mother didn't know it yet. Rachel wanted to get things off on the right foot – for their time left to be perfect, no matter the challenges they'd face. 'How are you feeling?'

'I'm fine.' Her mother snipped a branch with force, then put down the clipper and got to her feet. 'So, you're here. And you're staying?' Her voice was equal parts incredulous and doubtful, and Rachel swallowed. She couldn't blame her mum for being surprised. The last time she'd stayed overnight was maybe during uni? And now she'd be here for weeks. Months, hopefully. Her heart lurched again at the thought of leaving the kids for so long, but then she pictured them here, encircling her mother as the sun streamed in, their faces wreathed with smiles. God, she couldn't wait for that.

'I'm here. And yes, I'm staying.' She stepped towards her mum and put her arms around her, holding back the sadness as she felt her mother flinch in surprise. Her mum's embrace briefly tightened before she pulled back, and Rachel moved away too. This would feel more natural soon, she told herself to cover the ache inside – for both of them. It was a start, though, and at least her mum had hugged her back. She *did* want Rachel here, even if she'd yet to believe her daughter was truly here for good.

Her mother started snipping the branches again. Rachel watched, mesmerised, as one after another plunged to the ground. She tried desperately to think of something to say, but her mind went blank. Sighing, she bent to pick up the branches. One pricked her hand, and she flinched, thinking how she and her mother had developed thorny bits over the years: Rachel to protect herself from longing, and her mother to protect herself from Rachel's distance. Given time, though, she was sure they could prune off those parts that kept them apart and come together once more.

Hopefully, the time they had would be enough.

THREE

RACHEL

The sound of voices jerked Rachel awake the next morning. Her pulse quickened, and she swung her legs over the side of the bed. The kids were up already? She must have slept in! Oh God, she was going to be late for the school run, and Matilda would complain all the way. She had a headache just thinking about it. Then she breathed in slowly as the knowledge sank in. She wasn't home. She was at her mum's, miles from her children. For the first time in their lives, she wasn't there to jolly them along; to remind them to brush their teeth and tie back their hair.

She sighed, thinking of her call home last night. The kids were so busy fighting over the tablet that they barely realised she was on the phone, and Mo was stupefied by the amount of food he'd ingested from the meal his mother had dropped round. They'd felt so far away, and Rachel had only managed to drift off to sleep by conjuring up that vision of the kids around her mother's bed, the whole room flooded in light.

A laugh drifted up the stairs, and she cocked her head. Was that Victoria? Rachel rubbed her face, listening as her sister's and mother's voices rose and fell, twisting and turning in easy conversation. It was a stark contrast to last night, when Rachel had stayed with her mother until late, dredging up every topic she could think of while her mother stared at the telly. Rachel curled in bed now, memories flooding through her of all those times she'd stayed in this bedroom, loneliness and pain clinging onto her, while her mother and sister had been downstairs.

Not any longer, she told herself, throwing on a T-shirt and jeans. There wasn't time to hide away behind fear and guilt. If her mother and sister were a unit of two, it was because Rachel had let them. It was time to change that.

'Morning!' she said, rounding the corner to the bright and airy kitchen, where Victoria and her mum were sitting at the table with a cup of tea. She tried to hide her surprise at her sister's appearance. It had been months since she'd seen her, and she seemed to have lost even more weight. She'd already been skin and bones. In contrast, Rachel seemed to be working on a reverse diet principle, gaining a pound every month or so. She wasn't too fussed, though, and Mo didn't seem to have noticed the extra weight. He was on the same diet too.

'Hi, Rach.' Victoria pushed back her chair and put her arms around her sister. Rachel tried not to cringe at the fact that she could feel the bumps in her sister's spine as they hugged. They were still the same height, but that was all that was similar, despite how much they'd resembled each other when they were young. Even their hair was different now – Rachel's was a mousy brown, while Victoria's was a glossy chocolate with subtle red highlights.

Rachel had often wondered if her sister ever missed her – missed that closeness they'd had when they were young – but even as a youngster, Victoria had always moved a mile a minute, flitting from one activity to the next, seldom pausing except to cook supper with their mum before heading out again. She'd stayed equally busy all through university and beyond, filling any remaining space with their mother and then her own family and job. The sisters rarely spoke, and as with her mother, Rachel had learned to wall off that pain. But maybe... she swallowed. Maybe now, they could start to get to know each other again.

'You're looking well,' Victoria said.

Rachel smiled. She knew what that meant. 'Thank you,' she said. 'And you're looking very... slim.' She knew Victoria would take that as a compliment.

'Thought I'd pop round to make sure you'd settled in okay,' Victoria said, putting a hand on their mother's back. 'I wanted to say goodbye to Mum, too, before I head off on my trip. Terrible timing, I know.'

'That's all right,' her mother said, moving closer to Victoria. 'I do wish you could stay, but I know how important your work is. I'm so proud of all you do.' She held out her arms, and Rachel's heart twisted as she watched her sister step into her mother's close embrace. She wanted her mother to be proud of her too. She'd become an environmental consultant to do something good, but a small-buried part of her had also hoped it might foster a connection with her nature-loving mum – give them something to talk about, even if the distance between them was too great for more. But her mother didn't seem to even understand what Rachel did, and the job boiled down to companies yelling at her to change what she'd written so they could move forward with their conscience intact.

'Let me help you with your bath before I head out,' Victoria said.

'I can do it,' Rachel said, forcing herself to break in. 'That's why I'm here, after all.' She willed herself to stay smiling despite her mother shaking her head, clinging onto Victoria's arm.

Victoria looked at her watch. 'Could you? That would be great. I really should get going.' She drew her mother into a hug again. 'I'll be back before you know it.' She patted her arm, then hurried out the door.

'Right, let's get you sorted.' Rachel stepped forward into the space where Victoria had been. 'Do you like your water warm or hot? Bubbles, or—' Her phone started ringing, and she drew it out of her pocket. Shit – it was the project lead from Amgo, the client whose draft report had been due in yesterday. She stifled a gasp. *Amgo.* Oh, God. She'd forgotten to send the report! With everything that had been going on, it had been the last thing on her mind.

'One second,' Rachel said to her mother, trying to keep the smile nailed on her face. 'I need to take this and then I'll be right with you.' She hit answer and scurried into the lounge, trying to keep her voice level as she feigned surprise that they hadn't received the report she'd never sent. Then she rifled through her laptop bag and drew out the computer she should have opened up yesterday, frantically trying to start a hotspot so she could send it over. Fifteen minutes later and she'd eventually managed to send it through. God, she was going to need a drink after all of this.

She cocked her head at the sound of running water. Was that bathwater running? She'd thought her mum was waiting for her.

'Mum?' There was no response, and her heart lurched. '*Mum?*' Her mother still didn't answer, and Rachel rushed up the stairs and burst inside the bathroom, panic and fear gripping her as she spotted her mother lying in a flood of water on the floor, her clothes sodden and cold.

'Oh my God. *Mum!*' Rachel knelt beside her mother, moving her head off the floor and onto her lap. She'd be okay. She had to be. She... With shaking fingers, Rachel touched her mother's neck, relief flooding through her when she felt a pulse. She yanked herself up and turned off the water, then knelt back down beside her mother.

'I'm here, Mum. You're okay.' She levered her mother's head back onto her lap and her mum's eyes fluttered open, focusing up at Rachel. For a split second, something like terror flashed across her face, and Rachel took her hand to comfort her. 'It's okay, Mum. You must have had a fall. You're in the bathroom at home, and everything is going to be fine.' She swallowed, guilt rising inside. How could she have let her fall? Hadn't she just pledged to give her mum safety and comfort; protection and love? How could she show her mother she loved her when she hadn't even been watching out for her? Bloody Amgo! She never should have let work distract her. 'Are you hurt anywhere?'

Her mother shook her head. 'No, I grabbed onto the side of the bathtub before I passed out. I think it broke my fall.' Her voice was low and gravelly, but she sounded fine otherwise.

'Okay. I'm going to help you up. Be careful – the floor is a little wet.' That was an understatement if she'd ever heard one. At least a few good inches sloshed around her ankles. 'We'll get you settled into bed, and then I'll call the doctor.' Trying to be as gentle as possible, Rachel put her arms around her mother and hauled her to a standing position.

As she helped her mum the short distance to the bedroom, Rachel realised how light she was – how much weight she had lost – and her heart twisted as it hit once more that soon, she wouldn't have her mother around. Her mum protested as Rachel started to peel the wet clothes off her, but she was too weak to resist, and Rachel gently manoeuvred her into a fresh nightgown and settled her under the covers.

Rachel pulled the duvet up and tucked it around her mum's shoulders. Her mother's eyes sank closed, and Rachel collapsed into a chair by the bed, resolve pouring through her more powerfully than ever. She'd make this up to her mother. She had to. Nothing would distract her: she wouldn't let her mum down again. In fact... Rachel shifted, an idea floating into her

head. Sod Amgo. She'd tell them she had a family emergency
and that they'd have to find someone else to finalise the report.
She pushed aside the memory of how hard she'd worked to get
the account in the first place, never mind convincing them she
wouldn't let 'the kiddies' get in the way.

This was her mother. Nothing else mattered. Nothing else
but finding her way back again.

FOUR

RACHEL

'Thank you for coming,' Rachel said to the doctor as he went out the door. She loved that in this small village, GPs still made house calls for their regular patients. And it was even more a miracle that Dr Druckow, who must be eighty if he was a day, had the energy to do the rounds. Just seeing his familiar face and bushy grey beard calmed her.

'Of course,' Dr Druckow said, turning to face her. 'You did the right thing calling me. But you do need to make sure your mother understands not to overexert herself. There may be more of these incidents as she gets weaker and weaker. I know she may seem strong, but the coming weeks will be very hard for everyone. Don't hesitate to reach out if you need help, all right?'

Rachel nodded, but she knew she wouldn't need help. She could – she *would* – be everything her mother needed. She wouldn't let her fall. She'd never let that happen again.

Dr Druckow's eyes softened. 'You're a good girl, coming back for her. You know, your parents were so happy when you came along. They'd been trying for a very long time to have a child – they wanted one so much. You were quite a surprise to everyone!'

He smiled, and Rachel grinned back even though her mind was whirling. She'd no idea her parents had any difficulty having children, but then her mother never talked much about her early years. There weren't many photos – a few random ones of her first birthday, wide-eyed in front of a cake, and then a sprinkling as she grew older. Rachel's mum had always said she'd been too busy taking care of her to snap many photos, and with her father working such late hours, she was lucky to have any photos at all.

'Please call if you need anything,' the doctor was saying, and Rachel watched as he climbed into his car and drove away. She went back inside, closing the door quietly so as not to wake her mother, who'd fallen asleep again as soon as the doctor had left the room, thanks to the medication he'd given her. Sighing, Rachel stood in the middle of the kitchen, surveying the huge stain on the ceiling and the back wall from the water that had poured through from the bathroom above. The smell of damp was heavy in the room, almost like another presence. Even now, after she'd managed to mop up most of the bathroom water while waiting for the doctor, water was still dripping onto the kitchen floor and slowly trailing down the wall, the pool at the base growing wider every passing second. She bit her lip, wondering if it had gone into the basement below too. When Matilda had let the bath overflow last year, the water had travelled through cracks and crevices they hadn't even known existed.

Rachel shook her head, guilt pouring in as she thought of the job ahead, and at the worst time possible. The last thing her mother needed was home renovations; builders blaring their radios and plumbers clanking around. And her mum would never leave here to stay somewhere more comfortable while the work was being carried out. Rachel knew that much for sure.

She'd barely left at all since Rachel's dad had died. But maybe the damage wasn't as bad as it looked? Maybe they could wait until it all dried out and then paint over it? God, *how* could she have let this happen?

Right, she'd better go check out the basement. Snapping on the light, she stared around the dingy space. The whole thing retained the smell of diesel and grease from when it had served as her father's motorcycle workshop. He'd loved bikes, spending hours here and forbidding his daughters from coming anywhere near his precious toys. Rachel paused, remembering how she'd once crept downstairs when she'd heard him playing the radio and working on his bikes. He'd jumped in surprise when she'd tapped him on the shoulder, then his face had softened and he'd beckoned her forward to have a look at what he was doing, helping her onto the back of the bike and laughingly placing a helmet on her head. She'd breathed in his scent, shyly smiling, and he'd tweaked her cheek. That was one of the few memories she had of herself and her father alone, actually. She'd never really got the chance to know him.

Her heart dropped as she noticed that the far wall was sodden and stained, with droplets of water slowly forming on the surface before bursting and running to the floor. Rachel picked her way through discarded furniture – she remembered her father replacing everything with the best of the best, yet refusing to throw anything away – and over towards the wall, grimacing when she touched it and her fingers came away wet. She prodded it gently, yelping as her finger punched straight through the plaster. A huge chunk came away as she took her finger out, landing with a slap on the concrete floor. Ugh, this wall was so thin she could practically dismantle it now!

Well, if it was that easy, maybe she could do just that. At least it would give the wood behind it a chance to dry out. She knocked down another chunk and then another, thinking that this was kind of cathartic. It felt like she was peeling back the layers of her childhood, sloughing off the pain, the loneliness, and heading right to the heart of it all... back to her mother.

Wait. She stopped for a second, tilting her head as a swathe of black appeared. What was that? Was there something inside the wall? She pulled down more wet plaster, reaching in to touch it. It looked like a black bin bag. She stepped back, taking it in. It *was* a black bin bag, wrapped around something that was secured with thick duct tape.

She stared. What the hell? Why would that be in the wall? Was it something her father had wanted to hide from her mother – maybe a bike he'd bought that he didn't want her to go crazy over? She was always saying he already had too many, but then she'd shake her head and give in. She could never say no to her husband.

Reaching in, Rachel tried to lever it out, but it didn't budge. She tore at the bin bag, but the duct tape stopped her from ripping it open. Now more than curious, she dashed upstairs, grabbed a knife and scissors, then went back down. She cut the tape with the scissors, then sliced through the middle of the bin bag with the knife. Whatever was in here, it was very well hidden, she thought as she sliced through layer after layer. At last, she managed to get through them all, widening the hole.

She jerked back. What *was* that? A flash of red peeped out at her, the fabric of... she reached in. A T-shirt? Maybe this was just a bag of clothes? But why would it be here in the wall, secured so tightly? Shaking her head, she made the hole larger, tearing up the middle towards the top, then ripping it open.

Oh my God.

Oh my *God*.

The scissors and knife slid from her hand and clanked onto the floor, but Rachel barely noticed. All she could do was stare at the grotesque sight in front of her. It wasn't real. It couldn't be. It was like something from a funfair horror ride, and yet it was here, in this basement, hollow eyes staring out from a face that was no longer; tattered clothing falling from a body reduced to bones. Her stomach lurched, and she gagged as the scent of death and decay swirled around her. She stumbled back, then turned and raced up the stairs into the light once more. She snatched up her mobile and dialled 999.

'Police, please,' she said, her voice shaking. 'I think... I found someone. A... a body, in the wall.'

Then she sank into a chair and tried to breathe.

FIVE

SAM

May 1985

'Get that bloke a pint. The faster the better, before he screams the place down.'

Samantha Hughes nodded at her manager Will, then glanced towards the red-faced man bellowing at the football match. He clearly didn't need another pint. At this pub in South London, though, they only cared about how much they sold, not about the punters' welfare. With their clientele, they were lucky to get through a shift without a fight breaking out. Sam set the pint in front of the man, who barely even noticed her but to leer at her chest, then went back to the safety of the bar.

God, this *place*, she thought, wiping the grimy counter with an already grimy cloth. How on earth had she lasted here for the past few years? It was only supposed to have been a stop-gap to bring in extra money until she found a real job as one of those secretaries who went to work every morning dressed in a smart suit with killer heels, or even as a waitress in the upscale restaurant she'd seen on a rare day out in Covent Garden. Something that could carry her from this life towards the one she'd always dreamed of: as a mother with a beautiful baby and an adoring husband, with their own little house on a quiet, clean street. Of a family. Of *love*.

But no matter how many applications she filled out or how many CVs she distributed, either she hadn't the right qualifications or they took one look at her and shook their heads. Sam sighed, glancing at her reflection in the window. With her frizzy home perm and 'highlights' that were more orange than blonde – not to mention her thrift-shop outfits – she knew she didn't belong at those places... yet.

But she would, she told herself, trying yet again to smooth down her hair. She was only twenty, after all. She'd get an expensive haircut, buy a good, second-hand suit, and maybe even go back to school part-time. She wouldn't be this lowly barmaid who couldn't do anything but pour a pint; the kind of woman a decent man wouldn't look twice at. She'd be someone to be proud of – someone *she* could be proud of too.

'Right, you can knock off now,' Will said a few hours later, when she'd finished wiping down all the tables and gathering pint glasses swilling with dregs of beer, as well as spit, cigarette butts and, in one case, a whole load of vomit.

'Okay, great, thanks.'

'You all right to get home? Want me to walk you over?'

Sam smiled, thinking how it sounded much more chivalrous than it actually was, seeing as how she lived across the street. It was the main appeal of this place and one of the reasons she'd got the job: she was right next door if someone called in sick and Will needed someone to open up. It was probably why she'd stayed at the flat for so long, even though five girls crammed in the dingy, mouldy one-bedroom basement flat was almost as bad as the pub itself – especially when no one except her ever bothered to clean, and the smoke in the air meant that even if the windows hadn't an inch of grime on them, you wouldn't have been able to see outside anyway. She probably could have afforded something better, but she wasn't willing to spend her meagre savings on a place to simply sleep. She'd dealt with much worse, and she could deal with this now.

'I'll watch and make sure you get home all right,' Will said, when she didn't answer. 'Go on, now.'

'Okay, okay, I'm going.' Sam shrugged on her coat, then gathered up her handbag, thinking that even if Will was a little overprotective, that was no bad thing. As boisterous as the punters might be with each other, they were usually mild-mannered with her. But in the past few weeks, one man seemed to have taken a liking to Sam, hanging around the bar when Will wasn't there and asking her out, over and over – out for a drink, out for a ride in his car, out to see the new build he was working on. She'd force a laugh and continue cleaning up, telling herself he was harmless despite how uncomfortable she was feeling.

But then a couple of nights ago, she'd been closing alone, and he'd been waiting for her outside. He'd taken her arm with a grip that was more firm than friendly, but she'd shaken him off, then run home and locked the door. The thought of what might have happened had made Sam shudder and even more grateful that she lived across the street – even if this man did know now where her flat was. In fact, only this morning he'd left a wilted red rose and a card with the name 'Love, Alex' scrawled on it in what looked like a child's handwriting. Her flatmates had taken the mick out of her for a good hour, but Sam hadn't found a flower from a man who'd grabbed her funny. She'd looked around her carefully before daring to cross the street to work this morning, hating how uneasy she felt.

The pub phone rang, and Will answered. Sam turned to go, but something in his words caught her attention, and she paused.

'A manager? I can imagine it's hard, finding someone out where you are. It's all fields and cows!' Will laughed and made a face. 'No, I can't think of anyone, sorry. I'll let you know if I do come across anyone I think might be a good fit, though. Okay, talk soon. Bye.'

'Who was that?' Sam asked, trying to sound casual. She wasn't looking for another pub job, not really. But a manager... that was a step up, and even if it was in the country, it was sure to pay better than the pittance she earned now. The more she could save, the faster she could make a better life for herself. Maybe, eventually, she could even stop working for a bit and focus on finishing her A-levels. That might get her closer to the life she wanted.

'Oh, a mate who owns a pub up in the Chilterns,' Will said. 'She's looking for a manager to help out, but she's having trouble recruiting one.'

'Where are the Chilterns?' Sam's cheeks went hot, embarrassment filtering through her. She probably should know, but she'd barely been outside of London. That was what happened when you grew up in the care system: your world was limited to what your foster parents wanted to show you. In her case, that meant the four walls of her bedroom and the walk to school. Her foster parents had always kept her clothed and fed, but as for anything else... as for love...

'It's about an hour from London,' Will answered. 'Beautiful countryside – rolling hills, trees, lots of good walking – if you like that sort of thing.' He grimaced. 'Give me pollution and crazy punters any day.'

'And they're looking for a manager?' Sam asked carefully, trying to keep the hope and excitement off her face.

Will swivelled towards her. 'No, no, no,' he said, wagging a finger at her. 'I'm not losing one of my best employees. Forget it. Besides, you'd hate it there. It's where people go to retire. No clubs, no bars – you really will end up an old maid.' He nudged her with his shoulder to take the edge off his words, and she grinned. He was always joking about how she'd never had a boyfriend, but Sam didn't care. She wasn't going to settle for anyone. She wanted a man to make a life with, a man with ambition, a man who would make her feel special and not just a drunken one-night fling. And while available men might be in short supply in the Chilterns, she definitely wasn't going to meet that kind of man here. She wasn't looking right now anyway.

'Will...' She bit her lip. 'Could you put in a good word for me at your friend's pub? Please? I... I need a change. I need something different, you know? And this could be a big step up for me.'

Will's eyes softened, and he stared at her for a minute. 'I've always said you don't belong here – and definitely not in that shithole across the street. You're destined for better things.' He tilted his head, sucking on his lower lip. 'All right, all right. Decision made. You're going to the country. But don't get too comfortable there, okay? I'm only doing this because I believe you can do more, so don't let me down.'

Sam smiled, warmth flooding through her. She loved that Will believed in her. He always had, ever since he'd taken a chance on her when she'd showed up at the pub with no experience to speak of. Over the past couple of years, he'd taught her everything she needed to be a manager. 'I haven't got the job yet!' she said.

Will waved a hand in the air. 'You will, don't worry. Jean will go with what I say. But the question is, who am I going to get to replace you? You'd better run before I change my mind! I'll tell Jean to call you here tomorrow to discuss details, all right? Now go!'

Sam nodded and threw her arms around him, then pulled back and turned to go. As she crossed the street to her dirty, smelly flat, she barely noticed the rubbish swirling around her in the gusty wind – or the second red rose that had been hastily shoved through the post slot, lying trampled and torn on the doormat inside. Soon, she'd be miles away from all of this. In her mind, she was already in the countryside, breathing in fresh air.

Breathing in the start of a better life.

SIX

RACHEL

Rachel tried to stop shaking as she waited for the police to arrive, every fibre straining to try to make sense of what she'd seen; to absorb that this wasn't a nightmare. This was real: there was a body in the wall. She shuddered, the image flashing into her mind. By the looks of things, it had been there for a very long time. Likely since the house had been built, since her parents hadn't ever renovated. She remembered her mother saying it was such a perfect house that they hadn't needed to change a thing.

She rubbed her arms, picturing her parents happily buying this place years ago, never knowing what horror it was concealing; never realising what was lurking inside the basement all that time. Worry flooded through her at the thought of her weak, pale mother curled up in bed. How could she wake her to say the police were on their way to remove a *body* from her beloved house? This wasn't only a bit of damage caused by flooding. This was a person, buried in the wall. The shock could hurt her mother more than any fall.

Rachel shook her head. She couldn't tell her – not now; not after she'd already caused her mum so much pain by not being there. Dr Druckow had given her mum medication so she'd rest comfortably tonight. Hopefully, she'd stay sleeping, the police would remove the body quickly, and she'd remain oblivious. When she recovered from her fall and the body was gone, Rachel would tell her what had happened – if she needed to, that was. Because apart from where the body had been found, this had nothing to do with them. There was no reason to cause her mother such distress.

A police car pulled into the driveway, and Rachel raced to open the door before they knocked. Thank goodness they didn't have the siren on, although there was obviously no need for a siren anyway. Whatever had happened to end that poor person's life had been years ago. She shivered, wondering if she would ever be able to get that image out of her head.

'Lucas!' She gazed at the officer in front of her in surprise. It had been years since she'd seen him, but he still looked the same: sandy hair that curled over his ears, green eyes flecked with brown, and a large frame that she'd always felt so safe folded into. Lucas had been her boyfriend for almost a year in secondary school – they'd only broken up the summer before their last year when his family had moved to Edinburgh. That final year of secondary school should have been amazing, but instead Rachel remembered it as one of the loneliest of her life. She'd seen on Facebook that he'd joined the police, but she'd no idea he'd come back here.

Thank God he had, she thought, relief flooding in. He knew her family. He knew they could have no connection to this.

'How are you?' she asked, giving him a quick hug. His arms felt the same, even if his body was studier, more solid, than the boy she remembered.

'Rachel.' He pulled back, his eyes warm. 'What are you doing here? Last I heard, you were some bigshot in London.'

'Hardly.' Rachel couldn't help smiling, remembering how people here thought anyone who lived in London must be a millionaire with an amazing job. She'd thought the same. 'My mother's not well,' she continued. 'I've come back to help her for the next few months.'

'Oh.' Lucas's eyebrows flew up, not that she blamed him for being surprised. He'd seen how distant her mum had been with her and jokingly said that he wished his mother didn't care what he did. Rachel had nodded, responding stonily how lucky she was, but she hadn't been able to help the tear streaking down her cheek before she'd turned away. Lucas had patted her arm awkwardly, and she'd forced a smile, then changed the topic. They'd never spoken of it again, but she suspected he might have said something to his mother because whenever Rachel went round, Sue would make a fuss over her, inviting her for dinner and giving her plenty of hugs. Rachel had adored Sue, and sometimes she didn't know who she'd missed more when the family had moved.

'How's your mum doing?' she asked, realising this wasn't exactly the moment for small talk, but desperate to restore some normality and banish the terrible thing she'd seen.

'She's great, thanks. Loving being a grandmother.' He smiled, and Rachel could imagine how wonderful she would be; how she'd embrace the role. 'Right, so...' He cleared his throat, and Rachel could see him slip into police-officer mode. 'Tell me about what you found.'

'It's awful, Lucas.' The shudder swept through her again, and she breathed in. It would be all right. It was a dreadful tragedy, but Lucas would deal with it. It wouldn't have to even touch them.

'We had a flood in the bathroom, and the water went through the wall and down to the basement. The plaster was damp and soggy, and it began to crumble.' She paused, wishing she could turn back time... wishing she'd never uncovered what was in that wall. Wishing she'd been there for her mother, like she'd promised.

'I started knocking it down to dry out, and I saw something – something that looked like a bin bag, and I wasn't sure what it was. When I opened it up...' She covered her mouth, nausea rising. 'Go down the basement stairs and across to the back wall, and you'll see it.'

Lucas started towards the steps.

'Lucas?' she called softly. He turned around. 'My mum is sleeping upstairs. She had a fall earlier – she's all right, but she needs to rest. Can you keep things quiet? I don't want to upset her.'

Lucas held her gaze. 'Let me figure out what we're dealing with here first, all right? You might have found animal remains, or... Let's see what we've got. But I promise I'll do everything I can not to disturb your mother.'

'Thank you.' Rachel sank into a chair at the kitchen table, listening to Lucas poke around downstairs and praying that he was right: that it was animal remains and nothing more. But she knew what she'd seen. It wasn't animal remains. It was a person. A person who'd likely had a terrifying end to their life; a person someone had hidden here. Horror washed over her again.

She heard Lucas's footsteps on the stairs, and she got to her feet. As soon as she saw his face, she knew she was right.

'It is human remains,' he said grimly. 'I've called in more members of the team. They'll be here shortly to remove the body; do an initial inspection of the basement. We'll need you and your mother to stay out of it until the team has completed their work.'

'Of course,' Rachel said. 'I don't think my mother has been down there for years anyway. And after what I found, I certainly don't want to go back.'

Lucas's face softened. 'That must have been awful. I'm sorry you had to see that.'

Rachel swallowed, uncertain if she wanted to know more,

but part of her needing to. 'How long do you think it's been there?'

Lucas shook his head. 'I'm not sure. From what I could see, the remains looked mostly skeletal, but since it's been sealed in bags and inside a wall, it's hard to tell. I'm no expert, but I'd say it's been there for a while. How long has your family lived here? Since before you were born, right?'

Rachel nodded. 'My parents bought the place right before they got married, and they moved in straight after the wedding. I don't know when the house was first built, but they've never done any kind of construction, so the body must have been here when they moved in. They'd never in a million years have imagined something so horrific.' Who would? 'Would you like a cup of tea while we wait?'

Lucas nodded, and Rachel got down a mug and flicked on the kettle.

'It's so good to see you,' Lucas said as they waited for it to boil. 'I mean, apart from Facebook.' He grinned, and Rachel was glad she wasn't the only one who'd checked Facebook to see what he was up to. 'You have a beautiful family.'

Rachel smiled, suddenly longing for that family right now. They seemed further away than ever.

'And you?' she asked. 'How many kids do you have?'

'I've got two – a boy and a girl. They live with their mum, but I see them every weekend.' Sadness flashed across his face. 'Joint custody is hard when you're doing shift work. But I put my name in for a promotion that will hopefully give me more regular hours. Now I need to do everything I can to get it.' He lifted his head at the sound of cars coming down the drive. 'That didn't take long. Here they are.'

Rachel cringed as the team slammed doors, spoke loudly, and bustled into the house like they owned it.

'Sorry,' Lucas said, turning to her after directing them down to the basement. 'I know you don't want to disturb your mother, but I'm going to have to speak with her now.'

His voice was firm, and Rachel's heart sank. Of course the police would want to talk to her mother. Even if Lucas knew that her family could never be connected to what had happened to this poor person, as owner of the property, he'd have to inform her of what he found. He couldn't just take the body and go.

But he couldn't tell her now. She couldn't let him. She had to let her mother rest and regain whatever strength she could. Rachel couldn't begin to imagine rousing her mother to tell her such horror.

'Only a quick chat,' Lucas said, seeing her expression. 'I won't be long, I promise. It will give me a chance to find out if she knew the previous owners or anything about its history.' He squeezed Rachel's arm. 'I know it will be upsetting, but hopefully we'll only need to talk this once.'

No. The word rang in her head so strongly that for a second, she thought she might have said it aloud. 'Mum's pretty knocked out on medication right now,' she began slowly. 'Dr Druckow gave her a heavy dose of painkillers and sleeping pills, and you won't be able to get much out of her even if you can wake her. Can't you look up that stuff online? Who the previous owners were and everything?' She remembered all of that from when she and Mo had bought their flat. 'See what you can find out before you have to bother her?' She shook her head. 'The doctor says she may only have weeks to live, Lucas.'

'I'm sorry, Rach. That must be so hard.' She held her breath, praying he'd leave. 'All right,' he said at last. 'If she's on medication, any information we are able to get might not be reliable anyway. I'll hold off until tomorrow.'

Relief flooded into Rachel. *Thank God.*

'Right, I need to go and oversee everything.' He turned and

started down the stairs. 'Oh.' He swung around. 'We'll need to take a DNA sample from you since you touched the remains.'

'That's fine.' Rachel collapsed into a chair, trying to calm the flurry of emotions inside. She'd kept her mother safe from this terrible discovery – for now. And maybe... she breathed in, hope returning. Maybe tonight, Lucas's team would discover evidence that pointed in the direction of the previous owners. Maybe it would be enough to tell Rachel what they'd found, and they wouldn't need to talk to her mum, after all.

Then Rachel could put this dreadful mistake behind her – the dreadful past behind her – for good.

SEVEN

RACHEL

Rachel sat at the kitchen table the next morning, sipping her cup of tea. She'd only dozed fitfully last night, drifting off in a chair at her mother's bedside, then jerking awake as images of the body in the wall twisted through her mind. Forensics had spent all night carefully removing the remains and combing through every inch of the basement, finishing only as the sun started lighting the sky. The body was gone, and thankfully, her mother had slept straight through. The medication had kept her unaware of everything that was happening a couple of floors beneath her. Rachel prayed she'd stay that way.

Rachel rubbed her eyes, hoping Lucas and his team had managed to find something that meant she *could* keep her mother oblivious. Her head felt foggy, her eyes ached, and every inch of her longed to be back in her familiar cosy chaos with the children cavorting around her as she tried to get them off to school. She'd called Mo last night, eager to hear a friendly voice and to banish the horror of what had happened, but instead she'd ended up feeling even more distant.

'You sound really rattled,' Mo had said, his voice concerned. 'And I don't blame you. Finding something like that... wow. I can't even imagine. How did your mum react? My mother would have a heart attack.'

Rachel had cringed at his words. 'She doesn't know yet. She slept through the whole thing, thank goodness. I'm hoping...' She swallowed. 'I'm really hoping she won't need to find out.' She paused, listening to her kids shout in the background and Mo's pleas for them to be quiet.

'Look, why don't you come home this weekend?' he said, coming back on the line. 'Victoria can stay with your mother, can't she? The kids would love to see you.'

Rachel had bit her lip, realising she'd yet to tell Victoria the news of the discovery. Maybe later, when things calmed down, she'd give her a call. She'd be busy on her work trip anyway.

'I'd love that,' Rachel had responded, 'but Victoria's away, and I need to stay put and make sure all of this is wrapped up.' *Please God, may it all be wrapped up.* 'Not to mention fixing the damage from the water leak.' Even if her sister hadn't been away, though, Rachel wouldn't have gone. Her world was here now, at least for the time being. Her mother needed her more than ever, and nothing would distract her again.

Rachel sighed, thinking of the phone call she'd had with her client to tell them she needed to bow out. They hadn't been nearly as upset as she'd expected, which had both relieved and unnerved her at the same time. The project manager had wished her well, told her to send the invoice, then hung up – almost as if he'd expected her to bail at some point. She'd worked so hard to keep her private life separate from her work one, only for them to collide anyway. Guilt speared her as she thought of herself on the laptop while her mother lay on the cold wet floor. Never again, she told herself. She'd made the right decision.

'Daaaad!' Matilda's voice cut across the line, and Rachel smiled. The sound of her child's voice always made her feel warm inside, even if Matilda was an expert in the art of the perfect whine.

'I'd better go,' Mo said. 'Matilda's come out of the bath and dripped down the stairs. Why can't that child stay in the bathtub?'

'You shouldn't—' The phone had clicked off before Rachel could tell her husband to stay in the bloody bathroom with Matilda. She might be nine, but the number of accidents she'd already had climbing in and out of the tub 'to say one little thing' was worth the extra ten minutes in there with her. Rachel had put the phone down, wishing again that she could be there but knowing she was where she needed to be.

A banging on the door made her jump, and her heart lurched when she spotted Lucas. God, he must have only got an hour or two of sleep, if that. He wasn't here to talk to her mother already, was he? He might have a tragedy to investigate, but there was hardly any urgency, and surely he could have given her more time to rest before disturbing her. He knew how ill she was – he couldn't be *that* inconsiderate. Rachel tilted her head, remembering how he'd always been so sensitive to her feelings.

Maybe he didn't want to talk to her mum, Rachel thought. Maybe he wanted to talk to her. Perhaps he'd found something: something about the previous owners; something that meant he could leave her and her mother in peace now. That must be it. *Please God may that be it.*

She opened the door and eased outside, closing it behind her so she wouldn't disturb her mum. 'Good morning,' she said. Despite her fatigue, she couldn't help noticing how Lucas's hair was still wet from the shower, curling around his ears in the way it always had when he'd come back inside school after football practice. She'd be waiting for him in the library, surrounded by a stack of science books. They'd been a very unlikely couple, she thought now. It was a wonder they'd lasted as long as they had. If she was being honest, it was probably more about being less lonely than *him*.

'Morning.' Lucas smiled, then took a swig from the travel mug in his hand. She eyed it, recognising the eco-friendly label on the side. A policeman and environmentally conscious, she thought, impressed. 'Can I come in?'

Rachel hesitated, not wanting to let him inside – not wanting any more of this sad story to taint the space she was desperate to let the light into. 'Mum's still sleeping, so if you wouldn't mind staying out here.' She took his arm and propelled him further from the door. 'Did you find anything? A connection to the previous owners? Do you know what happened?' The questions burst out of her, and her heart sank when Lucas shook his head.

'No, there's no connection to the previous owners. But...' His face was solemn, and a seed of apprehension lodged inside of her.

'But what?'

'But there is a connection to your family.'

Rachel jerked in surprise. To her *family*? No. He must be mistaken. He couldn't mean them. The very thought was ridiculous.

'The body was placed there when your parents owned the house,' Lucas continued, and Rachel's mouth dropped open. Her parents had been living here when the body was hidden? 'We haven't been able to identify the remains yet. Our pathologist is still working on that. There haven't been any missing-person reports in the area for years, and there wasn't any ID on the body. But the one piece of concrete evidence we did find is a ticket stub, like the kind you get for a bus. We could only just make out the date.'

'And?' Rachel could barely get out the words through the disbelief swirling inside her.

'It's 1986,' Lucas said, and she froze. 1986. Her parents

were living here. They'd been here for a few years already, and her mother would have not long had her.

'I need to talk to your mother now,' Lucas continued softly. 'I can't wait any longer. I'm sorry, Rach, but with this link, she could be an important part of the case.'

'An important part of the case?' Horror swept through Rachel. 'But how?' Surely he couldn't think she was involved in this somehow.

'It's still very early, and we don't have enough evidence right now to get a clear picture of what might have happened,' Lucas said. 'It's possible that your mum remembers something. I need to see what she might know.'

'What she might know?' Rachel's voice rose, and she told herself to keep it down. 'Of course she doesn't know anything, Lucas. How can you even think that she might?' This could never – would never – have been her mother's perfect house if she had. This wouldn't have been the place she'd stayed in for so long... the place that provided such comfort after her husband's death.

Lucas held her gaze. 'Sometimes, people see things that they don't think are important at the time, but later turn out to be critical. Anything she can tell us could help.' He paused. 'I know you said your parents hadn't done any renovations, but you were only a baby when this happened. She might be able to tell me about any builders they had on-site, or prolonged periods they were away from the house. Friends who had access to the building or who might have been behaving suspiciously. She could have witnessed something without even realising it.'

Rachel stared at him, her heart racing. She'd been praying to keep this from her mother in the first place, and that was before the discovery of a connection to the family. And now... now, while her mum was still recovering from the fall, Rachel had to tell her not only that a body had been hidden here, but that it had happened when she and her husband were starting their journey together as a family – put there by builders, by friends, by people they had trusted? That somehow, unbeknown to them, their past had intersected with such a horrific tragedy? No. No *way*.

It would darken the place where her mother had always sought shelter; taint the sanctuary where her most precious memories lived. And Rachel couldn't let that happen. She might have let her mother down by not keeping watch once, but she wasn't going to now. Her mother had kept the ghost from her door when she was young, and Rachel would do exactly the same.

'My mum is still sleeping,' she said slowly, her mind frantically whirling. He couldn't force her mum to talk to him, could he? If she wasn't a suspect, then wasn't it up to her to cooperate or not? 'And actually...' She swallowed. 'Actually, I think it's best if you go now.' She needed him to go, so she could think. Think of what she could do now to keep this ghost at bay.

Lucas's eyes widened in surprise. 'Go?'

'I can't let you talk to her. I told you how ill she is. And this...' Rachel shook her head. 'I can't let you upset her.'

Lucas sighed. 'I understand, Rach. I do. But it'll be better if she talks to me now. Get it out of the way, and then you can both move on.'

Rachel held his gaze. *Move on.* He didn't understand, not at all. He'd no idea what this house meant to her mother. This would ruin everything. *She* would ruin everything, right when she was trying to repair all that had gone wrong.

'You need to go,' she repeated. 'Please, Lucas. Just go.'

They stared at each other for what felt like ages, and then he nodded. 'All right. I'll go – for now. But you can't keep me from your mother forever, Rachel.' His face was set, and she remembered how determined he could be when he wanted something. His words about the promotion flashed through her mind, and fear shot through her. He would be back again, that much she knew for sure. He would try everything he could to get her mum to talk, but Rachel was equally determined to protect her.

Only when the police car had disappeared down the road at the bottom of the lane did she go back inside. She locked the door, taking deep breaths to calm herself as Lucas's words rang in her ears. *Builders on-site, or prolonged periods they were away from the house. Friends who had access to the house, or who might have been behaving suspiciously.* Was there anywhere she could find evidence of that? Building plans or credit card expenses? Receipts or letters to friends, maybe? If nothing else, it could give Lucas's team another avenue to pursue besides talking to her mother. Or was she simply clutching at straws? Maybe she was, but right now, she had to do something. *Anything.*

She stood in the middle of the room, her mind spinning. Where to start? Her father had an office full of books and files to do with the business – as far as she knew, everything was still intact. Like the rest of the house, her mother hadn't changed a thing. Would he have kept anything to do with his personal finances there too? She tilted her head, hope filtering in as she remembered her mother rolling her eyes and saying he was worse than an accountant with all his files and records. But then Rachel's father had grown up in a poor family, unlike her mother's wealthy one. He always said that was why he worked so hard: because he never wanted to be poor again.

She went up the stairs, cracking open the door to her mother's room to check in on her mum. Thankfully, she was still fast asleep, chest rising and falling in a regular rhythm. Cool fresh air filtered into the room, and Rachel breathed it in. She'd opened the window earlier this morning, eager to let some fresh air into her mum's stuffy room, but now the room felt cool. She went to close it, stifling a gasp. This was right above where she'd been talking to Lucas! Could her mother have heard what Lucas was saying?

She spun to look at her mum again, her eyes closed and face peaceful. No. She couldn't have heard. She wouldn't be sleeping so comfortably if she had, not in a million years.

Rachel swallowed, picturing her mother's face if Lucas told her what had happened... picturing the darkness spreading over this place, enveloping everything. She shook her head, remembering her vow to let in light to the house; into the space between her and her mother.

She turned away and closed the door, then took a deep breath. She *had* to find something. She had to do everything she could to keep that ghost away.

EIGHT

SAM

May 1985

Sam gave Will a hug, unable to believe this was the last time she'd be serving in the pub – not that she would miss it. She *would* miss the man who'd taken her under his wing, though. He'd supported and encouraged her these past few years, but she needed to strike out on her own now. She swallowed, fear shooting through her when she thought of Alex. He hadn't left any more roses, thank goodness, but she was sure she'd seen him lurking around her flat a few times this past week. Once she'd been certain he was right behind her, and she'd spun around, heart pounding. There'd been nothing but the dark night, but still the threat hung heavy in the air. She might have talked to Will about it, but Alex hadn't returned to the pub – at least not when she was here – and since she was leaving soon, it didn't seem worth making a fuss. She was probably being silly anyway.

'Promise me you'll come visit?' she said, tears pricking her eyes.

'Oh, for God's sake, girl, you're not going to the moon!' He laughed, giving her a squeeze, then letting her go. 'Of course I'll come visit – but only to see you, mind. Don't think you're going to drag me on any country walks to experience the joys of nature and all of that.' He grimaced.

Sam grinned, trying to picture Will on a country walk but failing miserably. In fact, it was hard to picture him anywhere but behind the bar, but she knew that in his time off – rare in this job – he headed out to Broadstairs with a 'friend' that she suspected was a boyfriend, even if he never came right out and said it. It wouldn't have bothered her in the least, but in this rough and ready place, she knew it might have caused him problems.

In a way, it did kind of feel like she was going to the moon, she thought as she made her way across the Underground to catch the train to Great Missenden, the nearest station to the pub. She'd had a rather rushed interview with Jean, the harried owner, before Jean had told her that if Will vouched for her, that was enough for her, and to come as soon as possible – early next week, if she could. There'd be a room waiting for her above the pub. She'd rung off, leaving Sam staring at the receiver as her brain whirled with all she'd have to do. Emotions had swarmed through her: hope, excitement and nerves. Her little part of the world – the dingy streets, the flat and the pub – might be the lowest of low, but she knew them inside out. Now, she was leaving them for a foreign land.

A foreign land that was going to be better; a land that would help launch her in the direction she wanted to go, she reminded herself as the train flashed through green pastures with cows and sheep. Neat rows of trees marked the edges of the fields like picture frames, and in the distance, she could make out the stone spire of a church spearing up into the blue sky. It was like something from a dream, and as she wandered down the high street of Great Missenden to find the bus that would take her to the village of Sunhill where the pub was, she felt even further away from reality – from *her* reality anyway. The streets were shockingly free from any rubbish, the pastel houses untouched by the soot and grime that coated London buildings, and neat flower boxes lined their fronts.

She paused for a minute and took a deep breath, loving how the air seemed so fresh. This place was straight from her fantasies, when she used to lie in the dark, alone at night in strange houses with strange people tasked with taking care of her, and dream of another place. A place drenched in light and colour, with parents who loved her with all their might... of a family of her own. For a split second, an image of her, a beautiful baby and a handsome husband happily ensconced in one of these houses flashed into her mind, and even though she knew it wasn't real, happiness flooded through her.

You have a long way to go before that's your life, she reminded herself sternly as she climbed on the bus. *It's a step up, but you're still only a pub manager.* And the kind of man she wanted would want someone successful too; someone his equal in all things. She closed her eyes, imagining them sitting at a dinner table, chatting long into the night.

She leaned back in the seat as the bus bumped along the narrow roads, wending through more fields and trees until it came to a little cluster of houses gathered along a village green, as if waiting for a show to begin, with the pub right in the middle. The driver called out the stop and, heart pounding, Sam grabbed her bag and got off.

She stood for a minute, silence descending as the roar of the bus faded away. Will was right, she thought, surveying the village in front of her: this was the middle of nowhere. There were no cars and nothing moved. It was like the whole scene was frozen. She was so used to the frenetic movement of the city, where the headlights of cars and the screeching of buses washed over her consciousness even while she was sleeping. The silence was unnerving.

She picked up her bag and forced her legs forward across the green and towards the pub. It was huge: much bigger than she'd expected for a village this size. Its exterior was gleaming white, the black-framed windows peeping out like welcoming eyes. Flower pots hung from the door, and the car park stretched out to one side. The whole thing felt warm, as if it was a benevolent giant beckoning her inside, and somehow, she knew she would be safe here. She stared up at the second floor, which covered half the length of the structure, wondering if that was where her room was. She wasn't fussy – after living with five girls, she could deal with anything – but she hoped she wouldn't be sharing with too many others.

She went to push open the heavy wooden door, but it didn't budge. Frowning, she tried again, then glanced at her watch. It was just gone ten, and she'd arranged to meet Jean at half past. The pub didn't open for another hour, so maybe Jean wasn't here yet. She sank down on the step, resting her bag beside her, and closed her eyes, tipping her head up to the morning sun.

'Oh, hello!' A ginger cat curled around her legs, and she opened her eyes to stroke its soft fur. It jumped right onto her lap and settled there, as if it knew her already. She loved the warm weight of it on her lap, and it purred in response as she scratched its neck. She'd always wanted a pet, but the one time she was in a home long enough to even feel like she could dare to ask, she'd been told in no uncertain terms that it was more than enough to take care of one stray, thank you very much, and they weren't able to take on another.

'Are you Sam? I'll be with you in a second!' A voice called down from above, and Sam glanced up to see a middle-aged woman with a mad mop of greying curls leaning out of the window. She gently nudged the cat off her lap and got to her feet, her heart pounding again. She'd come all this way; she'd left her old life behind. What if Jean didn't like her? What if she couldn't do the job, after all? What if—

'There you are. Sorry. Come on in.' Jean swung open the door and beckoned her inside. 'No, not you, George! Shoo!' She made motions with her hands, and Sam tried to hide a smile as George took absolutely no notice and scurried inside.

'Typical male, does what he wants regardless of what I say,' Jean said, rolling her eyes and pushing the curls away from her face. They tumbled back again straight away. 'He does catch a mouse or two, so he has some use.'

Sam nodded, trying not to show horror on her face. Mice? 'Nice to meet you,' she said, holding out her hand. 'And thank you so much for giving me this job. I'm really excited to get started.'

Jean brushed aside her hand and folded her in a huge hug, wrapping her cushiony body around Sam's slender one. It was like being cuddled in a duvet, and despite Sam's surprise, she couldn't help feeling comforted by it.

'No handshakes here,' Jean said, pulling back. 'Right, let me show you where you're going to be sleeping, and then we can get started before the lunch rush. I know this village looks sleepy now, but give it another hour and we'll be overrun by day-trippers and walkers. There's a National Trust place nearby, too, and we get a lot of our trade from there. Come, follow me.'

Sam blinked, taking in the torrent of words, and trailed behind Jean through the pub. The whole space gleamed in the morning sun streaming in through the lead-paned windows, the polished wood shining like it was lit from inside. The old wooden floor creaked under her feet, as if singing a welcoming song, and Sam couldn't wait to get behind the huge bar, which arced out from the far wall. It was a beautiful place, and Sam could see that it had been lovingly taken care of.

'This pub has been in my family for the past century –

maybe even longer,' Jean said, as she led Sam through a door at the back and up some narrow stairs. 'And it's been in the village since the seventeenth century, although it's burned down and been rebuilt a few times!' She paused outside a door, huffing, and took a minute to catch her breath. 'Right, this is your room. It's not much, but it'll do you. You'll probably spend most of your time downstairs, anyway, like I do – even when you're not working. The people here are great, but I hope Will warned you: there's not a lot for you to do in the village.'

'That's fine by me.' Sam smiled. 'I didn't go out much, even in London.' Make that never, she thought. Her flatmates always tried to drag her to clubs, but she was too tired from working or too busy saving.

'Bathroom is down the hall to your right – you'll be sharing with me. Here's the key.' Jean dug in her pocket and handed over a keyring with two keys. 'Punters who stay have their own bathroom and rooms at the back of the ground floor. Don't worry – they can't get up here without a key. Right, I'll leave you to get your things unpacked and see you downstairs in about thirty minutes. Good to have you here.' She patted Sam on the shoulder, then went back downstairs.

Sam fit the key in the lock and swung open the door to her room, her eyes widening in surprise. With the cramped corridor, she'd expected a space as big as a broom closet, but this was huge, taking up what looked like almost half of the very top floor of the pub. And – she took in the double bed – it was all hers. She sank onto the mattress, gazing around the space in disbelief. A wardrobe was jammed under the slanted roof on one side, and on the other was a chest of drawers. A cheerful rug covered the old wooden floorboards, and a little desk and chair were slotted in beside the door. But best of all was the window, looking out to the village green and the rolling hills beyond. Sam got off the bed and jerked it open, breathing in the scent of cut-grass and greenery.

A meow made her turn, and she smiled as George pranced into her room as if he owned it, then jumped onto her bed, curled up and closed his eyes. And as she patted his soft fur, contentment echoed inside her. This might just be a stop on the way to even better things, but right now, she couldn't think of a more perfect place.

A place that actually felt like home.

NINE

RACHEL

Rachel opened the door to the tiny room her father had called his office, grimacing at the overstuffed files and boxes piled high around the space. Dust danced in the morning sun, and she pulled out a chair and sat down, wondering where to begin. There had to be something here – some evidence of work done to the house, builders who'd been on the grounds, trips away, *anything* – that could shunt Lucas off into another direction where he might actually find something productive, rather than fruitlessly probing her mother and destroying her peace when she needed it most.

Right. Where to start? Rachel opened a drawer and lifted out a stack of files, heart sinking as she realised that nothing here seemed to be in order of date, alphabet or anything else. She leafed through the papers inside, all relating to the car dealership that her father had managed. Her mother's father had owned it and made a real success out of it, expanding to the size of three car parks. Her mum and dad had met there when her grandfather had employed her father to service the cars. Her father had quickly caught the eye of her grandfather with his ambition and hard work, and soon he was selling cars on the shop floor and rising through the ranks.

When he and her mum had married, her grandfather made him manager and promised that when he retired, the business would be his – because he didn't have anyone else to give it to, her grandfather would say with a smile that even Rachel at age six knew wasn't genuine. Unlike her mother, who'd been raised in a household brimming over with luxury, her father had started out with nothing. But despite this gap in their childhoods, there was one thing they had in common: neither were close to their parents. Even though they lived nearby, Rachel had only seen her mum's parents a few times each year, and she'd never met her father's. Maybe that was why her mum and dad were so tight; they'd loved each other in a way neither of them had been loved before.

Nothing in this lot of papers would give her any answers, she thought, putting them back into the drawer and sliding out another stack. God, this was going to take forever. Why hadn't her mum cleaned out any of this? But then her mother hadn't cleaned out any of the house. It was like she was too afraid to face the fact that the man she loved was gone forever.

Rachel sighed, thinking back to that terrible day when her dad had died. Her mum had supper on the table, but her father had said he'd be home on time for once, so none of them were allowed to eat. Rachel had snuck away to phone him, telling him to come home quickly; that there was a family emergency and they needed him. Of course there hadn't been anything of the sort, she thought now, that old heavy guilt pressing down on her. She'd simply been hungry and impatient.

They'd waited and waited, and eventually her mum had caved in and let them have some toast to tide them over. They were about to bite into it when there was a knock on the door. All Rachel heard was a low voice, and then... silence. She and Victoria crept from the kitchen to the lounge to see her mother, staring like a statue, at a police officer. And then she'd dropped to the floor, rocking back and forth as if someone invisible was pummelling her, over and over. The police officer helped her up and onto the sofa, asking in a gentle voice if they should call someone. A few minutes later, Rachel's grandparents had arrived, and Rachel and her sister were bundled off with their granddad while their gran stayed with their mum.

Rachel had lain in bed beside her sobbing sister that night, unable to even cry. She didn't deserve to be sad because it was her fault their father was gone. *Hers*. She'd destroyed everything, and nothing would ever be the same again. And she'd been right: nothing *was* ever the same again. Not her family, not her mother. The only thing that had remained constant was this house, a refuge full of treasured memories that her mother still clung to.

A refuge Rachel needed to protect now with everything she had.

She slid out another folder and opened it up, heart jumping when she saw it contained documents to do with the house and the land. Could there be something here? Could she have got lucky so soon? She flipped through the papers inside, her eyebrows rising when she saw the house had been originally purchased by her grandfather the same year her parents married, before the deed was transferred to her father. She couldn't imagine her proud dad happily taking such a huge handout, but then he wouldn't have had the money to purchase a place her mother would want to live in either.

Wait, what was this? She drew a sheaf of papers from the folder and held it closer.

'The Last Will and Testament of Sean Norman' came into focus, and she pulled it out, curious what it might say, as if it could give her insight into the man she'd never really known. She scanned the legal language, noting most of her father's possessions were left to her mother, and— hang on, *what*? Her eyes bulged as she took in the words.

Her father had left Rachel the house?

She sat back in the chair, emotions battering her. Why had he done that? Why not leave it to her mother? She was the one who'd made their home what it was. It was her sphere, the place where she'd spent her days caring for her family. She loved this house – that was the reason Rachel was so desperate now to keep this discovery from her. Rachel's father would have known how much she loved it. Why would he give it to his daughter? And why just to her and not to Victoria, as well?

Rachel cringed, picturing her mother reading this in those raw, bleak days following the death. It would have been a huge blow, having that security taken away from her, even if it had been passed to someone close. Rachel tilted her head, wondering if *that* was why her mum pulled back after the death... why she still held herself at a distance. But no – she couldn't resent Rachel for that; wouldn't let that stand between her and her child at such a difficult time. Would she?

Anyway, she must have known, surely. It couldn't have been a surprise. Rachel's father held the power in their marriage, but even he wouldn't do something so huge without his wife's approval – especially since her own father had bought the property. Perhaps they'd been thinking of the future; how her mum would move to a smaller place if her husband died, and they'd thought that by then, Rachel might have a family of her own to move in here? They never could have imagined such a terrible accident could change their lives so early on. Warmth swept over Rachel that her parents had thought of her; had planned for her future like this. They must have something else planned for Victoria.

But why had her mother never told Rachel? Why had she kept this from her daughter all of these years? Why had she buried this will in an avalanche of papers, where the chances of anyone finding it were slim to none? Was she worried, perhaps, that Rachel would take the house away from her once she got older, once she did have that family of her own? Rachel could understand why her mum would want to stay in the property after her husband's death; the memories were all she had left. But now that she was about to die... why would she keep this secret? Did she not want Rachel to have this house at all? Yes, there'd been distance between them, but...

Rachel gulped in air, trying to breathe as that knot tightened, pulling at her insides. Maybe her mother didn't want her to have the house because... she swallowed, the thought forming in her head. Because her mother did blame her, after all. Maybe Rachel hadn't been wrong as a child – maybe she *had* interpreted her mother's distance correctly. Maybe, in the painful aftermath, Rachel had become a lightning rod for her mother's anger and pain. Maybe that was why her mum had never made much of an effort to cross the barrier Rachel had put between them: because she couldn't bear to look at the cause of her husband's death.

And now, even though her grief may have subsided and she may not even still feel that way, those feelings remained buried inside, preventing her from moving past them – in the same way Rachel's painful memories had held her back.

Yet, Rachel *had* finally managed to reach out, and though she could feel them tugging at her now, she wasn't going to let those long-held emotions stop her. If she could conquer the past, her mother could too. But perhaps being here wasn't enough. Rachel understood how deep those feelings could go. She needed something more – something big – to break through. Something to show her mum how much she really loved her.

The house.

Rachel put the will down on the desk. Whatever the decision that had been made in the past, this place should be her mother's now. Life had wrenched control from her mum's grasp – *love* from her grasp – and if Rachel could give her back a tiny piece of security in the time that remained, then that was what she'd do.

She picked up another heavy file, determination flooding through her. Now, she had to find something to stop this house and all it represented from being destroyed.

TEN

RACHEL

The ring of Rachel's mobile interrupted her thoughts as she rummaged through yet another drawer in her father's office. She glanced at the screen, guilt flooding through her: it was Mo, and it was almost ten o'clock. She'd missed the kids' bedtimes by a longshot. She hadn't even thought of the kids' bedtimes, actually. Back at home, sometimes, it seemed like the whole world revolved around getting them to sleep at a decent time. The next day would be hell if they were tired. But here that world felt so far away, in another place and time. All she was focused on was her mother – and finding something before Lucas returned.

Her mum had spent all day in bed, sitting up long enough to pick at the roast chicken and potatoes Rachel had prepared. Rachel had sat beside her, watching as she ate in silence and waiting for the right moment to bring up the will. But every time Rachel started talking, her mother's eyes would sink closed, and even though Rachel could tell she wasn't asleep, she was obviously exhausted. Rachel would creep from the room and resume her search in the office, desperately combing through document after document. Her eyes were gritty and dry from scanning so many papers, and her arms and back ached from shunting around endless boxes. But so far, she'd found nothing.

'Everything okay there?' Mo asked when she picked up the video call. She could see the concern in his dark brown eyes, the lines etched on his forehead whenever he was worried. 'The kids wanted to call and say goodnight, but I told them you'd ring when you could. I know you have a lot going on right now.'

Rachel nodded gratefully, thoughts turning to her family. She'd been so impressed with how quickly Mo had taken over her role, shepherding the children off to school with little apparent drama. It made her wonder why it took so much time and headspace with her. Because she let it, she answered herself. Because she *needed* it to – needed to feel wanted; loved. Because she never wanted to feel that loneliness again.

'Mum's still pretty out of it after her fall,' she said, guilt swamping her once more as she compared the vibrant woman when she'd arrived with the listless one now lying in bed. She'd yet to even get up again. 'The house is a mess, and the police keep badgering me to talk to Mum.' She swallowed, realising she hadn't updated Mo on the latest news. She almost didn't want to. Mo was her safe place, and this... Rachel cleared her throat. 'The body was put in the wall while Mum and Dad were living here.'

'Shit.' Mo's voice was low. 'So does that mean... does that mean they suspect your *parents*?'

'No.' The word emerged like gunfire. 'Lucas – the police officer – knows my family. He knows neither Mum nor Dad could be involved in anything like this. But he wants to talk to Mum to see what she can tell him about that time, and there's no way I can let him do that. Finding out something like that happened while she was here would be way too much.' She shook her head. 'I've been searching through my father's old papers to see if my parents went away, or if there was any building work or renovations around that time. If they were having work done on the house, it makes sense a builder might have done this. Maybe that will give Lucas the lead he needs. And Mo...' She paused. 'You'll never guess what I found.' She still couldn't believe it herself.

'What?'

'I came across my father's will. I'd never seen it before. And he left me this house. This whole place... it's mine.'

'Wow.' Mo gaped at her, and she could almost see the wheels in his brain turning as he absorbed the news. 'And your mum never said anything? Never even mentioned it?' She could hear the incredulity in his voice, and she bit her lip. She knew it was hard to grasp, but she couldn't tell him why. She couldn't say the words that had been ringing inside her head since she was young – the words that might explain her mother's distance too. The words she'd never told him, and the part of her heart that was wrapped in darkness, away from him.

It was my fault. I thought it was my fault. And Mum thought so too.

'No.' Rachel cleared her throat. 'But I reckon it was hard for her to even talk about. She never mentions Dad.'

'Maybe. But whatever the reason, this is amazing news.' Mo's face lit up with excitement. 'For us; for the family. The house is huge, isn't it? I mean, I haven't been for a while, but I remember the plot was massive.'

Rachel stared into her husband's eyes. Oh, God. She'd been so caught up in what this meant for her and her mother that she hadn't even thought of her own family. A bigger place, more space... but surely Mo wouldn't want to *move* here? This was miles from their life in central London.

'I know we don't want to live that far out,' he continued. 'But it should fetch a decent price once you sell it, right? That will give us enough for a good deposit on a proper place. The kids could each have their own room, and you could have an office for working from home. We could even have a bit of a garden.'

Rachel held his gaze, her heart sinking as his words tumbled over her.

'This is our chance to give the kids a place they can stretch out in; a place they can really call their own,' Mo was saying. 'A real house, in a great area, with even better schools. We make good salaries, but the way prices are, we may never be able to give them that.'

Rachel breathed in, thoughts swirling through her head. Mo was right. The money she got from selling her mum's house would buy the kind of place in London that they could have only dreamed of before. It *would* provide her family with a brighter future, and giving it to her mum might take that away. With their shaky relationship, there was every chance her mother would will the house entirely to Victoria now, not Rachel. And even if she did decide to include Rachel and leave the place to both her daughters, that sum of money wouldn't be enough to upgrade in the hot London market, as ridiculous as it seemed.

But how could she live in a place knowing all along she'd passed up the opportunity to really break through to her mum? How could she hug her own children each night knowing she could have done more to show her love and she'd chosen not to?

'Look, I know it's a lot to take in right now,' Mo said when she didn't respond. 'I understand. Take some time; absorb it all. We love you. I love you. We're here for you.' There was a sound in the background, and he turned away. 'Ryan's managed to spill water down his pyjamas,' he said, when he came back. 'I'd better go. Love you.'

'I love you too,' she said, even though the screen was now black. Tears filled her eyes, and she swiped them away as she hung up. She missed him so much. How would he respond when she told him she was giving the house to her mother?

How could he even begin to understand when she'd never told him the real reason for their distance in the first place?

His ignorance had always been a godsend. It had let her keep that darkness pushed down inside; let her live in light. But now, for the first time, the space between her two worlds wasn't a comfort.

It felt like a burden – like one more heavy weight she had to carry.

ELEVEN

SAM

July 1985

'A bottle of Krug? Let me get that for you straight away.' Sam smiled at the man in front of her, then reached into the glass-fronted refrigerator at the back of the bar and took out the dewy bottle. Even after two months, she couldn't believe how different the customers at this pub were to the last. Instead of cheap lager, here they were more apt to order pricey glasses of Chardonnay or bottles of champagne whose cost made her eyes water. When Jean had first showed her the stock, Sam had privately thought the woman was delusional. Who would order one of these to sit and drink at a country pub, even one as nice as this? But it turned out that this wasn't just any country pub. This was the place for the wealthy who lived in huge houses dotted around the hills to go on a weekend – or even a weekday – when they wanted excellent food in a casual place.

As manager, Sam had quickly got to know the regulars and their quirks: where they liked to sit, how they wanted their drink poured, and the very moment to lay a menu in front of them to fill up their stomachs. Jean would shake her head, saying that since Sam started here, the kitchen profits had almost doubled. Sam had laughed, thinking that whether you were in South London or the country, the signs of a drunk person were still the same, and the sooner you headed them off with a good meal, the better they'd fare the next day – and the happier they'd be.

Not that these punters would ever cause problems the way those in her old pub would, of course. They were the ideal customers, even saying 'please' and 'thank you', words that almost didn't exist in her last place. And when they got a little tipsy, they simply took themselves off home without any worry, asking her to call the local taxi service (one lone man with a beat-up car) and not even attempting to drive. They knew Jean would kill them, and everyone here – no matter how rich – seemed to look up to her. And as Jean's new hire, they had all taken her under their wing. A creepy pest like Alex wouldn't last a second here; he'd be chucked out by the other customers before she could even say 'no'. One woman had even brought in a blanket she'd crocheted to make Sam's new room 'nice and cosy'. That feeling of home when she'd first arrived had only got stronger.

'Excuse me.'

Sam swivelled from where she was opening up yet another bottle of champagne. 'Yes? What can I get you?' Despite the long list of drinks she had yet to pour for people waiting at the bar, she couldn't help pausing to take in the man in front of her. God, he was handsome. His long dark hair curled gently over the collar of his white shirt, and a dark-blue tie knotted around his neck made his eyes look even bluer. She stared, feeling something twist inside her – something like longing, maybe, desire. Something she'd never felt before.

'Could we have a bottle of your finest champagne, please?'

Her eyebrows rose. Finest champagne? With all the stock they had on hand, that would cost an absolute fortune. This man must be very successful as well as handsome. 'Of course,' she said, turning to get it for him. She made a mental note to order another bottle from the suppliers.

'We're celebrating today,' he said, as if he'd heard her thoughts. 'I got a promotion!' He gestured towards a nearby table, where another man wearing an expensive-looking suit was staring at his beeper.

She smiled at his excitement. It was nice to see someone who cared about their work, and it must be a very big promotion indeed if he could afford that champagne. She expertly popped the cork, poured two glasses, and set the bottle in a metal jug full of ice. She hadn't a clue what those were until Jean had shown her; they'd only sold champagne by the glass at her old place. Actually, scratch that, they'd only had cheap Cava. 'Here you are.'

'Thank you.' He smiled, and she felt her cheeks reddening. Don't be ridiculous, she told herself. Whoever this man was, like the rest of the clientele here, he saw her as a prop at the bar to serve him, nothing more.

He went over to the table and sat down with the man. She tried to busy herself with other customers, but her gaze kept being drawn back towards him. She watched him from the corner of her eye, impressed with his open and friendly laugh and the way he made sure to keep topping up the older man's glass. In her short time here, Sam had witnessed many people 'sharing' a bottle, which often consisted of one person guzzling most of it while the other sipped their drink. You could tell a lot about a person by how they rationed out a bottle, and she could see that this man was kind and generous. His eyes caught hers and she yanked her gaze away, her cheeks heating up once more. God!

She forced herself not to look his way again, telling herself that not only was she being ridiculous, she was also being very unprofessional. A true manager didn't go ga-ga over the customers, although she couldn't help remembering that was how Will had met his boyfriend. Still, this wasn't that pub – far from it, thank goodness. And when she glanced back again, the man and his friend were gone.

That was fine, she told herself through the haze of disappointment as she cleared away the empty glasses and bottle. That was more than fine. He was probably married – idiot that she was, she hadn't even thought to look for a ring. Successful men his age usually had a wife. She hadn't spotted a single man in this area since she'd arrived. Why would she bother trying? She didn't want a boyfriend. Not now. And that man would be bored by her in a second anyway. What would they talk about: how to pour the perfect pint? She needed to wait until she had more qualifications, more money, more... whatever it was that would make her the equal of someone like him.

'Okay?' Jean appeared behind her, and Sam nodded. 'You can knock off now, if you like. You've been here since ten! Go, have a rest and you can come back down for the supper rush.'

'All right.' Sam pushed through the bar and up the stairs to the top of the pub, then went into her room and lay down on her bed. George curled around her, and she patted his head, smiling as she thought that he was all she needed.

Even so, the man's face lingered.

TWELVE

RACHEL

Rachel awoke the next morning to the ding of her mobile. Blinking, she pushed her hair from her face and grabbed the phone. Mo had sent three WhatsApps already. Was there a crisis with the kids? She jolted awake when she spotted the time: 8.30 a.m. How could she have slept for so long? Yes, she'd been up most of the night sorting through her father's files, but she hadn't yet finished, and so far, she hadn't found a thing. Already a day had passed since Lucas had said she couldn't keep her mother from him forever, and given that look of determination on his face and the pending promotion, she knew he'd be trying his best to come up with something to get her to talk.

Rachel's heart dropped as she scanned the messages: they were all property listings. Unable to stop herself, she clicked on one of the links. A four-bedroom terraced house filled the screen, in a 'prime location with a huge back garden and a sunny, bright kitchen'. It was a dream house – the sort of thing she and Mo had aimed for, back in the day before they had kids... and before the property market went crazy.

Mo was right, she thought, guilt weaving into her. This *was* their chance. It might be the only chance they'd ever get. And she was giving it away on a hunch – a hope – of making things better with her mum.

Because it was just that, wasn't it: a hunch? She didn't really know why her mum had never told her about the house. And maybe she'd been wrong about the lingering blame. Maybe spending all this time here had brought back too many memories – maybe those ties were pulling her back into the past, no matter how hard she tried to escape. Maybe her mother *did* want Rachel to have the house and was staying quiet for a reason Rachel didn't know.

Maybe Rachel should give them more time together before making any final decisions. It was the least she could do for Mo – and for her family.

Rachel cocked her head as the low murmur of her mum's voice filtered through the air. Who could she be talking to so early in the morning? At least she was awake, and this was more words from her than Rachel had heard since her fall.

'Mum?' Rachel got out of bed and padded down the corridor to her mother's bedroom. 'Everything okay?'

Her mother put down the phone and pulled the covers up around her. 'Fine. I'm fine. I was just leaving a message for Victoria. I haven't heard from her since she left.'

'She'll be back soon, Mum,' Rachel said, remembering that she still hadn't filled her sister in on the body in the wall. She sat down on the bed and patted her mother's arm awkwardly.

But her mother didn't even seem to notice she was there. Instead, she turned to gaze at a photo on her bedside table. It was a picture of Rachel's parents standing in front of the house, soon after they'd moved in. It had lived by the bedside for years while her father had been alive, but Rachel realised she hadn't seen it for ages. Her mum must have brought it out again recently.

Her parents looked so young, she thought, staring down at their proud smiles in front of their new family home. They'd adored each other, and they must have been so excited for their future together; to grow their family and fill this place with love and laughter. Instead... Rachel breathed in sharply, the guilt ricocheting inside like a bullet with spikes. Instead, her father had died all alone on a country road, and her mother had been left nothing but memories.

'I saw Dad's will,' Rachel said, the words flying out of her. 'I know the house was left to me.' Her mother swung towards her, her eyes widening. 'But it's yours, Mum,' Rachel continued quickly before her mother could say a word. 'It should never have been mine. Not so soon.' Her stomach tightened with that knot inside, but she forced the words out. 'I can't change the past. I can't change...' She swallowed, her voice going low. 'I can't change what happened. I can't bring Dad back, but I can give you this. Mum, I need to give you this.' She bit her lip, thinking of Mo; thinking of her family. He'd be upset. He wouldn't understand, but she had to do this.

Rachel stared down at her mother, her heart beating fast as she waited for a response. For her to say something, anything. Anything that showed she understood her daughter was sorry; that she wanted to do all she could to make up for the past. But her mum was frozen, still locked away somewhere Rachel couldn't reach. And as the silence stretched, the empty space inside of Rachel gaped even wider. She *had* to get through.

'Mum, the house is yours,' Rachel said even louder, but her mother still didn't move. Rachel drew in a breath, her mind spinning. Maybe she worried that Rachel was upset that she'd never told her? 'And I'm not angry. I get why you didn't say anything,' Rachel went on. 'I understand. I—'

'What were you doing, going through his papers?'

Rachel jerked. Of all the things she'd thought her mother might say, she hadn't imagined that. 'I'm sorry. I...' She swallowed, trying to think of something plausible. 'I wanted to tidy things up,' she finished lamely.

'Don't touch his things.' Her mother's voice trembled. 'Don't do that again.' Her face tightened as if she was in pain, and Rachel nodded.

'Don't worry, Mum,' she said slowly. 'Things will stay the same from now on, I promise. Nothing will upset Dad's things; Dad's memories. I know how important that is to you.' Seeing her mother's reaction now made her even more certain she was doing the right thing. 'I'm going to speak to a lawyer and get the necessary documents drawn up, and then the house and everything in it will be yours. No one will change a thing.'

Her mother's eyes burned through her, then she turned and picked up the photo by the bed, lifting it closer to her face with unsteady hands. 'The house,' she said in a whisper, so quiet that Rachel barely heard her. Then her whole body started shaking, as if years of tension had been released... as if she could finally let go.

'It is yours now,' Rachel said, gripping onto her mother's hand. 'Yours, and no one else's. You deserve this, Mum.' And even though her mother stayed quiet, Rachel could feel how much this meant to her mother; feel the intensity of her emotion. Maybe she hadn't said many words, but this *was* something; something that showed Rachel had reached her. They sat in silence for a few more minutes until her mum's eyes drifted closed.

Rachel's phone pinged again, and guilt swept through her as Mo sent another listing. She should tell him what she'd done before he got his hopes any higher, but right now she needed to finish sorting through her father's papers before Lucas turned up again.

And maybe she wouldn't have to tell him, she thought, hope growing as she glanced down at her hand entwined with her mother's. Maybe once the distance between them had diminished, her mum would decide this house should be Rachel's again, after all – as she and Rachel's father must have agreed when the will was drawn up. Maybe they could return to that place once more, before this had all gone wrong.

A place that would let Rachel bring together the family she had now and the family she'd grown up with, just like she'd envisioned when all of this had begun.

THIRTEEN

RACHEL

Rachel ripped open the last box in her father's office, every muscle aching with exhaustion. Her mother may not have wanted her to disturb her father's papers, but she had no idea what was at stake. Rachel had been through everything now but one final box, and apart from the deed to the house and the will, all of the documents had either been old bills, household accounts, warranties, or endless paperwork to do with her father's business. And – her heart sank as she sifted through the contents – these papers looked exactly the same. She was about to close the box and shove it into the corner when a yellowed piece of old-school computer paper poked out of the stack of documents she was holding. She squinted at the dot matrix print. What was that? Her eyes widened as she took in the text. It was an itinerary: a flight itinerary for her mother, for a trip from London to Lyon, where her own parents had a holiday home.

Heart pounding, Rachel looked at the date, a slow smile spreading when she saw the numbers: 1986. Bingo! Granted, this only showed her mum had been away for a few weeks in December and Lucas hadn't said the exact date on that bus ticket he'd found on the body, but this was something. This was a chance, however small, that her mother might not have been here when the body was hidden. And if she wasn't here, then she couldn't have seen anything helpful, like Lucas had said. For God's sake, she hadn't even been in the country!

Rachel glanced through the itinerary again, noticing neither she nor her father were listed anywhere. Her father might have been too busy at work in the run-up to Christmas to travel, but surely her mum wouldn't have taken off without her? She would have been very young at the time. But then as an infant, she would have travelled on her mother's lap. She wouldn't have had a separate ticket anyway. It was a little odd that her mother had wanted to visit her parents, given they'd never been close, but Rachel remembered how having a baby made any new mother long for her own. She'd felt the same, wanting to show off her baby and yet feeling like a child in need of her mum's embrace.

She clutched the paper in her hand and went down the corridor to check on her mother before calling Lucas to tell him what she'd found. Her mum was curled into the blankets, the photo askew on the bedside table. Rachel reached over and straightened it, remembering how her mother had shaken with emotion after Rachel said the house was hers. They still hadn't exchanged many words since, but it didn't matter. It was a first step – an important one – and just knowing they might be starting to come together was everything. And now Rachel might have found the evidence she needed to make sure nothing would ruin that. Hopefully, she'd done something right at last.

A bang on the door interrupted her thoughts and she scuttled down the stairs, praying the noise hadn't awoken her mother. Her heart lifted as she spotted Lucas. Perfect timing! She couldn't wait to show him what she'd uncovered. She cracked the door open, adrenaline pumping through her. Please God, may this help. *Please.*

'I was about to call you. I wanted to show you this.' She handed him over the itinerary, watching his face carefully as he took it in. 'It says my mum wasn't here for the first few weeks in December 1986,' she said. 'I don't know when the body was put here, but if it was during that time, my mother wasn't around. She wouldn't know anything about what happened.' Rachel crossed her fingers, barely breathing. Maybe there wasn't a big chance the dates matched, but at least there *was* a chance.

Lucas nodded, then glanced up at her. 'Can I keep this?' he asked.

'Of course.' Rachel watched as he carefully folded it and put it into a front pocket. 'So... is the itinerary important, then?' Her heart was beating so loudly she could barely hear her words.

Lucas met her eyes. 'It's important, yes. We'll need to take closer look, but it does appear that your mother wasn't here.'

Rachel felt everything inside her loosen as the tension drained away. She gulped in air, feeling like she could breathe for the first time since she'd arrived. She *had* done something right. She and her mother could be left in peace. At last.

'But Rach...'

She shook her head. She didn't want to hear buts. There was nothing more he could say now. It was time for him to go; time to leave them alone. She went to close the door, but Lucas was holding it open.

'Rach, one minute. I know you believe your mum doesn't know anything,' he began. 'But while she may not have witnessed what happened to the victim or how the body was hidden, she may still be able to give us some important information.'

'What?' Rachel shook her head again. 'How? You just said she wasn't here.' God, why couldn't he let it *go*?

'We managed to find out more about the victim.' Lucas's face softened. 'Forensics are still working, but they have been able to determine the victim was a female, very likely in her early twenties.'

Rachel's heart twisted. A woman in her early twenties. She'd been so young. It was tragic, but to think that her mother might know anything...

'They were able to find something on the T-shirt she was wearing. It was the name of a pub, like the kind of shirt you'd wear for a uniform. The Red Lion, it said.'

Rachel stared, wondering where this was going.

'Our team created an e-fit from the remains,' he went on. 'They're not always accurate, but sometimes they can be useful. I took it to every pub in the area called the Red Lion. Well, you know how many pubs are called Red Lion around here?' He let out a breath. 'Countless. But I found one that would have been along the bus route the victim took, so it made sense to go there first. It was so long ago, but I figured there was a chance the owner might still be there, and maybe they'd remember something. An employee who had suddenly disappeared, or one who'd run off.'

Rachel was silent, waiting for him to continue.

'But when I went inside, the place had a new owner and was undergoing a refurbishment. It had been closed for years, and since he bought the place at an auction, he wasn't sure who the owner had been. I showed him the e-fit, but of course he had no idea since he'd not long bought the place. But he did say there was a whole load of photos he'd found in a back room – pictures of staff with customers, from all different years – and I was welcome to go through them if I liked. And...' Lucas blinked. 'And I think I found her. She's a dead ringer for the e-fit, and she's around the right age. The timestamp on the photo is the right time too. The same year as the bus ticket we found.'

'Okay,' Rachel said slowly. 'So you found a woman who

looks like the e-fit and who worked at the same pub as the victim. That doesn't prove it *is* the victim, though. And what does any of this have to do with my mother?'

Lucas held her gaze. 'This woman – she knew your father. Knew him very well, by the looks of things.'

'She knew my father?' Rachel took a step back, as if she could move away from the words. The victim had known her dad... *very well*? Did Lucas mean... He couldn't. Her father loved her mother. He'd never do anything like that to her. 'No. You're wrong. You must be wrong.'

Lucas didn't respond. Instead, he reached into his jacket and drew out a photo, then handed it over to her, watching her closely.

Rachel caught her breath as she stared down at the image. It was her dad – a much younger version, with longer hair and slimmer frame, but undeniably him – with his arms around a young woman. It wasn't a friendly embrace: she was pulled tightly against him, her lips pressed firmly on his. Rachel stifled a cry as she tried to take it in. Lucas was right. They were more than friends. God, she couldn't believe it. She'd always thought her parents were more in love than anyone she'd ever seen; that her dad would do anything for her mum.

How could her father do this? And who was this woman?

Rachel gazed at the photo, sadness, confusion and anger stirring inside. *Could* this be the woman in the wall? The links between the two seemed too many to ignore, especially since she'd known Rachel's father. A chill washed over her, and she met Lucas's eyes again. Rachel's mother had been away with her at the time. Maybe he'd had this woman over, and— *no*. Perhaps he'd had an affair, but he wasn't a murderer. For God's sake, he could barely stand the sight of blood. She remembered how Victoria had tripped over once and split her lip, blood pouring down her face. Her dad had taken one look, turned white and nearly fainted. He couldn't have done anything as horrific as this. He *couldn't* have. If her mother had been in France and he'd been at work for long stretches, it would be easy for someone else to have access to the house during the day. Builders, like Lucas had suggested, or...

'Your father is on the system from a former offence. He stole a motorbike and went joyriding, back when he was eighteen,' Lucas explained. 'From the photo we have on file, I thought I recognised your father in the pub picture. But the file photo was so old that I couldn't be certain.'

Rachel raised an eyebrow. Her father had stolen a motorbike? It wasn't that hard to believe, actually. He always said he'd been obsessed since he was young, and he wouldn't have had the money to buy one back then. It went a long way towards explaining why he'd purchased so many when he did have the money.

'So I checked the newspaper archives on the off chance there might be a more recent photo,' Lucas continued, 'and up popped a picture from when your father got a promotion at his business. I was sure it was him then.'

'Okay.' Rachel's voice trembled. 'Maybe he did know this woman.' She still couldn't believe it. 'But this doesn't prove he killed her. Not even close.'

Lucas nodded. 'You're right, this isn't conclusive evidence, but now we know that your father had a connection with the victim.' He touched Rachel's arm again. 'And the fact that she ended up here, well... You can understand why it's even more important that I speak to your mum. Maybe she was away when the body was hidden, but any background information she can give us might be vital. Your mother might recognise this woman. She could have been a family friend, or she might have lived in the area. Perhaps your mum knew of your father's—' He cut himself off at the look on Rachel's face. 'I don't want to upset her. You know that, but don't you think the victim's family deserves to know what happened to their loved one?'

Rachel breathed in. Of course they did, but she wasn't going to let her mum pay the price for someone else's evil. And if talking to her mother before was out of the question, now it was even more so. This wouldn't only ruin the house she'd held so dear; her place of shelter. This would ruin her *life*, both past and present. It would taint every memory of the man she'd worshipped, and Rachel had just promised to protect those memories. Even if her father hadn't been involved in the victim's death – even if Rachel knew her mother would never believe he could have been – finding out he'd been with another woman would devastate her.

Rachel had already taken her father away; cut his future short. She'd destroyed her mum's world then, and she wasn't about to again. Not now, not *ever*. They'd only started coming together, and there wouldn't be time to right it once more. Time was running short as it was.

'No.' Rachel shook her head. 'I can't let you. You know how unstable her health is at the moment. This news... *No*.' She stepped back against the door, as if she could block him. She *would* block him, if she had to.

But Lucas didn't seem to hear her. Instead, he moved towards her, and anger leapt inside. What didn't he understand?

'Lucas, you need to go,' Rachel said, the anger making her voice loud and strong now. 'Leave us alone.' She met his eyes, and for a second, she thought he would acquiesce. Then his face twisted.

'I didn't want to do this,' he said, sighing. 'I didn't want to have to. But you're not leaving me much choice.'

Do what? Rachel swallowed. *Was* there a way he could make her mum talk? No, she thought, standing her ground. Her mother wasn't a suspect. She wasn't even a witness. But even as Rachel told herself that, a seed of fear was growing inside.

'This photo.' Lucas tapped it, and she looked down, then

wrenched her eyes away. She didn't want to see that. 'If you won't let me speak to your mother, then I'll be forced to release it to the media to see if any of the public can come forward to identify this woman. To see if anyone knows anything.' He paused. 'But like I said, I don't want to do that, Rach. I'd rather talk to your mother and see what she can tell us first.'

Rachel tilted her head, trying to grasp his words. Was he actually *blackmailing* her? If she didn't let him talk to her mother, he'd release the photo to the media to be splashed across newspapers and screens? Her mother would be publicly humiliated, and everyone would know about the body that had been found here. It was a miracle they hadn't already.

'I've been very careful to keep things under wraps for you guys. I've told everyone to keep quiet about this, so we wouldn't upset you or your mum,' Lucas said, as if hearing her thoughts. 'But if you won't let us talk to her, then I won't have a choice. And you can bet it will get crazy. People love a good cold case, and when they see that photo of the woman with your father...'

Rachel stayed silent, desperately trying to think of a way out of this. She couldn't let her mother talk to Lucas and find out about her father. And she couldn't let Lucas release that photo to the media either. He was right: the whole place would be awash with rumours and gossip, and the way her mother was glued to the TV, she'd be sure to see it.

'Please, Rach. Let me talk to her.'

She barely even heard him as her mind whirled. What could she do? Because she had to do something. Maybe... Rachel bit her lip as an idea filtered in. Maybe she could take her mother somewhere away from here? Somewhere no one knew who she was; somewhere without internet or TV. They were under no legal obligation to stay in this house, after all – or to tell Lucas where they were going. He could release whatever he wanted and it wouldn't matter because her mother would never see it. It wouldn't touch her in her final days. Rachel would save her memories; save her love.

Save any chance of *their* love reaching the other again.

'Look, I know it's hard,' Lucas was saying. 'And I'm sorry. I really am.' His face softened into the boy she remembered. 'The boss will kill me, but why don't I give you some time – time to talk to your mother first and tell her what's been going on. She's going to find out anyway, so surely it's better coming from you, right?' He waited for her to agree, but there was no way she could. 'Call me when you've told her, and I'll come round. I'll tell the team to hold off on contacting the media until lunchtime. That's as much as I can do. And Rach, if I don't hear from you, then... I can't stop this story, you understand? This isn't my call.' He waited once more, but she still didn't speak.

'I'll talk to you later, then,' he said.

Rachel nodded, although she knew that even in a million years, she wouldn't tell her mother. She closed the door, then sank into a chair. Her head throbbed, but she had no time to relax. She may have found evidence her mum hadn't been here when that woman was hidden, but she still hadn't stopped the nightmare from closing in. She had to find a place for her and her mother to stay, far away from all of this.

And she had to do it fast, before everything came crashing down.

Again.

FOURTEEN

SAM

July 1985

'Why don't you go to bed,' Sam said to Jean as she wiped down the counter. It was a Monday night, just past nine, and the pub was practically empty. Outside, rain lashed down from the dark sky, and branches tapped against the windows. It was more like November than July, and only the hardiest – or hungriest – person would venture out tonight. 'I'll tidy up everything here.'

'You're a star,' Jean said, giving Sam one of her special hugs that Sam had come to know and love. 'I owe Will more pints than I can pull for recommending you to me. You've fit in so well. I'm lucky to have you.'

Sam smiled, warmth flooding through her. She was the one who was lucky, though. This was the first place she truly felt she belonged, and the longer she stayed, the more she loved it. George the cat had practically adopted her, and Jean was warm and affectionate. Sam loved the tiny village with the church bells that jarred you out of bed every Sunday, the green where the primary school held their PE classes, and the long walks over paths white from chalk where the air was tinged with the scent of smoke. It was like a dream. She closed her eyes for a second, an image flashing into her mind: her, clutching the hands of two dark-haired children as they ran down the path, towards a man with dark hair and blue eyes, and—

The creak of the pub door opening jerked her back to reality. She sighed, hoping it wasn't a big crowd of people who'd want to stay for hours that she'd have to gently coax to leave.

'What can I...' Her voice trailed off as she took in the man before her, a face from her past that she'd almost forgotten in her months here. He seemed so out of place that it took her a second to conjure his name. '*Alex.*' What was he doing here? She swiped the counter, trying to cover up the fear circling inside. She was alone. Jean was upstairs, but she'd never hear Sam shout if she needed to. Hopefully, she wouldn't have to.

'So you remember me, huh?' He leaned against the bar, so close that she could smell the cigarettes on his breath. His sweatshirt was smeared with dirt and his neck was speckled with flecks of paint.

'Are you working nearby?' she asked, remembering he was a painter and decorator. Maybe that was why he was in the Chilterns. It was miles from his usual stomping ground in London.

'Working nearby?' He ran a hand through greasy hair, and she tried not to recoil. 'No, not at all. I came to see you.' He leaned even closer, and she took a step back. He'd come all of this way to see her? The fear grew inside her.

'But how did you know I was here?' she asked, willing her voice to stay calm.

'Talked to one of your old flatmates,' he said. 'Took me a while to get it out of her or I would have been here sooner. Think she only told me because she got tired of me hanging around.'

Oh, God. Her poor flatmates. Sam breathed in, her pulse picking up pace as she pictured him 'hanging around' outside her flat all of this time. That wasn't normal. That wasn't normal at all. She eyed the phone on the other end of the bar, wondering how quickly she could get to it if she needed to.

'You never told me you were leaving,' he said, wagging a finger in her face. 'You should have let me know.' He came around the bar to where she was, and she backed away, her heart pounding. 'But it doesn't matter. I'm here now, and we can pick up where we left off.' He took her arm and she tried to wrench away, but he was holding her too firmly this time.

'Let go of me!' she yelled, but he was drawing her closer despite her struggling. She tried to push him away, swinging her torso back and forth, and—

'Get off her!' A shout came from behind her and a fist flashed by, striking Alex in the face and sending him flying in the opposite direction. He tumbled to the floor and Sam spun around, her jaw dropping when she saw who it was: the handsome man with dark hair and blue eyes; the man she'd kept an eye out for weeks. And now he was here. He was here, and he'd saved her.

He went over to Alex, then dragged him to his feet and away from the bar. Already, Sam could see Alex's eye swelling shut. That must have been quite a hit, and while normally she hated violence, she was grateful now. 'Get out,' the man said to Alex through gritted teeth. 'Get out, and don't come back. Don't bother her again.' He gave Alex a push towards the door, and Alex stumbled over to it. A minute later, he was gone, and Sam put a hand to her chest and collapsed against the bar, able to breathe again.

'You okay?' the man asked. He grimaced and flexed his hand. 'I haven't done that for a while. I forgot how much it hurts.'

'Let me get you some ice.' Her hands trembled as she scooped some ice from the freezer and wrapped it in a towel. 'Thank you so much. I don't know what I would have done if you hadn't come in.' She passed him the towel, noticing for the first time that his hair was sopping wet. He was wearing sodden jeans and a leather jacket that looked as if it had been through the wars. Up close, he smelt like wet leather and cologne. 'Here, sit by the fire.' Even though it was technically still summer, they'd lit the fire earlier that evening to ward off the damp chill in the air.

She pulled a chair in front of the grate and settled him into it. The pub was empty except for the two of them, but it didn't feel threatening any longer. Somehow his very presence calmed her nerves.

She cleared her throat. 'Would you like a cup of tea?'

'I'd love one, thank you. Then why don't you come have a seat here with me? You need a breather after that, I can imagine.'

She nodded. 'You're right about that.' She went into the kitchen and clicked on the kettle, using the extra time to absorb what had happened. A man from her nightmares had tried to hurt her, but then the man she'd been dreaming of had scared him away. It was like something from a Mills & Boon novel. But it wasn't a novel, she told herself, and this man would have done the same for anyone. She wasn't anything special. She carried the hot tea over, then pulled up a chair beside him. The fire warmed her arms, the golden light creating a glow around them. They sat in silence for a few minutes, and she felt peace wash over her, rinsing away any remnants of the fear she'd felt with Alex.

'I'll finish this and leave you in peace,' the man said. 'You probably want to close up now.'

She shook her head. 'Please, take your time. I'm so glad you came in when you did.' She met his eyes and smiled, that same strange feeling curling through her stomach. 'I can't say thanks enough.'

He slid off his leather jacket, draping it over the back of the chair, and she tried not to look at his solid arms and torso. 'I was on my way home on my motorcycle, but the weather was too bad to keep going. I could barely see the road in front of me. I was driving through, and I remembered this pub and how welcoming it is.' Her cheeks flushed. 'I thought it might be a good place to come in and dry off a bit, and hope that maybe the weather would let up.' He grimaced at the branches now slamming against the window. 'But I think it might be getting worse, by the looks of things.' He turned to face her. 'I'm Sean, by the way.' He held out a hand, and she couldn't stop herself from glancing at his ring finger. No wedding band! Not that it mattered, she told herself. She *wasn't* looking.

'Sam.' As his fingers closed around hers, a shock of desire went through her, surprising her with its force. It was like an electric current, jolting every nerve-end, and she reminded herself once more that this wasn't romantic fiction. But with the glowing fire, the empty pub, the storm outside and the man next to her, it felt exactly that.

'Would you like some whisky in your tea to warm you up?' she asked, remembering how one of her foster parents had always slogged whisky into whatever hot drink he was holding at the time, saying how it warmed you from the inside out. With the heating off most of the time and the whole place freezing, Sam had thought it made sense. It was only when she got older that she realised he'd been an alcoholic, and that was the reason he'd fallen down the stairs one night and Sam had been bundled away.

But that was behind her now, she told herself as she went to the bar to get the whisky. She was miles away from being that little girl, on the path to a much better life.

'Here you go.' She poured a generous amount of amber liquid into Sean's mug.

'Thanks.' He raised his mug and took a sip. 'But what about you?'

'No, I can't drink on the job. Jean would have my head.' Truthfully, she'd never been a big drinker anyway, having only a glass of wine here and there. Even the smell of alcohol was enough to bring back bad memories.

'Oh, come on. It's not like there's anyone around, and no one else will come with the weather like this. After what just happened, I'm sure you need it. Here.' He held out his mug, and despite herself, Sam took a tentative sip. She didn't want to come across as the prude her flatmates had sometimes laughingly called her when she turned them down.

Actually, it wasn't that bad, she thought, swallowing the liquid. It burned a bit, but it felt like someone had lit a candle inside of her. She could almost see why some people liked it.

One hour later, the bottle was half empty, and the whole room felt hazy and warm, as if it had wrapped itself around her. Sam glanced at the clock on the wall with surprise.

'Oh my God, it's almost eleven!' Where on earth had the time gone? She and Sean had been drinking and chatting, and the minutes had passed in a blur. To her surprise, they'd found loads to talk about, although she couldn't remember exactly what. 'I'd better start closing up.' She got to her feet, but the floor swayed beneath her. 'Whoa.'

'Steady on.' Sean took her arm, and she leaned into him, loving the feel of his hard chest against her slender frame. 'Listen, it's still too bad for me to carry on home, so I'm going to stay here tonight, if you can give me a room? I'll settle up in the morning.'

'Okay.' Even the words felt thick in her mouth, and her head was fuzzy. How much had she had to drink?

'You sit back down.' Sean eased her gently onto the chair again. 'I'll tidy these things away.'

She watched him gather their mugs and walk to the bar, loving the feeling that someone – practically a stranger, but somehow, he felt like more – cared enough to do this for her... cared enough to *save* her when she'd needed help. She might not know him, but she felt safe and protected by his side.

'Right,' he said a few minutes later, coming back over to her. 'If you can show me a room, then we can call it a night. Here, let me.' He took her arm and levered her up, and she managed to force her legs behind the bar where the keys were.

'You can take this one – it's the biggest room. It's through the door and down the corridor.' She fumbled with the keychain, trying to focus enough to get the key off, but she couldn't quite do it. Vaguely, she knew she should be embarrassed – and that tomorrow, she would be – but right now, all of her emotions were still wrapped up in that big hazy blanket. After her earlier fear and panic, it was kind of nice.

Sean took the keychain from her and slid off the key. 'This will be great. Thank you.' He put an arm around her as she swayed. 'Where do you sleep? Let me help you there first.'

'I'll be fine,' she said thickly, but part of her didn't want him to take his arm away; didn't want him to go away. 'But maybe you can help me up the stairs?'

Sean nodded, and together, they moved up the narrow staircase, giggling as she crashed into the wall. That was going to hurt later, she thought. She heard something, and she froze for a second. Hopefully, she hadn't woken Jean up. But then all went quiet, and she handed the keys to Sean to unlock her door. She couldn't even focus on the lock.

He opened the door and flicked on the light, then led her inside. George took one look at him, then streaked under the bed. 'You going to be okay?' he asked quietly as he gazed into her eyes, and Sam felt everything inside her focus on one thing only: this moment, right now, with him. She didn't want to think about the past or even the future. Right now, all she wanted was this.

She put an arm around his neck, and he reached down to touch her cheek. Then he closed the door behind them, and the rest of the world fell away.

FIFTEEN

RACHEL

Rachel sat at the kitchen table, trying to take everything in. She still couldn't believe her father had an affair, and that somehow, the woman had ended up here. What had happened? How had she died? *Could* he have killed her?

The thought was too horrific to even contemplate, and Rachel shoved the questions from her mind. She didn't have time to ponder the past – she didn't *want* to ponder the past. All she wanted now was to get away from here before Lucas broke the story. It would be a huge wrench for her mother to leave this house, but the memories it held would be worth nothing if she learned the truth.

Where could they go? Taking her mum back to London was out of the question – with the TV blaring and all the devices there, it was hardly a safe haven. They needed somewhere secluded; somewhere no one would find them.

An image shot through her mind of her and her mother, comfortably ensconced in a sun-drenched cottage, somewhere in the Lake District or the Yorkshire Dales. Nature would be on their doorstep, and even though her mother wasn't exactly up for walks, there'd be plenty of fresh air for the two of them to sit out in. Rachel bit her lip, thinking of taking her pale, weak mum miles from familiar Dr Druckow – and the myriad of other medical professionals who'd been caring for her. But she'd figure all of that out later, she told herself. There'd be doctors wherever they went, and right now, the most important thing was keeping her mother safe from her father's betrayal.

Rachel picked up her mobile and started searching Airbnb for a place that was available tomorrow. Lucas had given her until lunchtime, which meant the story would probably break sometime shortly after. They could leave as soon as she found a place and stay in a hotel tonight before checking in the next day. The sooner they got out of here, the better.

Summer was starting and many places were already booked, but after an hour of searching she came across a cottage in an isolated village in the Dales that was available for six weeks. It was set in miles of country, but it was only about an hour from Leeds if they needed the hospital. Hastily, she booked it, hoping she could extend it. If not, though, they could always try another place. The cost was astronomical and Rachel was forced to use her joint account with Mo, since her own was shockingly low at the moment, but it didn't matter. She'd do whatever she could to protect her mother from what was happening. Her stomach clenched as she thought of her father and that woman together.

She was about to go upstairs to begin packing when her phone started ringing: Mo. Was he calling because she hadn't responded to the many property listings he'd sent through? She'd been biding her time, leaning on the hope that the days and weeks ahead would continue to strengthen that spark of connection between her and her mum – hoping her mother *would* want her to have the house once more. She really didn't have time to talk now, but she couldn't help picking up. If it was something about the kids, she'd never forgive herself for not answering. She'd say hello quickly, then tell him she had to go.

She'd explain everything once she and her mum were safely on the road.

'Everything okay?' Mo asked, after she answered. 'I just noticed a huge amount come out of our joint account.'

Oh, God. She'd forgotten he had an app that flashed up any time money was deducted from an account. Now she'd have to tell him what had happened.

'I'm taking my mother away for a while,' she said quickly, heading up the stairs and into her bedroom. She hauled out a bag from under the bed.

'You're what?' Mo's voice was surprised. 'Why? It's not really a great idea to move her now, is it? Shouldn't she stay close to her doctors? And aren't you always saying how she hates to leave the house?'

Rachel swallowed, remembering the endless times she'd said that to Mo in order to excuse her mother's absences. It was true, though. 'You're right,' she said, opening a drawer and starting to pack. 'But I found out something this morning.' Was it only this morning? Already it felt like ages ago. 'The body they discovered in the wall... it was a woman.' The face from the photo flashed into her mind, and she shoved it away. 'And it turns out my father knew her. They were very close, by the looks of things.' She still couldn't believe he had done that to her mum.

'Wow.' Mo's voice was low. 'So was he the one who—'

'No, of course not,' she said quickly, before he could complete the sentence. She didn't want to think that. She couldn't think that. 'All the police have is this photo of him with her, and the fact that she was buried in the wall here. They don't have anything else.' She slammed the drawer closed.

'Okay,' Mo said, and she could hear that he was trying to sound neutral. For some reason, his tone made irritation spear through her, as if he was trying to humour her. But he hadn't known her father at all. She pushed aside the thought that she hadn't really known her father either – and particularly not if he could have been with another woman.

'Anyway.' She opened the wardrobe and threw some jumpers into the bag. 'The police want to talk to my mother to see what she knows, of course. But there's no way she could have known that my father was involved with this woman, and I can't let her find out now.'

'Okay,' Mo said again slowly. She could tell he was trying to absorb everything, but she needed him to get it quickly. She had to get off the phone fast.

'Lucas said that if I don't let the police talk to her, then they're going to release a photo they have of the woman and my father together to see if anyone else might come forward.' Anger swirled inside. *Damn* Lucas. 'The whole world will know my father was with another woman and that a body was concealed here for years. Lucas says the media will go crazy.'

'So your mother would find out anyway.' Mo swore under his breath.

'That's why I need to take her away from here.' She paused for a second, hoping Mo would understand, even if he could never begin to imagine her situation. 'I've managed to find a long-term rental in the Yorkshire Dales,' she continued, zipping up her bag. 'It's expensive – that's what the huge debit was – but it is beautiful. It's billed as off-grid – there's no wireless, no TV, no radio – but Leeds isn't too far away if we need anything. Mum and I will stay there, away from all of this. We'll stay there until...' She swallowed, unable to think right now about her mother no longer being here.

Mo was still silent, and impatience curled through her. She hadn't time to explain more. Maybe he didn't know the real reason why she was so desperate to protect her mother, but right now, it didn't matter. 'You and the kids can come visit. They'll absolutely love it, I'm sure. I know it's a lot of money, and that we might need to borrow from your mum for the mortgage this month. But I'm sure we'll be able to get back on track.' The words tumbled out of her. 'Right, I—'

'I don't care about the money, Rach.' Mo cut into her attempt to hang up. 'I care about *you*. Even if there is a hospital within reasonable reach, you'll still be on your own in an isolated location. Your mother might need minimal care now, but in a month or two – maybe even in a couple of weeks – she's going to need around-the-clock, end-of-life care to make her comfortable, so she doesn't suffer. It's a lot, Rach. And I know.'

His voice broke, and Rachel knew he was thinking of his father, who had died when Mo was a teen after a long battle with MS. 'I saw the toll it took on my mum, and she had nurses in to help at all hours. You won't be able to get that in the middle of nowhere. And I can't bear to think of you going through that alone. I love you. I don't want to see you suffer.'

Rachel sat down on the bed. She could hear that he meant every word, and he was partly right. It would be a lot to handle, but it wouldn't be too much, and she was strong enough to handle it. Being away from Mo – being on her own here, back in the past – made her remember how much she'd endured, from the death of her father to the intense loneliness she'd suffered. She'd been through so much, and she could get through this too. She could do anything to feel that love from her mother once more … to let that light back in.

But Mo didn't know that, of course. He didn't know her past; know what had made her strong or what was driving her forward. She breathed in, thinking how lucky she was to have him, and how he loved her so much. She knew he was only trying to protect her, but she didn't need it. And once more, that space between them wasn't a secure zone holding back the black, but a heavy weight she didn't have time to shift. She shook her head. Maybe once this was all over – when she and her mum had come together; when her family was one – she could finally tell him everything. But not now. Not now, when everything she'd been fighting for was about to collapse around her.

Rachel stood and picked up her bag, desperate now to get her mum to safety. 'We'll cross that bridge when we come to it. The most important thing right now is making sure she does have that peace for when the end comes. Everything else... we can deal with it. *I* can deal with it. Really, I can. And Mo, I *want* to.' She glanced at the clock. 'I'm sorry, but I have to finish packing. I'll call when we're settled in, okay? Give the kids a kiss for me. Talk soon. And Mo? I love you.'

'I love you too,' Mo said. And before he could say more, she hung up the phone.

SIXTEEN

SAM

August 1985

The pub door swung open, and Sam looked up from the pint she was pouring, her pulse quickening. Was it Sean?

'For the love of God, girl, will you focus on that drink!' Jean gave her a gentle nudge, and Sam glanced down to see the glass overflowing.

'Oh, sorry, sorry!' She mopped up the mess and got another clean glass.

'Don't worry,' Jean said, although she'd had to give Sam a few 'reminders' over the past week or two, so rare for Sam, who was usually more diligent than Jean herself. 'Look, I don't know who you're expecting, but if you're waiting for Prince Charming to walk through that door, you're going to be waiting a very long time.' She smiled, and even though Sam knew she was kidding and that she had no idea what had happened a couple of weeks ago (thank goodness), she was closer to the mark than she'd ever imagine.

Sam sighed as she poured the pint, thinking about that night. She still couldn't believe she and Sean had slept together

– right across from Jean's room, no less. What on earth had she been thinking? She hadn't been, she thought, her cheeks flushing. She'd been so drunk that her only thought had been desire. And once they'd started kissing, she'd never felt more alive; never wanted something more. Sean had seemed to feel the same, tearing her clothes off and devouring her as if he'd been waiting for her forever. It had been unlike anything else she'd ever known.

Afterwards, they'd both lain on the bed, sweaty and panting, and Sean had laughed and pulled her towards him. 'Well, I hadn't expected that with my pint,' he'd said, and she laid her head on his chest, thinking the same. She'd never, not in a million years, have expected that of *her*. She'd always been so focused on who she wanted to be in the future that she rarely let herself enjoy the present.

She'd awakened in the morning, her head pounding and her mouth dry, still unable to believe what had happened. She'd turned to make sure it was real, surprised to see the space next to her was empty. She hadn't imagined the whole thing, had she? No. She'd been drunk, but not *that* drunk.

Sitting up, she scanned the room, realising Sean's clothes were missing. Maybe he'd gone to the loo? She tidied her hair and threw on a shirt, but even after a few minutes, he didn't reappear. Perhaps he'd gone downstairs? She slipped on her jeans and went down the silent corridor – thankfully, Jean's room was quiet and she was still asleep – then down the stairs, but everything was still dark in the pub. She drew aside a curtain, the now-blue sky hurting her eyes, and looked out the window. The car park was empty; no sign of a motorcycle anywhere. He'd left.

She'd drawn in a breath, trying not to let the disappointment penetrate too deeply. That was fine, she'd told herself. It was better this way, in fact. She didn't want anything, and if nothing else, his actions only served to confirm what she'd believed: she wasn't the type of woman a successful man like Sean would take seriously – not yet anyway. Still, she couldn't quash the tiny bit of hope inside. Every time the door opened, her head snapped up, that hope flaring. It didn't make for a focused work day, and although Jean hadn't said much, Sam knew her boss was noticing more and more. At least Sam didn't have Alex to worry about too. He hadn't been back, and the way he'd left with his tail between his legs, she didn't expect him to be. Even if she never saw Sean again, she'd always be grateful for that.

Right, that's it, Sam told herself now. For God's sake, she didn't even know this man, and she shouldn't let him distract her from the real reason she was here. She was going to get on with it and stop looking at the bloody door.

And for the rest of the day and the ones after, she managed to keep her attention on the task at hand, burying herself even more in her job. She'd even asked Jean if she could start organising a pub quiz night, throwing herself into printing up flyers and starting to compile a list of questions. She was busy looking up the capital of Peru in Jean's huge atlas when she heard a voice in front of her.

'Hello.'

Her mouth fell open and she promptly closed it, telling herself to appear nonchalant. It was *him*. His hair was neatly combed this time – it looked like he'd had a haircut – and instead of a sopping leather jacket, he was back in a suit. But the masculine scent still lingered, and despite the fact that he'd run off that morning and hadn't returned until now – despite telling herself over and over that she wanted nothing from him – she couldn't help the desire sweeping over her.

'Oh. Hi.' Her voice sounded squeakier than the smooth tone she was going for, and the red of her cheeks deepened.

'I'm so sorry I haven't been in touch,' Sean said, his eyes drawing her in. 'And I'm sorry I ran off like that. I woke up later than usual, and with my promotion and all, my boss would have killed me if I'd gone in late. It was all I could do to get dressed and head to work. And then I had to go on a buying trip around the country to find some new stock. I'm in car sales,' he said, proudly flashing a grin. 'I'm not allowed to call long distance. I only got back last night, and I came here the first chance I could. Please don't be angry.'

He took her hand, and the niggling hurt and disappointment she'd told herself she hadn't been feeling faded away. So *that* was why he hadn't been in touch. He hadn't deserted her like she'd thought... like so many other people had in her past. Happiness flooded through her, but she damped it down. It was nice that he was here, but it didn't really mean anything.

Did it?

'I'm not angry,' she said, withdrawing her hand and trying to stay cool. 'Welcome back.'

'Can we chat once you're off work?' he asked, his eyes hopeful. 'I'd love to catch up.'

She held his gaze, emotions whirling inside. She'd love to, but... Well, he had come back to see her, and she didn't want to be rude. He was a customer, after all. 'Okay.'

He grinned, then grabbed the pint she'd poured him and went to sit by the table by the fire.

'Who's that?' Jean nudged her shoulder. 'Whoever he is, he's got you miles away. He's definitely a looker. Don't think I've seen him around here before, and I would have remembered.'

Sam busied herself with a glass. 'He's just a friend.' He couldn't have felt further from that, but Sam knew he wouldn't be someone significant. Even if she did want something with him, he'd be off as soon as he tired of her. She shouldn't really be wasting her time now. But her heart gave a little thrill as she met Sean's eyes again, and she couldn't help that hope rearing up.

At last, the pub emptied, Jean went up to bed, and Sam sat down beside Sean with a cup of tea in her hand. This time, she wasn't going to let alcohol cloud her mind. But even without the whisky, she couldn't stop the warm feeling growing inside as they chatted about her job here, how she was finding the area, and traded funny stories about their customers. She loved the easy, open feeling between them – she felt more relaxed with him than she had with anyone for a very long time. Then she realised they'd been talking way too much about her, and she knew next to nothing about his life.

'So tell me about your work trip,' she said, loving how the fire sparked in his eyes, making him look even more alive. 'Where did you go? What was your favourite place? I'd love to travel all over the country. I've hardly been anywhere.' That was a definite understatement, but she didn't want to tell him this was her first time out of London. One day, she thought, she'd travel the world.

He waved a hand in the air. 'Oh, you don't want to hear about that. Pure boredom, let me tell you. If you've seen the inside of one car dealership, you've seen them all.' His beeper went off, and Sam raised her eyebrows, impressed that he was important enough to need a beeper. He was exactly the sort of man she'd envisioned as her husband: friendly, kind and successful. Granted, she still didn't know him that well, but she felt like she did.

He checked the number, then met her eyes. 'Do you mind if I use your phone?' he asked. 'It's work.' He made a face. 'It never ends.'

'Sure.' She led him over behind the bar, then scooted away to polish some glasses, not wanting to make it look like she was listening. She wasn't, but even if she had wanted to, she wouldn't have been able to make out anything his low voice was saying.

'Sorry about that,' he said, coming over beside her a few

minutes later. 'One of the lads in the mechanical department has an issue. We stay open all night in case our cars need work. I'm afraid I'll need to go soon.'

'Oh.' Her heart dropped. She didn't want him to go, even though she knew she should. 'Okay, then I guess...' Her voice trailed off as he put his arms around her, slowly turning her to face him. Every inch of her was alive with that same longing she'd felt before – longing to be beside him, to feel his body, to be as close to him as she could.

'I don't need to go yet,' he said, running a hand down her back. She shivered, staring into his eyes, unable to pull away. So what if it was only a fling? If she wanted him as badly as he did her, what was the harm?

And maybe... the thought snuck into her head. Maybe she'd been wrong. Maybe he did like her, after all. Stranger things had happened, right?

Stop, she told herself as he led her to the bedroom. Tonight was enough. Tonight was all she wanted.

Right now, *he* was all she wanted.

SEVENTEEN

RACHEL

Rachel ran up the stairs, frenetic energy coursing through her. It was already eleven, and she'd spent the rest of the morning frantically gathering up everything she could think of – packing the car with as much as she could – to get ready for the long drive north. Finally, they were ready to go. She paused for a moment, staring at the family photo she'd kept on the bedside table as longing roared into her. God, she missed them. How long would it be until she saw them again? Would she even be able to video call from the new place? She should have said a quick goodbye to the kids when she'd talked to Mo, but it had taken so long to explain what was happening that she hadn't the time.

They'd be okay, she told herself, picking up her bag and bringing it out into the corridor. Everything seemed to be going like clockwork back home. Mo had it all under control. And thankfully, he hadn't called back to try to convince her not to go. Now she had to come up with a reason to persuade her mother to leave – and fast. Perhaps she could say the house repairs would be more extensive than she'd thought? That damp had been discovered in the wall, and it wasn't safe to stay here?

She bit her lip, thinking that her mum would wonder why

they couldn't go to Victoria's. Her place wasn't far, after all, and even if she wasn't yet home, it would make sense to stay there. Maybe Rachel could simply say they were on their way to the doctor's and then keep driving? Her mother would be furious, but they didn't have time to waste, and when she saw how beautiful the place Rachel had rented was, she'd be fine. Anyway, it was better than staying and facing the truth.

Rachel sighed, cracking open the bedroom door to peer at her mum. The doctor had said she'd have good days and bad, but it was clear her energy was continuing to wane. Mo's words about the amount of care she'd need drifted into Rachel's head, and for a second, hesitation shot through her. *Would* she be able to take care of her mother in the way she'd need? What if there was an emergency?

She pushed aside those thoughts. Lots of people lived in rural areas, and they coped fine. Like she'd told Mo, they wouldn't be too far from Leeds. If she really couldn't handle it, she could hire a care worker or something. No matter what, she had to get her mother away from here.

She was about to wake her mum up and bundle her into the car when she saw a car coming down the front lane. Who was that? It couldn't be... *No.* She watched incredulously as a blue people carrier pulled up in front of the house. Was that *Mo*? What was he doing here? Had he come to convince her in person not to go? Rachel breathed in, trying to calm the swirl of irritation inside. He knew they were on a deadline. He knew the consequences. In fact— she glanced at her watch. She and her mother should be in the car by now. She loved that he cared so much, but... She ran down the stairs and out of the house towards the car, thinking she'd give him a quick hug and then say she had to go. She didn't want to push him away, but right now, there really wasn't time for more.

'Oh!' She jerked in surprise as the doors opened and the kids tumbled out. For a second, she wondered if she was imagining things... if she was back in that vision where her worlds had come together. But then she remembered the darkness in the house behind her – the darkness she needed to escape – and she knew this was no happy ending. Not yet anyway.

'Hey, guys,' she said, holding out her arms. What on earth were they doing here? Despite the tension inside, happiness rushed through her at the sight of their faces.

'Come give me a cuddle.' The three of them ran towards her, almost knocking her over with the force of their hugs. She tightened her arms around them, breathing in the scent of the laundry detergent they used back home. For an instant, she was transported back to her old life: standing in the middle of the kitchen as the children cavorted around her. She missed them so much – missed her world back at home. That world had kept her safe and sheltered; helped pull the love around her so she didn't feel that lonely ache she'd lived with for so long.

The ache that she was even more desperate to fill now that she was here, with her mother, with time running out.

'Rach.' Mo's eyes were soft, and as she pulled back from the kids, he put his arms around her. He felt so familiar, so comforting, that her eyes welled with tears.

'I hope you don't mind us showing up like this,' he said into her ear. 'I know you're eager to get going. But the kids heard me talking to you about you leaving, and they wanted to come say goodbye. I did too.' His arms tightened, and that warmth surged through her once more. He hadn't come to stop her or try to convince her to stay. And while maybe he didn't fully understand, he supported her anyway, like he always had.

He met her gaze. 'And then I started thinking: maybe we don't have to say goodbye.'

Her brow furrowed. Not say goodbye? What did he mean?

'What if the kids and I go with you to the cottage? The school holidays are starting soon, and the kids can afford to miss the last week or two. I can work remotely. And I can be there for you, to support you and help you. You won't be on your own. You'll have us there every step of the way.'

'Please, Mum?' Ryan pulled at her arm like it was a piece of spaghetti. 'Dad said there are loads of sheep there. I want to make one my pet. Please?'

'Can we, Mum? It's so boring at home in the summer. Everyone else goes away. Can we go too?' Matilda tugged at her other arm, and Rachel turned to look at the kids again, her heart aching. She loved them so much, and she wanted to be with them. She was their mother, and they were her heart.

'What do you say?' Mo smiled, pulling her into his arms again. 'We can all be together. I know you haven't been gone long, but it feels like forever. The kids have really missed you. I've really missed you.'

Her heart wrenched as she stared down at her children's eager faces, and that image of the kids with her mother, full of light and love, flashed into her head again. Maybe this was the chance to make that happen. Maybe away from this place, together in such nature and beauty, they could.

'Why don't you kids go play for a bit?' Mo said, shooing them away when Rachel didn't answer. They streaked off, eager to stretch their legs after the time in the car. 'They're so excited, Rach. Even Tabitha wants to go hiking, and...' He carried on as Rachel stared at him, a smile growing on her face as she pictured the children ringing her mother's bed telling tales of their day; sinking into sleep beside Mo every night once again. She bit her lip at the thought that she'd need to tell him about giving the house to her mother, but with that darkness banished, she'd be able to explain why she'd needed to do it. At long last, he would know everything. There would be nothing separating them any longer.

She was about to ask him to grab the kids while she got her mother in the car when a sharp cry drifted from the window above them. Her heart lurched. 'Mum?'

She rushed inside and burst into the bedroom, relieved to see her mother sitting up in bed. But her face— her face was set in a deathly mask. Rachel followed her gaze to the TV, and everything inside froze. *No*. Oh no. Slowly, she sank onto the bed, her eyes glued to the telly and... she blinked, hoping the image wasn't real, but when she opened her eyes, it was still there.

The photo of her father and the woman in the wall, kissing.

She searched for the remote to snap it off, fury filling her. Lucas had said she had until noon, and it was only eleven-thirty! The very least he could have done was give them a warning, for God's sake. How could he do this?

It will be okay, she told herself, frantically trying to get a grip on this new situation. It had to be okay. Maybe it wasn't an affair. Maybe this photo had been blown way out of proportion. Maybe her mother *did* actually know this woman, and she was nothing more than a friend. Photos could be misinterpreted, after all, and—

Rachel had found the remote and was about the turn the TV off when something stopped her. A reporter was standing in front of the police station, saying that forensics had found a fingerprint on the bin bag the victim had been buried in.

A fingerprint belonging to Sean Norman.

The remote slipped from Rachel's hand and clattered onto the floor, but she didn't move. Oh my God. Her father. Her father *had* killed that woman. Why else would he hide her like that? He'd killed her, then put her in the wall. This wasn't just a photo gone wrong. This was *murder*.

'Mum...' She swallowed at her mother's stricken face. What could she say? It was too much for Rachel to absorb, let alone a woman of her mother's condition. She eyed her mum closely, praying she didn't faint or have another spell. She was staring at the black screen as if it was on, and a chill went through Rachel at the vacant expression on her face. It was as if she'd vanished, like she'd crawled inside herself. Seconds ticked by, and her mother still didn't move.

'Everything okay?' Mo asked quietly from the corridor. Rachel sprang up from the bed. She'd forgotten he was here, and everything about his presence inside this space – this world – felt wrong. He didn't belong here, and she needed to get him away from this nightmare. She closed the door behind her and propelled him down the stairs and out of the house, then turned to face him.

'My mum saw the photo of my father,' she said, horror and dismay swarming through her. 'It's on the news. It's everywhere now. And—' She stopped, unable to finish what else she'd discovered. She couldn't say the words. It was too awful to bear.

'Rach, I'm so sorry,' Mo said. 'I know how much you wanted to protect your mother from everything. I know how important it was to you.'

She met his eyes, despair circling inside. It *was* important to her – more important than he even knew. A cry rose up inside her, and she swallowed it down. Rachel had come here determined to show her mum how much she really did love her. Instead, she'd managed to destroy her mother's world once again... to destroy *her*. Her mum would never have peace. How could she, after learning this?

'Look, forget Yorkshire if it's too much for you now, after all of this,' Mo said. 'There's no reason to make such a big move. Why don't we stay here with you? There's plenty of space, and the kids would love it too.'

Rachel knew her answer before she could even speak. She felt it vibrate within her very bones. *No.* Her family would not stay here, in this place where tragedy and despair now reigned. They were the light that had saved her, and she couldn't bear to admit them into this circle of black. And she couldn't allow herself their light, because in turning towards her family, she'd left her mother unprotected to face a more horrific truth than she ever could have imagined. If she hadn't lingered to be with them, she and her mother could have been gone by now. They *would* have been gone by now.

Tears came to her eyes, and pain sliced through her. She wanted to be with her children: to laugh with them, to tuck them in, even to watch their annoying YouTube videos. She could tell by how they'd clung to her that they'd missed her too. But as much as she wanted to, she couldn't. Not now. Not yet.

'I'm sorry,' Rachel whispered. 'Tell the kids I love them, and I'll call them tonight.'

'You want us to leave?' Mo stared at her, an incredulous expression on his face. She'd never asked him to go in all of their years together, and every inch of her longed to throw herself into his arms; to feel the warmth he'd brought to her life. But he had to go now. Her family had to go. That was the only way she could hope to make things better, to even begin to reach that vision of togetherness she'd had.

'Tell the kids I love them,' she said again, opening the door of the house. She could feel the tug of pain, of anguish, pulling her inside – pulling her away from the man in front of her, away from her children. But she didn't fight it. She couldn't. 'I'll call. I'm so sorry, but I need to be with my mum now.'

And then she slowly closed the door and turned, trying to breathe through the agony. She went up the stairs and sat down on the bed beside her mother, still silent and unmoving. She tried not to think of her family travelling down the lane away from her, the light growing dimmer and dimmer.

Once again, she was here with her mother in the darkness. And somehow, she had to find a way to pull her out... to pull them *both* out.

EIGHTEEN

SAM

January 1986

'So tonight's the night?' Will jabbed Sam's shoulder playfully as they strode down the hill towards the village. Despite his objections, she'd managed to drag him out for a countryside walk. 'I finally get to meet lover boy? I'd better, after coming all this way.'

Sam laughed. 'Yes, he's going to join us here for supper once he gets off work around seven,' she said. 'And you've hardly come "all this way". It's only a quick train ride!' She hadn't seen Will since she'd left the pub in South London, and although they'd spoken on the phone a few times, there was nothing like an in-person conversation. She was so happy to see him, and she couldn't wait to introduce him to Sean.

She smiled, an image of Sean filling her mind. She'd been right to hope; right to let him in. Because he *did* seem to like her, even though she was only a lowly pub manager and nothing compared to his successful career. She'd been sure he wouldn't come back again after that second time, but he had, again and again. They'd been together for over five months now, and though they rarely left the confines of the pub – she was always working, and he was busy with his job – she loved every minute they spent together.

Jean was the only person besides Will who knew about them, and she'd told Sam that as long as she didn't disturb other guests, she could do what she liked. She and Sean hadn't talked about the future, but right now Sam was taking each day as it came. In fact, it was nice to be living in a suspended reality without worrying about what lay ahead. Dreaming about the future had always been an escape for her since her present had been far from ideal. But now her present was pretty idyllic.

Will grimaced as he clambered awkwardly over a kissing gate. 'It may not be far, but it feels like another world.' He turned to face her, cursing as he brushed dirt off his trousers. 'I have to say, I never thought you'd last here. But it looks like the country life suits you!' His gaze swept over her, and she flushed. She knew she'd gained a few pounds, but she didn't mind. She'd been too skinny before, and Sean said he loved her body. And when she gazed at herself in the mirror, sometimes she couldn't believe it was her staring back. The sallow cheeks, dark circles and pale skin were gone, replaced by a rosy blush and sparkling eyes. She looked alive, and it wasn't only the fresh air or Jean's loving embraces. It was Sean too. It was how special he made her feel… for the first time in her life.

'We're back, thank God for that,' Will said, as they came into the car park of the pub. 'Civilisation.' He looked around the deserted village green. 'Well, sort of.' They went inside, and he plopped down at a table as Sam scooted behind the bar to pour him a drink.

'Here you go,' she said, setting his gin and tonic on the table before sinking into a chair beside him. She had the evening off – Jean had forced her to, saying a girl her age should spend more time with her friends. She hadn't wanted to leave Jean on her own, though. She hadn't been well lately, constantly having to sit down 'to take a little breather'. Sam had asked her to go see a doctor, but she kept refusing, saying she hadn't the time. In the end, Sam had agreed to take the evening off, but she wasn't going to leave the pub in case Jean needed her. She, Will and Sean could have a wonderful meal right here.

'Oh, I almost forgot.' Will dug out a tattered envelope from his pocket. 'This came for you last week.'

'Thanks.' She took the long white envelope, wondering what it was. When she'd lived in London, she'd always used the pub's address – if any post had gone to her flat, it would be sure to disappear into the same abyss that swallowed most of her good clothes. Maybe it was a bill or something she'd forgotten to pay?

She opened it slowly, eyebrows rising as she slid out the paper. It was from Medhurst College, a school to which she'd applied to become a medical secretary. It had been a very long shot – way beyond anything she'd thought she'd be accepted for – since the application had specified a secondary school qualification in biology and a minimum typing speed, neither of which she had. But she'd loved the idea of sitting in a doctor's office, shooting smiles at babies and pensioners, doing everything she could to brighten up their day. As a child, she'd sit and stare at those pulled-together polished women in awe, perched behind a counter like a monarch reigning over their kingdom. Sometimes, their smile was the only pleasant thing she'd see in her day.

'What is it?' Will asked, sipping his drink.

She looked up to meet his eyes, shaking her head incredulously. 'I've been accepted onto a training course to be a medical secretary,' she said, still unable to believe it. 'I applied ages ago. It's been so long that I actually forgot about it.'

'That's amazing!' Will lifted his glass in the air. 'Cheers to you. When does it start?'

Sam scanned the letter. 'It starts next month!' she said. 'Back in London.' She bit her lip, a curious mix of emotions going through her. This was it: the very thing she'd been saving for; a real chance to gain some qualifications and get a job she'd be proud of; become a *person* she'd be proud of. But... she swallowed. This would mean going back to London. Where would she live? The same dive as before? Working in the same pub as before? And—

'You're coming back then?' Will asked, as if he had heard her thoughts. 'There will always be a place at the pub for you, you know – even if you only want to work a few hours here and there. Honestly, one hour with you is worth about five of the others.' He made a face.

'Thank you,' she said absently, staring down at the letter as her mind spun. She wanted to do this course. She *needed* to. But leaving this place, so cosy and homely with regulars she knew everything about, and Jean, who was like an older auntie, watching out for her – even George the cat! Could she work at Will's again, where cleanliness was an urban legend and 'regulars' were homeless people who popped in for a bit of warmth and a snooze on the stained banquettes? This pub might be the middle of nowhere, as Will had put it, but better to be in the middle of nowhere than somewhere you didn't like.

But it wasn't just that, she knew. It wasn't that at all. It was *Sean*. If she went to London, that would be it. She'd be far away, and he was way too busy with work to come see her. And these past few months, well, they'd been like a fairy tale for her. She'd been happier than she'd ever known. But maybe the fairy tale wouldn't last. Maybe Sean would tire of her and move on to a woman with a better education, better employment, a better life. Could she give up this opportunity for something so uncertain?

Didn't fairy tales have happy endings, though? And didn't they deserve to see what their ending would be? Because even if they didn't last, right now, the present with him appealed a million times more than the thought of a future in London.

Sam breathed in, trying to buffer herself from the warring thoughts inside of her.

She needed to see Sean. She needed to tell him about the offer and see his reaction. Would he encourage her to go or ask her to stay? Her gut clenched as she realised that this was the moment it would be clear if they had a future together or not. If he asked her to stay, then she'd know he was serious. And then... she let out her breath. Then she'd stay. He was the kind of man she'd always wanted, and if he thought she was enough, maybe she was.

A couple of hours later, she had on her very best dress, her hair was curled, and she was even wearing high heels. It was a bit much for a meal at the pub, but since she and Sean always met after work, she never had the chance to make an effort and show him how nice she could look, without the scent of spilled pints and damp washcloths clinging to her. As she glided mascara onto her lashes, the desire to see him grew. Thank God Will had agreed to keep quiet about the offer until she'd had the chance to talk to Sean in private. Nerves flickered through her at the thought of the conversation ahead.

Right, time to go. Sean should be there by now, and God knows she didn't want to leave Will with him for too long. She smoothed down her hair, gave George a pat, then went down the stairs.

'Don't you look nice,' Will said as she sat down, surprised to see that Sean wasn't beside him. It was already quarter past seven, and he hadn't called to say he'd be late. 'You must really like this bloke. You certainly never dolled yourself up like that for me!'

'Wasted effort,' Sam bantered back, unable to help laughing. She pushed back her chair. 'Shall I get us a few drinks?'

Jean swooped in, gently pushing her back down. 'No. Tonight, I want you to relax and enjoy. God knows you deserve it.' She shook her head. 'I don't know what I would have done without you these past few weeks.'

Sam smiled, glancing up at her boss. It was a kind gesture, but she seemed as if she was about to keel over. Will shot Sam a concerned look. 'That's all right, Jean. I'm getting up to call Sean anyway.' She went to the phone, dialled Sean's beeper number, then poured the drinks as she waited for him to call. But the phone stayed silent, and she brought the glasses over to the table.

'I hate to say this, but Jean looks awful,' Will said in a worried tone, so low that Sam almost didn't hear. 'Is everything okay?'

Sam sighed. 'She's been feeling quite weak these past few weeks, but she won't see the doctor. Maybe you can get her to go.'

'She's as stubborn as a mule, that one. I'll have a word.' Will craned his neck to take her in, leaning against the bar. 'She looks like she's lost some weight too.' He made a face. 'I mean, she could afford to lose a fair bit, but...'

Sam rolled her eyes. Typical Will. Despite herself, she couldn't help laughing. She'd missed his biting wit.

'Anyway, where's your man? I'm starving!'

Sam shrugged, wondering that herself. It was coming up to quarter to eight now, and irritation was starting to niggle. Sean knew he'd be meeting Will tonight and how much Will meant to her. So where was he? Besides, she was desperate to talk to him about the offer and see what he thought... see about their future.

'He must have got caught up at work. Ever since he got a promotion, he's been on call 24/7,' she said, thinking of how often the beeper went off and how much he was needed. She kept wanting to go visit him at work, but he always told her he'd be run off his feet and he didn't want her to waste the trip out to the car dealership. 'Let's order, and he can get some food when he arrives.'

'So tell me how you two met.' Will grabbed the menu and smiled as Sam relayed the tale of how he'd come into the pub that stormy night, dripping and cold.

'And what do you do together here in this backwoods? There's only so many walks through the fields you can take, no? Do you go into High Wycombe often?'

Sam bit her lip. 'Actually, we pretty much stick to the pub.'

Will cocked his head. 'You stick to the pub? Why? I mean, it's nice, of course. But don't you spend enough time here?'

'Well, Sean comes by after work and stays until I finish,' Sam said, feeling desperate to justify the reason but not quite sure why. 'Then we have a drink, and...' She flushed, and Will let out a whistle.

'Well, I'm glad you're getting some.' He paused. 'But honey...'

'What?' Sam took a sip of her drink, watching the door. Where on earth *was* Sean? He must have got her beep by now. He could have at least called! Fear flashed through her. Unless he'd had an accident or something?

'How much do you know about this man?' Will asked, leaning in.

Sam met his steady gaze. 'I know he works in a car dealership. That he's very successful, and...' Her voice trailed off as she realised that, actually, she didn't know many details of Sean's life. Their world was the pub, a magical place that had cocooned and comforted her. That had been enough for her.

'Have you even been to see him there? Does he live nearby?' Will shook his head at her silence. 'Look, I don't want to be the one to burst your bubble,' he said gently. 'But someone needs to watch out for you. I know you haven't had a lot of experience with men...'

Her cheeks burned. What was he trying to say?

'A man who only wants to see you in the pub at night, has a quickie and then goes home... a man who hasn't told you anything about where he lives or takes you out anywhere, well...' He looked at her, and unease curled through Sam. His words echoed her exact fear: that she wasn't someone a man like Sean would ever seriously consider. That she was only a fling – that she wasn't enough.

'In my mind, that's a man who's trying to hide something. Something like a *wife*,' Will continued.

A laugh burst out of her despite her worry. Will was so far off the mark it was funny. Whatever else she might be to Sean, at least she wasn't his mistress. 'He can't be married,' she said. 'He doesn't have a ring, for one thing.'

Will raised his eyebrows, looking at her as if she was a child. 'Those things can be removed, you know.'

The smile dropped from her face in an instant. Of course they could – she'd never thought of that. But Sean would never do something like that, would he? She shook her head. There still might be a lot she didn't know about him, as Will was only too keen to point out, but Sean was a good, kind man. She'd witnessed that first-hand when he'd saved her from Alex. And she knew – she *knew* – that he didn't belong to anyone else. She'd have felt it, somehow, if he had. And as for everything else, their future... she swallowed. She guessed she'd find out when she told him about the offer.

She nudged Will playfully, trying to lighten the mood. 'Thanks so much for watching out for me, big brother. But honestly, you don't need to worry. Sean is a wonderful man. You'll see yourself when he gets here. You can ask him whatever you want.'

But the hours passed, and Sean never showed up. Sam had beeped him several more times, but there hadn't even been a phone call. She'd been worried before about being enough in the future, but as she traipsed up to bed, an even worse fear gripped her. Maybe he'd left her now. Maybe he was gone for good, disappearing from her life without a goodbye, like so many people had.

She stared at the crumpled letter on her bedside table, trying to work up a bit of enthusiasm, but all she could think about was Sean. *Would* she ever see him again?

George meowed and curled up around her legs, but for the first time, he didn't give her comfort. Instead, she felt lonelier than ever.

NINETEEN

RACHEL

Rachel sat in her mother's room an hour later, the weight of everything that had happened pressing down on her. Her father was a murderer. A *murderer*. She shook her head, thinking that she could say the word forever and still have trouble connecting it with her dad. The man she'd believed could never stand the sight of blood had taken someone else's life away – and not just anyone, but a woman he'd been in a relationship with. Rachel had continued to rack her brain to think of something to say to her mum... of *anything* to make it better. But what words could there be to even begin to bandage such gaping wounds? She tried to explain how she'd found the body and how she'd attempted to protect her mother from it all, but her mum didn't even turn towards her. In the end, all Rachel could say was that she loved her and she was sorry, over and over, in a brutal echo of the past. And again, all her mother could do was stare with empty eyes that made Rachel shiver.

But Rachel wasn't going to look away this time. She wasn't going to leave. She'd find a way to haul herself and her mother from this pit. She only needed to think of how.

A loud bang sounded at the door, and Rachel jerked. Who

could that be? Surely not Mo again? She clattered down the stairs and opened the door, stopping short as a camera flashed in her face. What the *hell*?

'What's it like to have a skeleton in your wall? Was it a skeleton? What did it look like? Were you the one who found it? Did—'

Rachel slammed the door, her heart beating fast. *Oh my God.* She risked a peek out the window, her jaw dropping when she spotted a cluster of media with cameras out front and what looked like a satellite truck coming down the lane. She raced to the windows and yanked the curtains closed as one tried to get a photo. She leaned forward slowly, putting her head in her hands. Her poor mother. She didn't deserve this. No one did, especially not when they only had months – weeks, maybe – to live.

'Rachel?' Lucas's voice came through the door. 'Rachel, can you let me in?'

She strode to the door, eager to give him a piece of her mind and expel some of her anger. 'How could you? How could you go back on your word? The least you could have done was give me some warning. My mother had to find out everything on the *news*, for God's sake! She could have fainted from the shock – or worse. You could have killed her!' Her words sounded dramatic, but they were true.

'I'm sorry,' Lucas said, coming inside and closing the door quickly. 'I'm so sorry it happened this way. I wanted to call and warn you first – to give you a heads-up, and to be here to make sure no reporters bothered you. But then...' He sighed. 'You've probably heard that our forensics team found something else.'

'The fingerprint.' Rachel's voice trembled. How could he do that? How could he kill someone and then hide them in the walls of his family's home? She shivered, remembering that night she'd crept downstairs when he'd been working on his bikes. It had been one of the only times she'd really connected

with her father, and the body had been mere feet from them –
the woman he had murdered and disposed of. Nausea churned
inside, and she took a deep breath to keep it at bay.

'Yes, the fingerprint,' Lucas said. 'We checked it against
the record we had from when your father stole the motorbike,
and it matched. When my boss found out, he went over my
head and released the photo to the media without telling me.
It's evidence that your father was directly involved in
disposing of her body, and my boss wanted your mum to see
that photo; to put pressure on her to talk. I really am sorry.
I've cleared all the reporters from your property,' he continued, 'and I'll stick around outside to make sure none of them
come back up here. I've threatened them with trespass if they
try.'

Rachel nodded, her heart still pounding with anger.

'I won't be able to keep them from the main road outside,
though,' he said. 'So if you want to go somewhere, let me know
and I'll make sure to escort you out.'

She shook her head. She couldn't believe it had come to
this: she and her mother, trapped in a house where her father
had murdered his mistress and buried her in a wall. She'd come
here to help her mother die in peace, inside her sanctuary.
Instead, they were confined now to a grotesque morgue – all
because of her.

Somehow, she had to fix this.

'Rachel...' Lucas swivelled to face her. 'Since your mother is
aware of everything now, will you let me speak to her? I understand she's had a terrible shock, but maybe talking about it will
help.' He paused. 'And if she does know more and has been
keeping it secret all of these years, then perhaps getting it off her
chest will give her some peace.' His voice was low and soft.

Rachel held his gaze. Her mother didn't know anything;
that much was clear. The look on her face when she'd heard the
terrible news was evidence enough. She wasn't in any fit state to

see any strangers, let alone speak to them. She hadn't even said a word to Rachel.

'She's not talking at all right now,' Rachel answered. 'I've tried to get through to her, but like you said, it's all been such a shock. I'm not even sure how much she absorbed.'

Lucas was quiet for a minute. 'Now that we have solid evidence of your father's involvement, my boss is even more determined that we get her to cooperate. With the media aware of the case, he's under a lot of pressure to solve it quickly. While there is a chance someone may answer the media appeal, that can take ages. Your mum is here now.' He paused once more. 'Honestly, I don't want to keep coming back any more than you want me to. I know you want me to leave you in peace. I want to leave you in peace. Let me have a quick word, and then I can go.'

Rachel breathed out as his words filtered through her mind. Maybe it was better for Lucas to talk to her mother and get it over with. Lucas was right: she knew everything now anyway. There was nothing left to protect her from. Once he'd spoken to her, the police would leave them alone, and the media interest would die out when there were no new developments.

And then... Then what? What could she ever do to make this up to her mother? Could she ever find peace again?

'All right,' Rachel said. 'But only if I'm there.' No way was she going to let her mother face the past alone.

Lucas nodded. 'Of course.'

Rachel led him up the stairs and opened the door.

'Mum, Lucas is here. Remember him? He's a police officer now, and he wants to have a quick chat about...' She swallowed, unable to say the words. 'About what we saw on TV. It won't take long, I promise. And I'll be right here too.'

'Hi, Mrs Norman.' Lucas came inside the room, and she saw him try to hide his surprise at her mother's haggard appearance. 'I know this must be a very difficult time for you, and I'm so sorry if I'm making it any harder. But I need to ask you a few questions, all right? Anything – anything at all – you can tell me would be great.'

Silence echoed in the room, and Lucas looked quickly at Rachel.

'You know now that we found the body of a young woman in the basement wall of the house. That body would have been put into the wall about thirty-five years ago,' Lucas said. 'Rachel discovered it a few days ago after your bath overflowed.'

Rachel's mother's eyes flitted towards her, then back to Lucas. He took out a large blow-up of the photo in the pub. Thankfully, he slid his arm over Sean's face, hiding him – and the kiss – from view. He held it in front of her mother's face, and she slowly turned her gaze towards it, taking in the image in front of her.

'Do you recognise this woman? Have you ever seen her?'

Rachel's mother shook her head. She let out a long breath, and Rachel reached out to take her hand. She couldn't even imagine what her mother must be going through. Right now, though, she couldn't be prouder of her strength.

'Did you know...' Lucas's voice trailed off. 'Did you know that your husband was in a relationship with her?'

'No.' The word shot out of her mother from her very depths. '*No.*' Her face twisted, and Rachel squeezed her mum's fingers. 'Sean loved me,' her mother said, her voice shaking as she shifted in the bed. 'He loved me. Whatever he did, I never doubted that. Not in a million years.'

Rachel grasped her mother's hand harder, then pressed her down as she tried to sit up. 'It's okay, Mum. I know he did. I know he loved you.'

'I know it was a long time ago, but did you notice him acting strangely before you left to visit your parents?' Lucas asked.

Her mother's brow furrowed, and she shot Rachel a look of confusion. 'Visit my parents?'

Rachel swallowed, remembering how her mother hadn't wanted her to go through her father's things. She'd never told her she'd found the flight itinerary.

'Back in 1986, after Rachel was born,' Lucas said. 'Did he seem agitated or more distressed than usual? Was he behaving any differently? And what did he tell you about the new work he'd done in the basement? Did he say anything about the wall?' Lucas was speaking quickly now, as if he was as desperate as Rachel to get this out of the way. And while Rachel could understand that, she wished he'd slow down. Each question was like a blow to her mother, pressing her down more and more as the weight of the past piled upon her.

'I... I...' The words trickled from her mother's mouth, and she twisted in the bed. 'I don't know,' she said. 'It was so long ago.' She closed her eyes, collapsing against the pillows. 'I can't remember. I'm sorry,' she said. 'I'm so sorry, but I really can't remember.'

Her voice was a whisper now, as if the life was draining out of her, and Rachel glanced at Lucas. 'That's enough for now, all right?'

Relief flooded through her when he nodded. 'I'll let you get some rest,' he said. 'If you do remember anything, please get in touch.'

Rachel took his hand and propelled him out the door before he could say more.

'I told you she wouldn't know anything,' Rachel said, anger stirring inside again as they went down the stairs. They'd been thrown into this nightmare for nothing.

Lucas sighed. 'At least now I can tell my boss that I spoke to your mother and that she couldn't give us any information.' He tilted his head to look at her. 'Nobody in the community seems to know anything either. I've spoken to quite a few people about your father, and they all remember him as a very dedicated family man and a successful businessman. But there was some hint that your parents may have had trouble conceiving before you came along.' Rachel blinked, remembering what Dr Druckow had told her. 'And for a couple who wants children, that can be a big strain. I speak from personal experience.'

'I'm sorry.' She touched his arm. She could see that whatever had happened had a huge impact.

'Apparently, your mother became something of a recluse – signs point to a period of depression. And when she did fall pregnant, she was so worried about her pregnancy that she stayed in bed for most of it. Your father was seen around the village, but no one can remember him being with the woman in the photo. It sounds like he did a good job of hiding it from everyone, not just your mother.'

Rachel breathed in, the anger inside expanding. How could her father do this? His wife had been depressed because she'd been having trouble getting pregnant, and he'd been off with another woman – another woman he'd killed.

Why? Why had he done that?

Lucas glanced at his watch. 'Right, I'd better get back to the station.' His eyes softened. 'Take care of yourself, okay?'

Rachel sank into a chair as he went out the front door. It was over. Her mother had talked to Lucas, told him she knew nothing, and he'd left. Except... Rachel stared at the basement door, feeling the yawning blackness beyond. It wasn't over, not at all. The body was gone, but the secrets it had unleashed haunted them still. What could she do to banish them? To roll back the darkness, and begin to seek the light once more?

To *somehow* find a way to piece her mother's world back together?

Before she knew what she was doing, she snapped on the basement light and went down the stairs. She hadn't been here since she'd found the body, but now she felt drawn to it, as if by embracing the dark, she might discover something to put all of this behind them. She gazed at the empty hole in the wall, the young woman's face floating into her head. That woman was as much a victim of her father as she and her mother were. Whatever she had done – whether she'd known Sean was married or not – she hadn't deserved this, the same way Rachel's mother or Rachel didn't deserve what was happening to them now.

Rachel reached out to touch the wall, feeling the cold dampness beneath her fingers. 'We didn't know you were here,' she said quietly. She knew it was silly, but somehow she felt that the woman who'd been in the wall for so long could hear her. 'I'm sorry. I'm sorry for what my father did to you, but...' She swallowed. 'But that's enough now. My mother is dying. This is the only time I have left with her. You've been found, and now, please, *please*, let us be.'

Silence filled her ears, and Rachel snapped off the light and went back into the warm glow of the kitchen.

But still, it felt like the darkness had followed.

TWENTY

SAM

January 1986

Sam smiled at a customer as she mixed a vodka cocktail, but she felt anything but happy. Will had left earlier that morning, and although he hadn't mentioned Sean again, his words still rang in her head. Where had Sean been? Why hadn't he called? *Was* he gone for good? Her stomach lurched and her head throbbed, but she knew it wasn't anything to do with the cocktails she'd downed with Will. It was because... she drew in a breath as the realisation hit. It was because she was in love with Sean. Despite telling herself over and over it would never be anything serious – despite trying to steel herself against it – somehow along the way, she'd fallen in love with him. And now she might never see him again.

She thought of the acceptance letter upstairs and how she'd wondered if she could give up that opportunity for Sean. Now that she might have lost him, she wondered how she could have even *contemplated* leaving. Maybe their future together was uncertain, but she'd give up anything to spend one more minute with him – to hold him in her arms; to smell his cologne. She'd never felt so strongly about anyone before. Would he call? Tell her where he'd been?

Or would he discard her like almost everyone else in her life?

The lunch rush felt endless, and by the time the crowd petered out, she was absolutely knackered. She was about to sink into a chair when the door swung open, and there he was.

The rush of happiness that went through her almost knocked her off her feet, and she could feel a smile growing on her face – genuine this time. He wasn't gone. He *had* come back.

She hurried out from behind the bar, despite the fact that punters were waiting for their drinks. Nothing else mattered but Sean.

'Hi!' she said, throwing her arms around him.

He gave her a quick squeeze and pulled back. 'So you're not angry with me?' he asked, a hesitant expression on his face. 'I came as soon as I could – I wanted to apologise in person. I'm so sorry I wasn't here last night. I ran out of petrol driving from work and had to wait ages for someone to come along. By the time I got home, it was too late to call.'

The happiness grew even bigger. She knew there had to be a reason. On the dark, windy roads, she didn't doubt it would take ages for someone to come along. And the fact that Sean had taken time out of his busy day to come here in person and apologise... he had nothing to hide. He did care. And the notion that he had a wife? Ridiculous. What wife would let her husband out, day and night, until the early hours? There was no way. *Damn* Will for putting those thoughts in her head in the first place.

'Right, I'd better get back to work before they notice I'm gone.' Sean glanced at his watch, and love swelled inside her even more. He'd put her above his work, and she knew how important that was to him. Even though the pub was full of punters, she couldn't help drawing him in for a kiss.

'Cheese!' A bright light flashed, and Sean pulled back.

'Christ!' he said, practically pushing her away in surprise.

'I'm sorry to scare you,' Jean said, putting down the camera. 'I'm trying to get some candid photos around the pub for posterity, you know?'

'What a great idea!' Sam said, pleased to see Jean up and about and full of energy. 'Can I have a copy of the picture when you get it developed?' She turned to Sean. 'I don't have any photos of you at all! Maybe we should take some more?' She expected Sean to nod and agree easily, but instead his normally relaxed face was tight, his teeth clenched. 'What's wrong?' she asked, Will's words hovering at the edge of her mind. *Something to hide. A wife.*

No. She shoved them away.

'I'm not a fan of having my photo taken,' Sean said, turning to smile at her, and relief whooshed through her. God, she had to banish Will's words, once and for all. 'I've never liked it.'

'That's okay. I understand.' There was nothing suspicious about that. Not everyone liked having their picture taken. One of the girls she'd flat-shared with used to cover her face with her hands whenever a camera was in sight.

'Hey.' Sean's voice was soft, and she felt her insides melting. 'I need to go now, but I want to make up for last night.'

Sam shook her head. 'You don't have to do that. It wasn't your fault.'

'I know, but I want to.' He grinned. 'I've made reservations for us at a wonderful restaurant next weekend. I know you'll love it.'

Sam couldn't help the huge smile crossing her face. They'd never made plans before for something like this – something ahead of time; something in the outside world together. It was exactly what she needed to put Will's words to rest for good.

She didn't need to tell Sean about the offer to set things straight. *This* was what she wanted: this man in front of her right now, filling her with such happiness; such love. She'd write to Medhurst College tonight and tell them she wouldn't be coming. How could it begin to compete with what she had now?

She had more than one minute. She had a future. And even though she didn't know how much of one – even if Sean did get tired of her, or want someone with more to offer – right now, she was enough.

And that was enough for her.

TWENTY-ONE

RACHEL

Rachel gazed from her mum's bedroom window into the dim evening light. In the distance, the glow of the cameras and phones of the gathered media illuminated the night sky. Almost a week had passed since the story had broken, and with no one coming forward and no leads in the case, the group was thankfully diminishing every day. But even though things were quieting, her mother seemed as distressed as the very first day she'd heard the news. She barely spoke, spending most of her time sleeping, watching her favourite soaps, or staring into space.

Rachel had tried to convince her mum to leave, thinking it might be easier to be away from here. But her mother had shaken her head, saying this was still her home, and no one was going to drive her away. Rachel had nodded, thinking how she'd done the right thing by giving her mum the house. This *was* her home, and once she signed the papers the lawyer was almost finished drafting up, she could do with it what she liked.

She heard a rustle behind her, and she turned from the window. 'Mum?' She sat down on the bed, where her mother was now awake. 'Do you want something to eat? Do you want... do you want to talk about anything?' Rachel didn't want to upset her, but now that time had passed, maybe talking about what they'd learned would help her mother absorb the lingering shock; help them both absorb the shock. Rachel bit her lip, her father's face filtering into her mind. It was still so hard to believe this man she'd known had been so violent; had ended someone's life – the life of a woman he'd been having an affair with. And if it was this hard for her, she couldn't begin to imagine what it must be like for her mother.

But her mother closed her eyes again and moved away from Rachel, as if she was something threatening. Rachel sighed. Clearly, her mother needed more time, and the last thing Rachel wanted was to put more distance between them.

Maybe she'd been wrong to try to keep the body from her mother. Maybe if her mum had known, it would have helped cushion the later blow – maybe it would have been easier to find a way out of this darkness. She shook her head, thinking that despite the days that had passed, she was no closer to coming up with anything that might help. Things back at home weren't making it any easier either. The kids were calling and texting every day, begging and pleading to go away, and Mo continued to send through property listings... his only real form of communication with her right now, which showed how hurt he was that she'd asked him to go. It felt like both her worlds were straining, and she had to do something fast.

She would, she told herself, trying to stay calm. She'd hit on something. Until then, Rachel was doing the best thing she could by staying here beside her mother; holding her hand – a steady presence until she could make things right again.

A knock sounded on the door, and she jumped. Who could that be at this hour? Had one of the media made their way through? Despite the police presence, the small group that was left had become more brash, with one member even trying to sneak through the hedgerows. She peered through the window in the door to spot Lucas on the other side, and her heart sank.

Why was he here again? Hadn't he said he'd leave them alone? Right now, he was the last person she wanted to see.

'What's going on?' she asked slowly, cracking the door open.

'Can I come inside?' Behind him, three or four police cars with their lights flashing lit his silhouette. Rachel motioned him in, then stood facing him, her heart beating fast. Something had happened. Something big, by the look of things. She prayed this wasn't something more her mother would have to deal with before Rachel had even thought of how to make the last blow better.

'Someone who knew the woman in the photo came forward,' Lucas began, leaning against the kitchen counter. Rachel let out her breath. Okay, then. They could deal with that – it was one more piece to lay everything to rest. She tilted her head, wondering why Lucas was so sombre. Surely this was the break in the case he'd been looking for. 'Who was she?' Rachel wasn't sure she wanted to know, but she was keen to put all of this behind her.

'Her name was Samantha Hughes,' Lucas responded. 'She lived and worked at the pub for a year and a half. We've never been able to track down the pub's former owner – she fell ill, and we're not sure where she went after being discharged from hospital – but a man rang who knew both this woman and the pub owner. Samantha worked for him in his pub in South London before she moved up here, and he was able to identify her from the photo.'

Rachel felt something inside relax for the first time in ages. Now that this woman was identified, her family could be told and she would be buried in a proper grave. They might never know the true story of what had happened, but at least her family would have some closure. Maybe now, the darkness that the ghost had brought would begin to withdraw, and they could start to heal. Maybe this was what they needed to start to reach to the light.

Thank you, Rachel said in her head, glancing towards the basement door. It felt like the woman in the wall had heard her earlier plea.

'I'm so relieved you've been able to find out who this woman was,' Rachel said. 'But...' She peered over his shoulder at the flashing lights from the cars in the drive. 'Is there a reason for the cavalry? The media are going to think there's something more going on.'

'I'm afraid there is.' Lucas met her eyes, and she leaned back at the serious look in them.

'What?' she asked, her heart dropping. Her eyes flitted towards the basement door again. Maybe she'd been premature in her thanks. But she hoped not. Oh, God, she hoped not.

'This man told us that...' He fell silent, and impatience shot through her. *What?* 'He said that Samantha and your father had a baby together.'

Rachel flinched. 'A baby?'

'Yes.' Lucas nodded. 'According to this man, the baby was only a few months old when Samantha disappeared. Actually, when they both disappeared. That's the reason Samantha was never officially reported missing – because both she and the baby were gone. All the belongings from her room above the pub had been cleared out too. The pub had been in a state of flux because the landlady had been ill and taken into hospital, so people thought Samantha had left for another job.'

'And the baby...' Rachel swallowed, almost unable to even form her next question. 'The baby was never found?'

'No.' Lucas took a paper from his pocket and held it towards her. 'I'm sorry, Rachel, but I have a warrant to search your property.'

Rachel backed away from it. 'You don't think... you can't think...' Her voice trailed off. Her father couldn't have. He couldn't have killed a child. An innocent baby, who couldn't even speak. His *child. No.* She stared around the kitchen, horror rushing through her again at the thought of an infant somewhere in the house, its life snuffed out, all of those years ago. It couldn't be true. Could it?

'I'm sorry,' Lucas said again. 'You and your mother might want to consider staying somewhere else tonight, and maybe even for the next few days. Depending on...' He swallowed. 'Depending on how long this takes. I'll be in touch if we find anything, or if I need to speak to your mother again. We can have someone escort you past the media.' He sighed. 'They're going to have a field day with this.'

Rachel's stomach twisted at the very thought. 'Can't you just not tell them?'

'They're going to make their own assumptions when they see us digging up the property,' Lucas said. 'We can try to keep things under wraps, but in my experience, it's only likely to fuel more rumours and gossip. It's best to be straight up with them. I think my boss is releasing the news within the hour. He's anxious to show we've been making progress.'

Rachel put her hands to her temples, as if she could keep her reeling thoughts in order. It wasn't enough that her father had been with this woman and murdered her. No, he had to have a child with her, something her mother had been longing for. It was one more heavy load on top of everything she'd been carrying. How much could one woman sustain before breaking? Rachel had been proud of her strength and dignity when Lucas had told her about the affair, but how could she cope with hearing he'd fathered a child with this woman – a child he might have killed?

How could she ever recover from the blow she'd suffered if the past wouldn't let her rest?

'Can you give me an hour to pack and get out of here?' Rachel asked. Maybe it was time to get away, like Lucas had suggested. In the absence of something better, it was the least she could do for her mother now.

But Lucas shook his head. 'I'm sorry, Rach, but I can't do that. The team is here and ready to move, and I can't ask them to hang about. It's costing us a fortune as it is, and we can't waste time.'

She nodded, her heart squeezing as she watched him go back out the door, listening to the shouts and the sound of car doors slamming. How could she begin to explain why their house was being ripped apart? Her mother would find out, and — she swallowed, pain ripping through her. Rachel would be the one to deliver the hit.

Again.

She glanced at the basement door, anger mingling with the pain. It wasn't this woman's – Samantha's – fault, she knew. It was her father's. And her own, for uncovering all of this in the first place and for failing to protect her mother. But why couldn't this ghost leave them alone? Hadn't enough damage been done? Despair welled up inside her, and for a second, Rachel felt all the energy drain from her body.

But she wouldn't give up, she thought, straightening her spine. She couldn't. The darkness might be getting stronger, but she was strong too. And she'd hold her mother tightly against it until they both could breathe again.

TWENTY-TWO

SAM

March 1986

'I'll get it!' Sam lunged for the ringing phone behind the bar. You could barely hear it through the noise in the pub – it was a Friday afternoon and the whole place was packed to the rafters. But Sam had been waiting for what felt like years for this call, ever since she'd made the journey to the doctor's surgery in High Wycombe – ever since realising that she hadn't had a period in... well, she actually couldn't remember. She'd never been regular and she'd always been rubbish at keeping track, but she knew it had been a while. Plus she'd been feeling very tired and a little bloated, and even her loosest trousers were beginning to feel tight.

At first, she'd chalked it up to all the overtime she'd been putting in to help Jean. Of course she'd be tired. She'd been eating a lot, too, late at night when she finished working, so that accounted for the extra weight. She and Sean were always careful – he very much so, and she really appreciated that – so the other option never even crossed her mind. But when she spotted the unopened pack of pads in the cupboard underneath the sink – the pack she'd bought months ago – the thought had hit her that it might be more. Keen to put her mind at rest, she'd booked an appointment to have a test and then gone into the surgery early in the morning before the pub opened.

And now, she might be about to find out. She drew in a deep breath and picked up the phone, emotions swirling inside. She wasn't ready for a baby. She hadn't planned for a baby – not for at least a few years anyway; not until she had that perfect life all set up. But if she was pregnant, she'd give this baby everything she could. She'd give it all she'd never had growing up: stability, safety and, hopefully, *family*.

Her heart beat fast when she thought about telling Sean they were having a baby. Two months had passed since she'd turned down the Medhurst offer, and she hadn't regretted it once. But although they spent almost every evening together and most of the weekends now too – although Sam had never felt so happy – they still hadn't talked about the future. She knew Sean wanted children at some point. She'd seen how he looked at kids in the pub with longing, exactly the same way she did. He would make a great father.

'Hello?' she said into the receiver, her heart beating fast.

'This is Dr Gray's office calling,' a prim voice said. 'I have the results of your test.'

Sam swallowed, her hand shaking. 'And?'

'It's positive,' the nurse said, and Sam's mouth fell open. *Positive*. 'You're pregnant. Congratulations. You'll need to book another appointment to come along to the office.'

'Thank you,' Sam said numbly, then hung up the phone. She stood for a minute, the noise of the pub wrapping around her. She was pregnant. She was going to have a baby! Without even knowing she was doing it, her hand drifted down to her stomach, and everything else faded away. This was what was important now. This was what mattered. This was the future now – her future.

Did Sean want to share it?

'Everything okay, love?' Jean was looking at her with concern, and she jerked. 'You're as white as a ghost.'

She smiled. 'I'm fine. No, actually, I'm better than fine.' She was dying to tell someone, but she wanted Sean to be the first to know. They were going to be parents! Nerves washed over her again at the thought of sharing her news with him.

The minutes felt like days until the pub started to empty and Sean came through the door. She smiled and served him his pint with a kiss, then tidied up the bar as fast as she could before sitting down beside him at the fire.

'So.' She lay her head on his shoulder, loving how her head fit perfectly in the crook. 'I have some news.'

'You do?' Sean turned to face her, an easy smile curving his lips. 'Let me guess. You're going to organise another quiz night!' Her love of pub quizzes was a running joke between them.

'I'm pregnant.' The words slipped out quickly, but she couldn't keep them back anymore. She was bursting to tell him. She needed to see... needed to know what he'd say.

'You're pregnant?' Disbelief flashed across his face. 'And it's...' He swallowed. 'It's me? I'm the father?'

She drew back, forcing a laugh to cover the hurt that gripped her. What did he think, that she slept with all the men who came through here? 'Of course it's you! Who else would it be? You're here practically every night!' It must be the shock, she told herself. There was no way he could think that.

'No, it's just...' He laughed incredulously. 'I can't take it in!' He stared at her with an expression she couldn't make out, and a tiny bit of fear pricked her insides. Will's words of warning swarmed into her, as if they'd been waiting for a chink in her armour. Did he care for her enough to start a family together? *Was* there something stopping him? Her legs trembled as she waited for him to say something more.

'This is wonderful news!' he said at last, gathering her in his arms. She slumped against him, relief shooting through her. He *was* happy. She took a big gulp of air, savouring his scent.

'But look,' Sean said, his face serious. 'I think it's best if we keep this between ourselves for now, until we sort out what we're going to do.'

'What do you mean?' The relief was threaded now with doubt. Why would they keep it quiet? Unless... Will's words scrolled through her mind again.

'This is a conservative place,' he said. 'And we're not married. Not yet anyway.'

Not yet? He wanted to marry her? An image of him standing there in a suit and tie, sliding a ring on her finger, came into her mind, and happiness swelled inside. Oddly, she hadn't even thought of getting married. All she wanted was to be a family; to be together. She was still getting used to the idea of being a mother, and the thought of being a wife...

'We might be in the 1980s, but here we might as well be living in the 1950s,' Sean was continuing. 'I don't want to make things difficult for you with Jean.'

She squeezed his hand, loving him even more.

'And my boss is a very traditional man. I want to do things right: have everything lined up before we share our big news, all right?'

'That makes sense,' she said. The last thing she wanted was to disrespect Jean or cause her any problems. 'But, well, we'd better do it quickly. The rate my stomach is growing, I'm not sure how long we'll have until it's pretty obvious. And what do you mean, "lined up"?' She bit her lip. *Did* he mean getting married?

He put an arm around her. 'I want to have the house ready for you and the baby. And I want us...' He drew her closer. 'I want us to get married. To be a family – a true one – for when the baby arrives.' He took in a breath. 'How does that sound?'

A smile grew on her face, so wide it felt like it was going to split open and happiness would come pouring out. Sean wanted her. He wanted a future with her. She wouldn't let Will's words torment her anymore. They were going to be a family, and it was time to lay any worries to rest. She pulled back and gazed into Sean's eyes, the true joy she saw there extinguishing them.

'That sounds wonderful.' A baby. A husband. A family. A house. It was everything she'd dreamed of, the future she'd craved. For the first time, the dream was within reach.

It was only when she was lying beside Sean in bed later that evening that she realised he'd never said he loved her, but she batted that thought away. Of course he loved her. You didn't start planning a life with someone if you didn't love them. She didn't need to hear it said. She'd rather actions than words anyway.

Everything was perfect. And she was sure that from now on, it would stay that way.

TWENTY-THREE

RACHEL

'Mum?' Rachel eased open her mother's bedroom door, cringing as the sound of a digger reversing rang through the night air. The police had only been here for half an hour, but Lucas hadn't been joking about them not wanting to waste time. Already they were knocking down walls in the basement and digging up the back garden. Rachel bit her lip, looking at her mother's sleeping form in bed. She dreaded having to tell her mum about the missing baby, but they couldn't stay here while the house was ripped apart around them. She only hoped she could get her mother out quickly, without witnessing the full horror of what was happening to her home.

'Mum?' Rachel sat down on the bed, touching her mother's arm. 'I need you to wake up, okay? I'll help you get dressed. I'll tell you why in a second.' She yanked open the drapes, eyes widening as she spotted several spotlights illuminating a small tractor digging up the front garden and her mother's favourite flower bed. Hastily, she jerked the curtains closed again, praying that her mother hadn't seen, but it was too late.

'What...' Her mother's face was white, contorted in horror.

'What's happening?' She shot out of bed as if propelled by some invisible force. 'My rose bush! What are they doing? They can't do that!' She pulled on a robe and went down the stairs, not even seeing the chaos in the lounge as she went through the kitchen and out the front door before Rachel could grab hold of her.

'Stop!' She waved a hand at the man digging up the rose garden. 'Stop that now. You need to stop!' But the man couldn't hear her, and Rachel's mum sank onto the ground beside a rose bush, as if the sudden burst of energy had left as quickly as it had come. 'My baby,' she was crying, sobbing as if her heart was breaking. 'My *baby*. Stop, please. Stop.'

'Come on, Mum.' Rachel took her arm and got her to her feet, her heart aching at her mother's reaction. Her mum had planted those bushes years ago and tended them with such love ever since. They *were* her babies. 'Let's go inside and have a cuppa.' Eyes wide, her mother let herself be led back through the lounge, up the stairs and into bed, where Rachel settled the covers around her. God, she was absolutely *freezing*.

'What's happening?' Her mum's face was white, fear and tension pulling it even tighter over the bones. For an instant, her mother's face traded places with the body inside the wall, and Rachel shuddered. It was as if the ghost of the woman was expanding to fill this whole space, demanding that finally, after all these years, the full truth come out... that her child was found.

'Lucas came by with a search warrant.' Rachel swallowed, sitting down on the bed. She hated doing this, but there was no way to hide it now, and it was better that her mother heard the news from her than from someone else. 'They found the woman's identity, and they discovered she had a baby, only a few months old. When the woman disappeared, the child did too.' She paused as her mother's face went even whiter. 'The police think there's a possibility the baby might be buried here, either inside the house or somewhere outside.' Her voice was a whisper, but the words seemed loud – like rolling thunder, growing in intensity, using up every bit of air in the room.

'No.' Her mum drew back, and Rachel's heart twisted. '*No.*'

'I'm sorry, Mum,' Rachel said, tucking the covers tightly around her, as if that could protect her. 'I'm so sorry.' She touched her mum's arm. It was still ice cold. 'We can stay somewhere else for a while. We can go right now. You don't need to be here in the midst of all this.'

Her mother was shaking her head. 'No. I told you. I'm not going. I'm not going anywhere. They won't find anything. They won't. Your father – he wouldn't do that. He wouldn't kill anyone. He didn't. Least of all a child. He *didn't.*'

Rachel squeezed her mum's hand. Of course she would think that. Rachel didn't want to think it either. But if it was true, then she didn't want her mum to be around if they did find the child's remains. 'It'll be calm and peaceful. We can let the police get on with things here and come back when they're done. Lucas will tell us the second they finish.'

But her mother met her eyes defiantly. 'No. You can go if you want to, but I'm staying.'

Rachel sighed, but she could understand. No matter what had happened here, this was her mother's home. Her phone bleeped, and she pulled it from her pocket. Oh, God. That must be Mo. All of this was bound to be on the news – he must have heard by now. A curious mix of emotions swirled inside when she noticed the text was from the WhatsApp school group and not her husband.

Rachel breathed in, Mo's face filling her mind. After this latest discovery, she longed to be with her family and to hold them close; to banish the horror and pain. But she couldn't, now more than ever. Her mother needed every little bit of her to get through this.

'You sit tight and I'll grab a cuppa to warm you up,' Rachel said, sliding her phone back into her pocket. She'd bring the tea up, and then they could watch some soaps; try to block out what was going on around them. This room would be their safe haven. In fact... Rachel glanced around the space. Maybe until all of this was over, she could camp out right here beside her mum. If she awoke in the night from the noise, Rachel would be there to soothe her back to sleep. If she needed anything, she wouldn't even have to call. Rachel would literally be by her side until this final dark tidal wave receded, doing her best to keep the ghost at bay like her mum had when Rachel was young. The news was awful – beyond awful – but Rachel would show her mother now the real strength of her love. Maybe this was how they would find light at last: just the two of them, together.

'Ouf!' Her breath left her in a huff as she collided with someone in the hall. She drew back in surprise. 'Victoria! Oh my God. What are you doing here?' She hadn't known her sister was due back from her trip. So much had gone on since she'd left. Did she know any of it? Surely not, or she would have been here in a heartbeat. Rachel bit her lip. She'd kept meaning to fill Victoria in, but she'd been so busy trying to be there for their mother that she hadn't even called.

'What the hell is happening?' Victoria's face was white. 'How's Mum? Is she okay? I heard everything on the news on the way back from the airport.' She was shaking. 'It's not true, is it? It can't be. Dad wouldn't hurt anyone. Not a woman. Not a *baby*.'

Rachel took her sister's arm and propelled her a few feet away from their mother's room. 'I don't know about the baby, but it does seem clear that he had an affair with someone, and then...' She couldn't finish the sentence.

'I had no idea about any of this,' Victoria said, shaking her head. 'All of this was going on, and I knew nothing. I could have been here. I would have been here.'

Guilt flooded through Rachel. 'I'm sorry,' she said. 'I—'

'That bloody spa.' Victoria's face twisted, and Rachel stared in confusion. Spa? 'They took my phone and said I couldn't have it back until I left.'

'I thought you were on a business trip?' Rachel stared at her sister incredulously, remembering her saying that the trip couldn't be moved. She'd been at a spa this whole time? How could she have even considered going after finding out their mother was terminally ill?

'It was a business trip,' Victoria explained quickly. 'The spa is a client, but they said I had to behave like one of the guests: no electronics allowed. Anyway, I need to see Mum.' Victoria pushed past her. Rachel followed her into the room, watching her sister snuggle up to their mother, her arms around her.

'I'm so glad you're here,' their mother said, turning to Victoria. 'Didn't you get any of my messages? I've been trying to reach you every day. It's been so awful.' The look on their mum's face was calmer than Rachel had seen for ages, and Rachel felt that old knot inside tighten as her mother's words rang in her mind. *It's been so awful.* It *had* been awful; Rachel couldn't deny that. But she'd been trying... she was trying... and the whole time she'd been doing all she could to get their mum to talk, their mother had been reaching out to Victoria.

'Everything will be fine now,' Victoria said, patting their mum's arm. 'I'm going to give these police a piece of my mind and get them off the land. They shouldn't be here in the first place. God, I should have been here. I'm so sorry I wasn't.'

Rachel bristled at her sister's words. She had no idea how hard Rachel had tried to protect their mother. She'd just come swanning in from a spa, for God's sake – even if she did say it had been for work.

'And you don't need to worry about the house,' Victoria was continuing. 'I'll pay for all the repairs – any damage done. I don't want you to even have to think about that. You can relax now, Mum.' Rachel's heart lurched at the mention of the house, and she remembered her hope that maybe her mother would give it to her ... not because she wanted it, but because of what it represented. Would that ever happen? *Could* she ever get back to that place? With Victoria here again, the space between her and her mother seemed even more obvious. What Rachel had with their mum was nowhere near close to Victoria's connection, despite all she'd tried to do. *Nowhere.*

'It's not the house I care about,' their mother said, and pain shot through Rachel. She didn't care about the house? 'It's you.' She clutched Victoria's hand, then closed her eyes. 'I'm so happy to see you. I love you. Please remember that. You need to remember that.'

Rachel took a step towards the door, desperate now to escape, to gulp in air as that knot tightened. To curl on her bed once more, to make herself as small as she could and disappear. But then the memory of loneliness and longing rushed into her, and she turned back to face her mother. *No.* She wouldn't go – not this time. Not while the darkness was still choking both of them. Not when she had to do something to fix it.

Not when she wanted – needed – to hear her mother say those words to her.

'Right, time for your medication.' Rachel forced out the words, trying to get a grip on the hurt and desire still swirling inside. Victoria squeezed their mother's hand, then slipped from the room, and Rachel counted out the pills, struggling to push through the smoky haze of emotions surrounding her. She poured her mum a glass of water and handed her the medicine. She waited until her mother had taken the pills, then sat down beside her. Silence fell, and Rachel's mind whirred. What could she do? What could she say?

'Rach?' Victoria's voice came from the bathroom. 'Do you have a tampon?'

'I'll be back in a sec, Mum.' Sighing, Rachel levered herself off the bed and went into her bedroom, pawing through her things until she found one. She handed it to her sister, then stood for a minute in the corridor, trying to right herself once more. Then she went back to the bedroom and sat down in the corner of the room. Her mother was sleeping now, her back turned away from them.

'She's asleep,' she said to Victoria in a quiet voice when her sister came back into the room a few minutes later.

'There's a pill on the floor here she must have dropped.' Victoria picked it up, and Rachel tilted her head. That was odd; she was sure her mother had taken all the pills she'd given her. 'She needs to take all her medication, right? Let's wake her up so she can do it.'

Before Rachel could say it was fine, Victoria was gently shaking their mother. 'Mum! Mum? Wake up. You need to take this.'

But their mother stayed sleeping.

'Mum? Mum!' Victoria's voice rose in urgency. 'What's wrong? Wake up!'

Fear shot through Rachel and she grabbed her mother's hand, feeling for her pulse. It was weak, but it was still there. Oh, God. What had happened? All of this had been too much, Rachel thought. Of course it was. It was too much for anyone, let alone a woman who was terminally ill. 'Call 999,' she said to Victoria, who snatched up her mobile and punched in the numbers.

Rachel took her mother's hand, but this time, her eyes stayed closed. She didn't look at her daughter; she didn't turn towards Victoria. She remained deathly still. And as Victoria clutched their mother's other hand, Rachel thought of how she'd struggled to stay here – struggled with her mother, struggled with her family, struggled with herself. She'd overcome all of that, and she was still by her mother's side, where she needed to be. And now, after facing her own demons, she couldn't let her mother leave her. She *wouldn't*.

'I love you, Mum,' she said, grasping her mother's cold fingers. 'We love you.' She met Victoria's eyes. 'And we'll always be your daughters. We'll always be here. Nothing will change that. I promise.'

TWENTY-FOUR

SAM

May 1986

Sam jerked her hand away from her belly, making a mental note for the millionth time to stop stroking her bump. Even with the loose dresses she was wearing to disguise her pregnancy, she was going to give it away. Every so often, Jean would gaze at her through eagle eyes, and Sam was sure she knew. But Jean hadn't said anything – yet, anyway, there were still four months to go – and Sam hoped she could spill the beans before Jean twigged.

She understood why Sean wanted to keep things secret, of course. He didn't want people to look at her differently; any less respectfully. He didn't want to jeopardise his good relationship with his boss either. She appreciated that, but she was so excited to get married. She'd come up with lots of different ideas for the romantic wedding they both wanted, with just the two of them present. But Sean had been so busy at work that he'd barely had a chance to grunt before making love to her. He'd fall asleep, then roll out of bed a couple of hours later to go home. She'd asked him a few times to bring his things here so he could stay the night, but with his crazy work schedule, he kept forgetting. The more time she had to plan, though, the more special she could make their wedding, and she didn't want to push him. He was under enough pressure as it was, and it was enough to know that their future was each other – and their baby.

She smiled, thinking of the wedding dress hanging in her closet upstairs. Sean was away on a work trip this week, and she'd managed to duck into High Wycombe when things were quiet one afternoon at the pub. Only to look, she'd told herself firmly. She'd wandered through the high street, popping into boutiques half-heartedly. In her condition, with her budget and with the wedding so small, a traditional wedding gown probably wasn't the most appropriate choice. But in her heart, that was exactly what she wanted... what she'd always pictured when she closed her eyes and thought of her wedding. And since this would happen only once, why not go for it?

She'd pushed into a wedding boutique, an excited smile on her face, then spent a wonderful afternoon combing through the dresses on hand. With her burgeoning bump, anything too form-fitting was out, but the second the sales assistant brought out an ivory empire-waist satin gown with puffed sleeves and huge skirt, she was in love. As she slipped it over her head and stared in the mirror, she knew straight away that this was it. In this dress, she wasn't simply Sam Hughes. She was Mrs Sean Norman, wife of a successful businessman, and a *mother*. This was the person she was going to be – the person she'd always wanted to be – and she couldn't be more ready.

'You look gorgeous,' the assistant cooed, and Sam grinned. 'You're absolutely glowing.' Sam knew they were trained to say that, but she was right: Sam was glowing.

'Thank you.' The assistant hovered, and Sam knew she was waiting for her to slip out of the dress, but she didn't want to take it off. Steeling herself, she glanced down at the price tag, wincing when she saw the numbers. It was way over her budget, but she wanted this more than anything. She wanted to hug this feeling close to her forever. And she did have the money, even if it would pretty much halve her savings. But what was she saving for anyway? Sean would be there for her, she reminded herself, her smile growing even larger. Finally, she would have someone.

Finally, she wouldn't be on her own.

'I'll take it,' she said, sliding off the dress and handing it to the assistant before pulling on her own clothes.

'Perfect.' The assistant hung it up and slid the garment onto a rack. 'Would you like to pay for it now, or shall I set it aside for another viewing? Most brides come in with their mothers or bridesmaids to show them their favourite before purchasing. Not that I'm trying to put you off or anything, of course.'

A pang went through Sam's heart, but she pushed it aside. She'd never had a mother in her life, and when she'd pictured her wedding, it had been only her there, no one else. It would be nice to have Will as a witness, though, or maybe Jean. Will certainly wouldn't judge her, and she didn't think Jean would either. Maybe she'd talk to Sean about it, but right now she didn't want to wait. She was buying this dress.

'I'll buy it now.' She'd given the assistant her credit card, trying not to cringe at the thought of the huge bill coming in the post. It was worth it, though, she'd reminded herself. *Sean* was worth it.

A hand on her arm jerked her back to the present, and Sam nearly dropped the pint she was holding. She turned to see Jean, who'd returned from an appointment with a specialist in High Wycombe – at long last, Sam had convinced her to go to the GP, who'd referred her to have more tests. Jean was worried, Sam knew, but she refused to talk about it, pasting on a cheery smile whenever she noticed anyone looking at her.

But right now, her face was serious, and fear shot through Sam. Jean was her anchor. She couldn't bear it if anything was wrong.

'Everything okay?' Sam asked, trying to keep her voice steady.

Jean took her arm and propelled her out from behind the bar and over to a table in the corner. Sam's heart pounded as she met the older woman's eyes. Whatever she was about to say, it couldn't be good news.

'You know I was in High Wycombe for my appointment today,' Jean began. Sam stayed silent, unable to speak. 'Well, I saw your man there.'

'My man?' Sam echoed, trying to make sense of it. She'd thought Jean was going to talk about her appointment, not Sean. What was she on about? Anyway, she couldn't have seen him. He was away on a buying trip until tomorrow.

'Yes.' Jean nodded. 'I think he saw me, too, because he crossed the street before I could talk to him.'

'All right,' Sam said, her brow furrowing. Why would he do that? He liked Jean a lot, always laughing and joking around with her.

'Sam, he was with another woman,' Jean said gently. 'He had his arm around her, and they looked... well, they looked together. I don't want to be the bearer of bad news, but I thought you should know. Especially since—' She cut herself off, and Sam's cheeks flushed as Jean glanced at her swollen tummy. Did she know?

'Especially since you're pregnant, honey,' Jean finished. 'I know you wanted to keep it quiet, and I understand that. You don't have to say anything, but I want you to know that I'm here for you, no matter what.'

'It wasn't him,' Sam said quickly, eager to move away from the fact that Jean knew her secret. Sean wouldn't be best pleased. 'It couldn't have been him. He's still away on business.'

'It was.' Jean touched her arm, and Sam jerked away, as if Jean was poisonous. She couldn't let doubt reach her again. She *wouldn't*. It wouldn't taint her perfect future. 'I'm sure of it.'

Sam shook her head. 'You're wrong.'

Jean's eyes were sympathetic. 'I think you should talk to him and see what he says. And perhaps you are right, but I thought you should know.' She held Sam's gaze. 'You can talk to me about anything, whenever you're ready. No judgement. And I meant what I said: I'm here if you need me. Okay?'

Sam nodded, warmth seeping into her. In a way, she liked that Jean knew her secret. Even if she wasn't going to talk about it, she didn't want to hide it any longer. And Jean was only trying to help, she knew that. She didn't know that Sean had asked her to marry him – to be with him forever. He wouldn't have done that if he wanted someone else, that was for sure. He was committed to her, as much as she was to him. Whoever Jean had seen today, it wasn't him.

Sam didn't even need to ask.

TWENTY-FIVE

RACHEL

Rachel stared at the door in the hospital waiting room, as if by looking at it she could make the doctor emerge faster. Thankfully, her mother had hung on until they'd reached the hospital and the doctors had whisked her away. That had been over an hour ago, and they were still waiting for an update. Across the room, Victoria was on her phone, furiously tapping away on the screen as she tried to rearrange her schedule for the next few weeks 'to be around as much as possible'. An image of how she and her sister had clutched their mother's hands – clutched each other's hands – as they waited for the ambulance flashed into her mind, and emotion rushed through her. Maybe Rachel had separated herself from them for years, but in the end, they *were* all connected... they were all family. She would always be her mother's daughter. Nothing could take that away.

'You can see your mother now.' A doctor's voice cut into her thoughts, and Rachel glanced up to meet the woman's kind eyes. 'She's resting at the moment. We've had to pump her stomach, and she was in quite a bit of discomfort. We gave her some medication to help her rest.'

'Pump her stomach?' Victoria and Rachel looked at each other in surprise. Why would the doctor have to do that?

'She had an excess of morphine in her system,' the doctor responded. 'I saw from her notes that she'd been prescribed that, presumably for the pain and discomfort she was facing. But the amount that she took, well...' She looked at them sympathetically. 'Would it help if she spoke with someone? Once patients realise they can face the end of life comfortably, they're often more at peace. Their families are too.'

'Spoke to someone?' Victoria's face twisted. 'You're not implying she took too much medication on purpose, are you? She wouldn't do that. She'd never do that.'

Rachel listened, every bit of her twitching in shock. Victoria was right: her mother hadn't overdosed – at least not on purpose. Because Rachel had been the one who'd counted out the pills for that night's medication. She'd been lost in a daze of hurt, trying to shake off the past's hold on her so she could stay at her mother's bedside. She hadn't really been paying attention, had she? She'd done it all on autopilot. For God's sake, she'd even dropped a pill on the floor, and she hadn't even noticed. And now... oh God. She could have killed her mother. The very woman she was trying to protect – the woman she was desperate to have a relationship with; to hear her say 'I love you' like she had with Victoria.

How could she do that? How could she be so caught up in herself that she'd given her mother an *overdose*?

She followed the doctor down the hallway, feeling the hardened core of guilt and blame in her stomach again. Ever since she'd arrived, all she wanted was to protect her mum; to reach through to her. And yet ever since she'd arrived, all she'd done was unleash horror. She'd fought so hard to stay, but maybe she shouldn't have because the only thing she'd managed was to put her mother through hell. Sure, she'd given her mum the house, but... she breathed in, remembering her mother's words that she didn't care about that. She certainly didn't seem to: even with all Rachel's urgings, she still hadn't signed the legal documents the lawyers had drafted. Despite Rachel's efforts, nothing had really changed – for the better anyway.

Rachel shook her head, thinking once more of how they'd all held hands. She *would* always be her mother's daughter. Maybe that would have to be enough. Maybe it was time to stop fighting; time to leave her mother in peace. Rachel had always believed she could repair their broken relationship, but perhaps there were no pieces left to repair, and all her attempts were causing more harm than good. Victoria would be the light her mother needed to lead her out of this darkness Rachel had brought onto them, not Rachel.

Never Rachel.

Rachel sighed, feeling emptier and more tired than ever before. Could she accept that this was it – that she'd never reach through to her mum; never fill that longing inside? *Was* it time to go back to the people who did love her, before something worse happened?

'Right this way.' The doctor ushered them into the room, then turned to face them. 'I forgot to mention that your mother is very anaemic. It's a side effect of the cancer, and we gave her a transfusion. She may need to do this quite often over the course of the coming weeks, but her blood type – O negative – is in short supply here at the moment. Do either of you know your type? It would be very useful to have it on hand, and you can do it while you're waiting today.'

'I'm type A,' Victoria said, and the doctor shook her head.

'I'm afraid that's not going to work. And you?'

Rachel tilted her head. She was certain she'd been told at some point when she'd had the babies, but she couldn't remember. It was all a blur, with one moment standing out clearly: when she'd held each of her children in her arms, gazing down into the tiny face. Even after the 23-hour labour with Ryan, she'd still been in awe. 'I'm not sure,' she said, straining to remember.

'That's all right. I can get a nurse to do a quick test after you've seen your mother.'

'Okay.' Rachel breathed out. At least she could do *something* now to help her mum.

'Right, here's your mother.' The doctor pulled aside the curtain to a cubicle, then turned to go.

'Mum!' Victoria hurried over to the bed, and Rachel's eyes filled at the sight of her sister's emotion. She went over to the bed and took her mother's cold fingers, shuddering as she registered that with her pale skin and lying there so still, she almost looked lifeless. Rachel leaned in until she could feel her mother's breath on her skin; the warmth from her body. She ached to feel her mother's arms around her, the same way she'd ached when she was a child, and her earlier questions echoed in her mind. Could she accept that she'd never have that? Could she go back home with that piece still missing?

'Excuse me?' A whisper behind her made her turn. 'I've got the blood-type test ready for you, if you want to come with me.'

Rachel followed the nurse out of the ward and over to a little room that resembled a supply closet. The nurse made a face as she unwrapped the test and prepared to prick Rachel's finger.

'Sorry about this,' she said. 'Not exactly inspiring surroundings. I'm always tempted to bring in a poster of the Caribbean to liven up the place.'

Rachel laughed, realising that she hadn't even felt the nurse prick her finger. They waited in the tiny room, staring around at the walls.

'Okay, it's ready.' The nurse squinted at the test. 'Oh. You're AB.' She glanced up at Rachel, eyebrows raised. 'Did you say your mother is O negative? Are you sure?'

Rachel nodded. 'Yes. Apparently, it's in short supply or

something. That's why the doctor wanted me to do the test.' She stared at the nurse. 'Why?'

The nurse shifted, looking uncomfortable. 'It's just... an O negative blood type can't have a child with an AB type.' She frowned. 'Let me check again.' She looked down at the test. 'Yes, you're definitely AB. Maybe you didn't hear the doctor correctly.'

'No.' Rachel shook her head. 'I'm positive she's O negative.' She paused, trying to absorb what all of this meant. 'So, you're saying my mother...' She swallowed. 'That she can't be my biological mother?'

'Er...'

'Please. Tell me.'

'Well, um, no. She can't.' The nurse gathered up her things. 'I'd better get back to work.' She opened the door and nudged Rachel out, then locked it behind her and scurried away.

Rachel leaned against the wall, the bright lights searing her eyes. Her mother was O negative. She was AB. It wasn't possible that the woman lying in that bed was her mother. *It wasn't possible.*

She blinked, trying her best to take everything in as her mind spun. Maybe she was adopted? But hadn't Lucas said her mother had had a difficult pregnancy? Rachel had assumed that was her, but maybe it wasn't. Could her mother have lost that baby, then thought she couldn't have a healthy pregnancy? She knew now that her parents had had fertility issues, but Victoria was definitely her mother's daughter. Everyone always said she was the spitting image, and the older she got, the more she resembled her mother. Rachel didn't look like her mother at all, but she did have her father's dark hair – not that that meant anything, really.

Had her parents believed they couldn't have children, adopted her, then got pregnant with Victoria? She'd heard stories of that happening – it'd happened to Mo's sister, actually.

But why hadn't her parents told Rachel the truth? Why keep it quiet? She blinked again as an idea filtered into her mind: maybe they'd wanted to protect her, especially after they'd had Victoria. Maybe they hadn't wanted her to feel any different. And until her father's accident, she hadn't in the slightest. Whatever her mother did for Victoria, she did for Rachel. Rachel had felt her love and never for a second had she thought it was any less than for her sister. Would she have if she'd known she was adopted? She pictured those hard years after her father had died. Maybe, but her mother had continued to protect her, despite the distance between them. And now – even in her last days – her mother continued to keep the secret.

That showed something: that showed love. A love that existed still. A love that meant she wanted her daughter to feel a part of this family. She wanted to be her *mother*.

Rachel felt warmth growing inside her. She *was* her mother's daughter, and her mother loved her. Maybe her mum hadn't said the words, and maybe she hadn't been able to show it. But for the first time since arriving, Rachel knew beyond a shadow of a doubt that her mother wanted her here.

Perhaps sometime she would tell her mother she knew she was adopted, but strangely, it didn't seem to matter. She'd never known any other mum; never felt any other love. The woman who raised her was her mother… no one else.

And in what little time that was left, they could be mother and daughter again.

TWENTY-SIX

SAM

September 1986

Sam drew in a sharp breath and leaned onto the bar in the pub, trying to catch her breath as her stomach squeezed. She was three weeks from her due date, and she'd been experiencing what her GP called false labour pains for the past couple of weeks. There was nothing false about the pain, though, and every bit of her trembled when she thought of going through labour for real. Thank goodness she'd have Sean by her side. He'd promised to have his beeper on at all times during the next month.

He'd been so busy trying to get the house ready that she'd barely seen him, and only yesterday he'd dropped off a whole load of things for the baby that he'd wanted her to set up in her room at the pub in case the house wouldn't be ready. Jean had watched with raised eyebrows, and Sam had flushed. She knew what the older woman was thinking: that this house was as much a pipe dream as the wedding that had never taken place – not yet anyway. The dress was still hanging in Sam's closet, all her plans fading now that her due date was closer.

But maybe they could have the baby be part of the wedding, Sam thought, sucking in air. It wasn't traditional, but it would be a nice way to unite them all. A family, now and forever.

'You all right?' Jean touched her back, and Sam straightened up as best she could and wiped the sweat from her face. *God*. The room felt about a hundred degrees.

'I'm fine. Just these false labour pains.' She really should be asking Jean if *she* was all right. Though the landlady had insisted that the tests she'd taken months ago showed everything was normal, she was slower and weaker than ever, not to mention the weight that continued to drop off her.

'Okay. Well, you let me know if you need to take a rest. I can handle things here,' Jean said.

Sam nodded, even though she knew Jean couldn't handle the rush on her own. It was a Saturday, and the place was packed. It would only get busier. 'I'm—' She gasped again. She'd been about to say she was okay, but she couldn't even get the word out.

'Right, that's been about, what, five minutes since the last one?' Jean shook her head. 'I don't think these are false labour pains. How long have you been feeling them?'

Sam tilted her head, trying to remember. With the pub so busy, the day had been a bit of a blur. 'Maybe since noon? But I think it's because I've been on my feet so long.' She wasn't ready for the baby to come now, with the house still in disarray and the stuff in a pile in her room. This was nowhere near how she wanted to welcome her baby into the world.

'I think you'd better go pack a bag,' Jean said. 'I can take you to hospital.'

Sam breathed in. Was Jean right? Was this the real thing? Despite everything, excitement leapt through her. 'Thank you, Jean. But I told Sean I'd call him when the time came, and he's standing by his beeper. He won't want to miss out on a second, I know that much for sure.'

'All right.' Jean gave her a quick hug. 'So exciting. A new baby! I can't wait to meet it.'

Sam picked up the phone, punching her number into Sean's beeper. A baby. Her baby. Her and Sean's baby. Her life was starting. Okay, so maybe it was in the wrong order: mother then wife instead of wife then mother. But her baby would still have two parents who loved him or her more than anything – who loved each other more than anything – and that's what was really important.

She gasped as another contraction hit, keeping her gaze firmly locked on the phone. Sean was at work today, she knew, and Saturdays were one of the busiest at the dealership. Maybe he was closing a deal or drawing up some paperwork. He'd call. Any minute now, the phone would ring and he'd be on his way. The contraction eased and she grabbed the phone again. Maybe she'd beep him again to be on the safe side. Once more she punched in the numbers, glancing up to see Jean's eyes on her. She forced a smile. Sean would come. He'd never miss anything to do with the birth of his first child.

But thirty minutes later, she still hadn't heard from him. The phone stayed silent, but she wasn't sure she could talk anyway, as her contractions were gripping her stronger and more often. Finally, Jean came over to where she was huddled in the corner of the bar and wrapped an arm around her.

'Right, enough is enough. I'm taking you to hospital.' She put up a hand before Sam could even let out a protesting noise. 'I own this pub, and if I want to shunt everyone out for an emergency, then so be it.' She lifted her head. 'Everyone! We have an emergency situation, and I need to close. Please, feel free to take your pint outside if you haven't finished yet. You can leave your glass by the door.' She took Sam's arm. 'Now come, let me help you up the stairs to get your things. By the looks of it, we have no time to waste.' Sam was sure she heard Jean mutter something under her breath, but another pain hit and she couldn't think of anything but the giant hand squeezing her belly. 'We'll beep Sean from the hospital.'

Sam nodded, breathless now as she tried to make her way up the stairs, trying not to notice the boxes full of baby equipment that were still leaning, unassembled, against the walls. She gathered a few of the things she'd been told to bring, George curling around her legs as if he wanted to come too. By the time they went back down the stairs, the pub had emptied. Sam glanced inside, hopeful the phone would start ringing. But it remained silent, and she followed Jean across the car park and into the car. As the car pulled away, she looked back to see some of the regulars lifting their hands in a wave, calling out good luck and best wishes.

Her mouth fell open, and she swivelled to Jean. 'People know I'm pregnant?'

'They aren't blind, love. Of course they know, but they respected your right to keep quiet about it.' Her eyes met Sam's briefly before turning back to the road. 'Nobody here would ever judge you. We support each other. Besides, they know I'd give them a right bollocking if they ever dared say anything against you.'

Sam smiled, thinking that even if this wasn't the way she'd wanted to arrive at the hospital – where the *hell* was Sean? – it was wonderful to know that so many people were behind her. Sean would be so happy to hear that he hadn't a reason to worry about her, after all.

Fifteen minutes later, Jean pulled up to the entrance of the small hospital and stopped the car. 'Right, first thing's first, let's get you inside.'

Sam took Jean's arm as she tried to heave herself out of the car. A contraction hit again, and she doubled over in pain. Thankfully, a nurse inside spotted her and hurried over with a wheelchair.

'Here you go. Take a seat on this and I'll bring you up to the labour ward. How far apart are your contractions?'

Sam was about to answer, but she was gripped by another wave of pain. Through the blur, she heard Jean saying she'd park, then come back as quickly as she could.

'By the looks of things, we haven't long to go,' the nurse said cheerily as she wheeled Sam down the corridor. 'Is this your first?'

'Yes.' Hers and Sean's first. And if he didn't get here soon, he was going to miss it. She squeezed her eyes shut against the pain that threatened. He'd be here. He had to be.

'You're very lucky,' the nurse said, wheeling Sam into a ward full of women moaning and groaning. 'Sometimes, it can take an absolute age! Right, get yourself up onto the bed and a midwife will be over to check on you straight away.'

'Please, can I—' The rest of the sentence was cut off by another contraction. And by the time she'd recovered enough to lift her head, the nurse was gone. She swore under her breath. She'd wanted to ask if she could use the phone to try to beep Sean again. If he called the pub now, no one would be there to answer it.

'Hello, I'm the midwife on duty today and I'm going to check and see how far along you are.' Sam nodded, praying it wasn't much. 'Oh my, you're already eight centimetres,' she said, eyebrows rising in surprise. 'We'll take you through to labour now. I think this baby is ready to be born!'

'No.' Sam's voice came out loudly, and the midwife looked at her, brow furrowed. 'Not yet. Not until my...' She cleared her throat. 'My husband gets here.' It felt funny saying those words, but it also felt right. Maybe they hadn't married yet, but in her heart, Sean *was* her husband. And after today, he'd be a father too.

The midwife shook her head. 'I'm afraid this baby isn't waiting for anyone. Come, let's go.'

Sam swung her legs slowly around the bed and hobbled after the midwife down the corridor. It was only a short distance, but the walk felt endless as she tried to make her way through the contractions. All around her, women were holding onto their partner's hands, and she felt that pain clutch her again. Where was Sean? Where was Jean? She was alone.

Once more, she was alone.

'Right, get yourself comfy on here.' The midwife patted the bed. 'I think you're almost ready to push, aren't you, love?'

Sam didn't respond. She wasn't ready to push. She wanted this baby more than anything in the world, but she needed Sean. This wasn't how it should be. She lay on the bed, unmoving, her eyes trained on the door as if he would magically appear.

'Samantha? Are you all right?' The midwife cast a worried glance at her. 'Is there someone else here with you?'

But Sam didn't answer that either. Through the haze of pain, the midwife's words were floating in another place, unable to reach her. She'd wait, she decided now. The baby would wait for its father to come. Sean couldn't miss this moment – this time they'd become a family. All she had to do was lie here and wait.

'Okay, I can see a contraction coming on.' The midwife's voice was loud and firm. 'You need to give a really good push when I count to three. One, two, *three*.'

Sam didn't even blink. She didn't have to listen to this woman. She wasn't going to listen to this woman.

'Where is she? In here?' Jean's voice cut into Sam's daze, and her eyes slid over to take in her friend's face. Jean rushed to the bed and took her hand.

'Oh goodness, I'm so sorry it took so long. I couldn't find a place to park, and they told me you were in a different spot, and...' She squeezed. 'Well, I'm here now, and it looks like this baby is coming!'

'Sean.' Sam's voice was a whisper.

'I called his beeper and left the hospital number,' Jean said. 'I'm sure he's on his way right now.'

'Right, shall we try this again?' came the midwife's cheery voice. 'I can see the baby's head. This one is so ready to come out and meet Mum! A really big push, please. You can do it! One, two, three! Push!'

But Sam shook her head. If Sean was on his way, she would wait.

The midwife gave Jean a look, and Jean took Sam's hand again. 'Come on, Sam. You can do it. Imagine how proud Sean will be of you!'

A monitor started beeping, and the midwife swung towards it. When she turned back to Sam, the cheery expression was gone, replaced with a serious one. 'Your baby's heartbeat is getting weaker,' she said, and fear leapt through Sam. 'We need to get this baby out as quickly as possible. A few really big pushes can do it, Sam. Let's help the baby, all right? I know you don't want to put your child in any danger.'

Sam sucked in her breath. As much as she wanted Sean to be here, she would do anything for this child. It hadn't even been born yet, and already it was her world. 'Okay,' she said, and relief slid over the faces of both the midwife and Jean.

A few pushes later, and Sam was holding the baby in her arms. It was a girl – perfect in every way, with two cheeks like juicy rounded peaches. She and Sean had never really talked about names, and she would never dream of naming their child on her own. Until then – until their child had a proper name – Sam would call her Peaches.

'Thank you for being here,' Sam said, looking up at Jean. Thank goodness she had her in her life.

'It's my absolute pleasure,' Jean said, smiling down at Sam and the baby. 'She's beautiful. And you were amazing.'

Sam breathed in, knowing she would never forget the sheer,

jagged pain as Peaches came into the world, so quickly, as if she was eager to see what was waiting there for her. As if she was eager to see her mother.

'I'm so sorry.' Sean's voice cut through the silence, and Sam glanced up from Peaches to meet his anguished eyes. 'The one bloody time my beeper runs out of batteries! I couldn't believe it when I returned your calls and saw one was from the hospital. I got here as fast as I could, I swear.' His words came to a halt as Peaches yawned, and Sam smiled down at her.

'Meet your daughter,' she said. 'Isn't she gorgeous?'

'Oh my God,' he said in a low voice filled with awe. 'Can I hold her?' He stretched out his arms, and the midwife carefully took the baby from Sam and positioned her in Sean's arms. He stared down at her as if he couldn't believe she was here at last. 'She's beautiful.' Silence fell, and then he looked over at Jean. 'Thank you,' he said. 'Thank you for being with Sam when I couldn't be.'

Jean nodded stiffly, and Sam could see the tension in her body. But she didn't care what Jean thought. She didn't care what anyone thought. Sean may have missed the birth, but he was here now. This moment – watching him as he gazed down at their daughter – was enough to make up for any of that.

'Shall we give the new family some quiet time together?' the midwife asked softly, and she and Jean backed out of the room.

'Call me if you need anything,' Jean said, holding Sam's eyes as if she was trying to send a secret message. But Sam just smiled.

'I won't,' she said. 'Thank you, but I won't.'

Sean waited until the door closed behind them, and then he drew a necklace from his pocket. Sam's eyes widened: it was beautiful. Gems sparkled on a gold chain, and she'd never seen – or owned – anything like it.

'I know it's not an engagement or a wedding ring,' he said. She'd told him not to get her one anyway, as they needed to spend all the money on the house. 'But I wanted to give you something to show how special you are; something to mark this wonderful event: the birth of our daughter. And I hope...' He swallowed, and she could see his emotion. 'I hope that one day, she'll grow up to be as brave and as beautiful as her mother.'

Sam's eyes filled as he put it around her neck. She loved the necklace, but she loved what it represented even more. Her daughter and the man she loved, right here in this room, together forever.

Family.

'How are you feeling, Mum?' Rachel's voice was loud in the hushed hospital room, and her mum blinked slowly, as if still trying to figure out where she was. Two days had passed since the accidental overdose, and in those two days, Rachel and Victoria had taken it in shifts to sit by their mother's side. They were both exhausted, but they didn't want their mother to be alone. Victoria refused to believe their mother had taken too many pills on purpose, saying she'd probably got confused. Rachel had nodded, guilt sweeping through her at what had really happened, but determined to focus on the present. She'd made mistakes – so many – but that was all behind her now, and telling her sister would do no good. All she wanted was to be with her mother.

'I'm all right,' her mother responded, her voice raspy. 'When can I go home?' She tried to lift her head. 'Where's Victoria?'

'Victoria's nipped out for a second,' Rachel said. When she wasn't here, Victoria had been busy trying to restore order to the house before their mother returned home. Although the search outside was continuing, the police had finished inside the house without finding anything, thank goodness. She'd been working day and night overseeing a team of tradesmen to try to fix the plumbing overflow and nail down anything Lucas's team had torn apart in their search.

Over the past few days, Rachel had spent more time with her sister than she had in several years, and she couldn't help admiring Victoria's drive and efficiency. She was a force to be reckoned with, and Rachel was proud to be her sister. Knowing how their parents had tried so hard to ensure Rachel felt an equal part of the family – and knowing how her mother had kept the secret of Rachel's adoption – had erased any lingering hurt and envy, and even though they might not be related by blood, Rachel felt closer to her than ever.

And late last night, when they'd been having a cup of tea as their mother slept, Victoria had turned towards her.

'Rach...'

'What?' Rachel had raised her eyebrows, thinking she'd rarely seen her sister look so hesitant.

'I know it's under terrible circumstances, but I'm so thankful that we're able to spend all this time together. And I'd love to see you more often,' she'd said in a rush. 'If you want to. I know we're both busy, but it'd be great to do things together every once in a while. I've really missed you.'

'Of course I want to!' Rachel had said, realising that her sister wouldn't have understood why Rachel had been so distant for so long. She'd simply have thought that Rachel didn't want to be with her, which couldn't have been further from the truth. 'I've missed you too. I love you.' Rachel had held out her arms, feeling another piece of the puzzle slotting into place. She was her mother's daughter, and she was a sister too. Together, they were a family, and even though their mother didn't have much time left, they *would* be a family again, in the days and weeks remaining.

Rachel stared down at her mother now, the conversation with Victoria ringing in her head. Like her sister, her mum wouldn't have understood why Rachel had kept such space between them; why she'd ruptured their relationship. She'd never have imagined that it wasn't because Rachel didn't love her mother, but because she *did*. And Rachel needed her to know that now. She was ready for her to know why she'd held back. She didn't need to run or hide away in guilt and blame any longer. Whether her mother *had* blamed her for the accident or not, it didn't matter. She knew their love was stronger, and this would only serve to strengthen it more.

'Mum...' Rachel squeezed her mother's hand, her heart pounding. This was it. No more fear. 'I'm so sorry. I'm sorry I wasn't around more. That I stayed away.'

Her mother blinked. 'What do you mean?'

'After the accident... after Dad...' Rachel's throat caught, and she cleared it. 'After Dad died, I blamed myself. And I thought that you might have blamed me too.' Her mother opened her mouth to speak, but Rachel carried on talking. She had to get this out now. 'I know I didn't cause the accident. But I couldn't – I can't – help feeling like that. And it's led me to try to stay away from you, to try to hold myself apart. Because I couldn't bear it. Couldn't bear seeing what I did to you. And then you and Victoria got so close, and I felt like... like I wasn't a part of the family any longer.' She breathed in. 'It didn't mean I didn't love you. It could never mean that. You are my mother. You are my mother, and I love you.'

Her mum winced as if something had hit her, and she doubled over, her hands wringing the bedclothes. Rachel's heart dropped at her distraught expression, and she remembered what she'd discovered about the adoption. Was that what was upsetting her mother? The thought that someone else was Rachel's mother?

'Nothing else matters. No one else matters,' she said quickly, but her mother's face was collapsing now, and she was shifting restlessly in the bed, like she couldn't get comfortable any longer.

Maybe she should tell her mum she knew about the adoption, Rachel thought, desperate to ease her mother's distress. She knew, and it made no difference at all. Maybe that would help calm her. Maybe that would help her believe Rachel's love.

'I know,' she said softly. 'Mum, I know.'

Her mother twisted towards her with fear in her eyes, and Rachel's heart went out to her. Why was she so afraid of her daughter finding out? She must have really thought Rachel would be upset. And she wasn't. She was surprised, yes, but not upset. She was even more determined now to show the strength of her love.

'You *what*?' Her mum's eyes were wide with panic, and Rachel bit her lip. Had she done the right thing? 'But how? How could—'

'It's okay, Mum.' She squeezed her mother's hand again, anxious to put her at ease. 'Really, it's all right. The nurse did a blood-type test – she wanted to know if I could donate blood. When my type came up, it was obvious that you aren't my mother. My biological mother,' she added. 'Because, Mum, you *are* my mother. I love you. What I found out – it makes no difference. None at all.'

'Oh.' Her mum's body relaxed against the pillow, and Rachel could see the fear draining from her eyes. Finally, she was calm again. Finally, Rachel had done something right. Happiness flooded through her, and she gazed down at her mother's now peaceful face.

'So, no more secrets,' Rachel continued quietly. 'Nothing more to keep us apart. I'll be here, with Victoria, by your side, no matter what.'

They stayed silent for a few minutes, but this time it wasn't awkward; wasn't something Rachel was struggling to fill. This time, it was comfortable, as if the air had been cleared and they could both breathe again. Her mum's eyes drifted closed. Rachel sat by the bed, watching her sleep and waiting for the moment she would open her eyes again. When she did, Rachel would still be there.

This time not to protect or stand guard, but to simply be with her, the way families should.

TWENTY-EIGHT

SAM

November 1986

Crying filtered through the baby monitor, and Sam sighed. She'd been up all night with Peaches, and she'd hoped the baby would sleep at least a few hours this afternoon so Sam could finish putting in orders with the suppliers.

'Right, I'm coming.' She put down her pen and climbed the narrow stairs to her bedroom. The space had seemed so big when she'd first moved in, but now with the cot and playpen, there was barely enough room to even open the door.

'Hey there, little one.' Her heart melted as she stared down at her daughter's chubby cheeks, big blue eyes gazing up at her as if she was the only thing that mattered in this world. Sam scooped her up, rocking her back and forth, relishing the solid weight of her baby in her arms until Peaches's eyes closed and she sank back to sleep.

Sam wandered over to the window and looked out, not yet ready to relinquish her baby to the cot. That was the hardest thing: leaving Peaches up here on her own while Sam worked downstairs. Luckily, Sean had sprung for the latest baby monitor so she could hear if Peaches cried out, and she was never far away. Jean helped too whenever she could, and even Will had taken a turn babysitting when he'd come up to visit one night. But sometimes, if the pub was busy, she couldn't hear the monitor. Once she'd even gone to check on Peaches and found her soaking and cold, having sicked up most of her nightly feed onto the front of her baby-gro. George had been in the corner of the room, looking at her accusingly, and guilt had rushed through Sam as she hurried her daughter to the bathroom to give her a quick bath and change her into fresh clothes.

She loved Peaches with all her heart and never in a million years would she regret having her, but she had to admit that things weren't exactly how she'd envisioned – yet. Her daughter was coming up to two months old now, and instead of bringing her and Sean together, if anything she saw him even less. They'd yet to even register their daughter's birth: Sean was adamant that he wanted to do it himself, but whenever Sam asked if he had the time, he always said he was busy trying to finish the house and support them all. Sam had asked over and over when the house might be ready, and Sean would respond that there was 'one more thing' to do, and that he wanted to make it perfect for them.

And it wasn't only the house she was waiting for. Sam's wedding dress was still hanging in the closet, mocking her each time she opened the door. They hadn't spoken about the wedding for weeks, and the more time that passed, the more Will's words – the words she'd thought she'd laid to rest – loomed up again, gaining strength and power.

The more she couldn't push aside what Jean had told her about seeing Sean with another woman.

But no, she told herself for the millionth time, touching the necklace she never took off. Sean wouldn't do that to her. He loved her – she felt it. They were a family now, and Sean was doing everything he could to provide for them, just like he'd said. After all, it wasn't as if they'd planned for this. Peaches was welcome and loved, but she had changed everything.

Sam dropped a kiss on Peaches's forehead and gently lay her back down in the cot, pausing for a moment to make sure she settled before heading back downstairs into the din of the pub. She hated to leave her baby alone in the dark, but all of this was temporary. She was used to waiting for the future.

She could wait a little longer.

TWENTY-NINE

RACHEL

While Victoria sat with their mother, Rachel tiptoed into her room for a little lie-down. She'd brought her mum home a few days ago, helping her through the door and up the stairs into bed. Lucas's team was still searching outside, but the inside of the house was immaculate: Victoria had restored everything to how it had been when Rachel first arrived. It was as if the slate had been wiped clean, and Rachel couldn't wait for a new chapter in their lives as a family. Even though she and her mum hadn't exchanged many words since Rachel had told her that she knew about the adoption, Rachel knew her mother felt her presence by her side. It was in the way she'd open her eyes and cast her glance about the room, her eyes closing once more when her gaze landed on Rachel. It was how she'd reach out a hand, like warding off ghosts, then let it drop to the bed when she saw her daughter there. With every day that passed, Rachel felt that bond between them grow more and more. And that was everything.

Her gaze fell upon the photo by the side of her bed, her eyes tracing her family's happy faces. God, she missed them. The kids' constant texting had petered out, and even Mo had stopped sending property listings. She'd only spoken to him in snatched conversations between hospital and home, and so much had happened that she hadn't told him. He'd found out about the child who'd gone missing, of course, that Victoria was back and that her mother had been in hospital. He'd no idea about her adoption, though, and that was huge. So much space lay between them now, more than at any other time. Pain ricocheted through her, and the urge to talk to him filled her. She wanted to explain the distance between her and her mother. She *could* now. Finally, she was ready.

A knock on the door sounded through the house, and Rachel wiped her face, then went down the stairs to see who was there.

'Oh, hi,' she said to Lucas. There'd been diggers and men on the grounds ever since they'd returned from hospital, but she hadn't seen Lucas around. 'How's it all going? Are you done?' It would be great if they were leaving. God knows they could all do with some peace and quiet. The media were still camped out at the bottom of the lane, although with every day that went by without any news, they were growing fewer and fewer. If nothing was found, they'd move on for good.

'Almost.' Lucas ran a hand over his face. He looked as exhausted as she felt. 'We've finished the outbuildings, and we've only one quadrant left of the grounds to search.'

Rachel tilted her head. Outbuildings? Oh yes, she'd forgotten about the row of rickety sheds at the very back of the property, where her father had kept old bits of broken-down machinery and junk. He'd had huge padlocks on them, and she'd never even thought of trying to go inside.

'You may want to buy some new locks to secure the contents,' Lucas said. 'I'm afraid we had to destroy one of them to get in there.'

'Okay.' There probably wasn't much inside of value anyway.

'Your mother all right?' Lucas took off his cap, as if to signal this was a question in his personal capacity and not as an officer. Without it, he looked so much like the boy she knew that Rachel softened inside.

'She's... well, it's all taking a toll, really.' She sighed. 'The illness, and then finding out what my father did and...' She swallowed. 'But I'll be here for her, and I'll do whatever I can to help.'

Lucas touched her shoulder, then jammed his cap back on. 'Right, I'd better go. I'll be back with the team tomorrow morning. We have one more day's search and then we'll be out of your way.'

'Great.' One more day. One more day and this nightmare would be over. Rachel closed the door behind him, then made the tea and brought it up to her mother.

'She's sleeping.' Victoria put a finger to her lips, motioning for Rachel to set the tea down on the bedside table.

'Do you want to go home for a bit and get some rest?' Rachel whispered. 'I can stay with Mum.'

Victoria looked at her watch. 'I'll stay for another hour or so, and then I've got to go. The nanny is ill today, and I need to pick up Felicity from school.' She met Rachel's eyes. 'You're so lucky to have Mo. Honestly, I don't think Grant even knows where Fe's school is.'

Rachel nodded. Victoria was right. She *was* lucky, and she couldn't wait to talk to him and tell him everything. Maybe she'd call him tonight, when the kids would be in bed and they wouldn't be interrupted. 'Okay, I'm going to go check what kind of locks we need on the outbuildings. Lucas said they had to break one of them to get in.'

'Oh yes, I saw him go in there,' Victoria said. 'He took away a few boxes. He wouldn't tell me much when I asked, but they looked like old clothes. I had a quick look around what was left inside, but all I could see was Dad's tools and stuff.' Victoria shook her head. 'They've really ripped this place apart, haven't they? I'd forgotten those buildings were even there. I think Mum did too.'

Rachel squeezed her sister's hand, then went down the stairs. The evening air was fresh and birds were chattering as she made her way across the huge garden and towards the back field, where the rickety outbuildings stood. One of the doors was wide open, swinging in the breeze, so she headed towards it. God, it was a wonder the building was still standing, she thought, eyeing the rotted wood and splintered door. Forget breaking the lock: all they had to do was pry a loose board from the wall.

A few boxes were piled in the corner of the room, and Rachel eased one open. Victoria was right, she thought, gingerly picking up a broken wrench. The contents were a tangle of grease-stained cloths and rusty tools. Why had her father bothered saving all of this? She closed it back up and set it on top, nudging the stack with her foot to make sure the boxes were firmly against the wall. She nudged too hard, though, and the box toppled over, everything spilling out onto the dirt floor. Hurriedly, Rachel scooped up the smaller items, wrinkling her nose at the smell of oil even all these years later.

As she shook out a stained drop-cloth to refold it neatly, a swathe of satin spilled out from where it had been bundled inside it. Rachel stepped back in surprise. What was this? It looked like... she drew in a breath as she pulled out a dress, yard after yard of ivory fabric unfurling as if a tightly closed flower was seeing the light for the first time. Rachel held it up to her body, marvelling at its size. The poufy dimensions might not be fashionable now, but it was a wedding dress fit for a princess, the kind of garment every little girl dreamed of wearing. Miraculously, despite where it had been stored, it was in pristine condition. But what was a wedding dress doing in with her father's old greasy things?

She fingered the fabric, still soft under her fingers after all of this time in the box. This definitely wasn't her mother's wedding dress – she'd seen countless photos of her mother and father's wedding day, where her father was looking absurdly handsome in a black tux that even to this day still looked stylish, while her mother was wearing an elegant lace number with a flowing train. They'd seemed so happy. She shoved away the thought, her heart aching. If only her mother had known what her father was really like.

If this wasn't her mother's dress, then whose was it? Rachel caught her breath as a rogue thought filtered in. Could it have belonged to the woman in the wall? Lucas had said that her room had been cleared out, and that was part of the reason she hadn't been reported missing. Could Rachel's father have brought her things here? Maybe those were the boxes Victoria had seen Lucas taking away. They must have missed this dress, wrapped up as it was under broken tools in a greasy drop-cloth. If it was the woman's dress, that would explain why it had been hidden here all of these years.

But why would the woman have a wedding dress? Had she been planning to marry Rachel's father, maybe? Was he going to leave her mum and start a new life with her and their baby? Rachel winced, thinking of her mother, depressed and desperately longing for her own child. Surely, her father wouldn't do that, would he? He'd done much worse, though, she reminded herself, still trying to absorb the fact that he'd murdered someone.

But why would he kill her if he'd been planning to marry her?

Rachel stared at the dress a minute longer, then slowly bundled it back into the box. Then she combed through the other boxes, almost not wanting to but at the same time needing to know if any other secrets were concealed inside. Thankfully, they only held more broken tools and various random bits of machinery. She let out her breath and restacked the boxes. Should she tell Lucas about the dress? But what was the point? It wouldn't bring back the woman or say what had happened to the child. It would only open more questions; more probing. It would only draw out the darkness again.

She'd get rid of it when she had a chance, Rachel thought, closing the door behind her. It served no purpose. The past was the past, full of brutal secrets she may never know the answer to. She didn't *want* to – none of it mattered.

At last, she was able to embrace the present.

She went out of the building and closed the door, warmth spreading through her as she stared at the house in front of her. It wasn't the cold, lonely place of her past. Inside were her mother and sister, and finally she felt connected to them. And now, her worlds could come together. Not only could she talk to Mo and banish the emotional distance between them, but she could also bring her family here, into this light that now existed. That image of the kids by her mother's bed could come true. She grabbed the mobile and hit Mo's number, excitement leaping inside. Lucas had said there was only one day left of searching. Mo and the kids could come straight after. God, she couldn't wait to see them.

'Hey,' she said when he answered.

'Hey yourself.' His rich tone echoed through the handset, and longing went through her. 'Have they found the baby yet?'

'No, thank goodness.' She prayed they wouldn't; that the baby was safe and well. But whatever happened – whatever the police found – nothing would drag them down again.

'And your mum?'

'She's better now that she's home again,' Rachel said, thinking how odd this conversation was. It was almost like they were strangers. And in a way, as much as she didn't like to think about it, they always had been because she'd always kept something hidden away.

She drew in a breath. It was time. Time to tell her husband what had happened. Time to open up that buried part of her to the man she loved most.

But before she could say anything, Mo started talking.

'Look, Rach,' he said. 'I'm glad you called. I was going to call you anyway tonight. I'm taking the kids away tomorrow – I booked us a cabin for a week in one of those holiday parks in France.' Rachel drew in a breath, remembering how they'd looked at that last year and wanted to go, but thought it was too expensive. And now Mo and the kids were going? Off on a family holiday... without her? 'We won't be gone long, and we'll come back if you need us.'

Rachel was silent, gripping the mobile as the excitement ebbed away and pain twisted through her. This was her family; her husband. They needed her now, didn't they? And she wanted to see them. She missed them so much.

'I wanted to be there for you,' Mo continued, as if he could hear her pain. 'I want us to be with you. But you made it clear that you needed to do this alone. I've tried to understand, but the kids... well, they're just kids. I need something to distract them.'

Rachel's eyes filled with tears. They were just kids. Of course they wouldn't understand. She hadn't meant to hurt them, but there was no way she could have let them into this dark place. But now the dark was gone. She didn't have to keep them away anymore.

'Can you cancel it?' she asked. 'Can you all come here instead?' She held her breath.

Mo sighed, and her heart sank. 'I can't do that to the kids; can't yank away something again. They're so excited, Rach. Tabitha's actually in her bedroom learning French right now.' He paused. 'Supper's ready. I've got to go. We'll call once we're settled, okay? Take care. We love you.' The line went dead, and that image of togetherness in her head slowly faded away.

Rachel slid the phone into her pocket and started towards the house, disappointment swirling inside. After so many years, she'd been ready. Ready to tell Mo the fear she'd clutched so close to her; ready to bring those two families together. But before she could even begin to explain, Mo had hung up. He'd hung up, and tomorrow he and the kids would be far, far away, in another country without her – just when she'd been about to bring them closer than ever before.

Had she managed to piece together one family again only to have another fall apart?

No, she told herself, taking deep breaths. Her family was stronger than that, and she'd only been gone a short while. And maybe some extra time with her mother and sister would do them good before bringing others in. As soon as Mo and the kids came back, she'd call and explain everything.

Then at last, she would be whole.

THIRTY

SAM

December 1986

Sam smiled as she placed the last sandwich into the picnic box, then stood back to survey her handiwork. The spread she'd put together looked like something from a magazine: roast-chicken sandwiches, cheese she'd bought from the posh cheesemonger that opened last month on the high street, a bottle of champagne (the most expensive she could afford, which wasn't much), and some grapes and strawberries. She'd even bought a red-checked picnic blanket to lounge on. She wasn't sure if there was a table or not, and if they had to eat on the floor, then at least they could do it in style.

She wrapped her arms around herself with excitement, feeling downright giddy. She couldn't wait to see the house! Actually, she couldn't wait to see Sean. He'd been working non-stop for ages, originally hoping to get them in for Christmas, his face full of disappointment when he'd told her that it wouldn't be possible. She knew he wanted to show her the house only once it was completely finished, but she couldn't wait any longer... for the house or for him. So what if the downstairs toilet still didn't work, or the sliding glass door from the kitchen to the patio wasn't smooth? She didn't care! After three months of living in a cramped room with a baby, even the thought of a downstairs toilet and sliding glass door was sheer bliss!

So, she'd put together a plan to surprise Sean: a gorgeous picnic supper at the house after he finished work. He'd told her last night that he was going straight there to put on another coat of paint in Peaches's room, so she knew for sure he'd be around. And if the mountain couldn't come to Muhammad, then... Bursting with anticipation, she'd decided to doll up her and Peaches, make Sean a meal he couldn't resist, hop on the bus and claim the space as her own – as *their* own. Their first family meal at their new home! God, she couldn't wait.

There'd been a minor hitch when she realised with surprise that although she knew where he worked, she didn't actually know the street address of the house. He'd talked about it in such detail that she felt like she could recite each room dimension off by heart, but he'd never told her the exact location. All she knew was the name of the village, nothing more.

Shaking her head at her subterfuge, she'd rung up his work, pretending she had a delivery for him and that she needed to check his home address. Thankfully, his secretary had given it out with no problem, and Sam had jotted it down, committing it to heart. This would be her forever home. She could feel it in her bones.

'Come on, little one.' She tweaked her daughter's cheek, straightening the bonnet on her head and brushing a speck of dirt off the cherry-red dress Jean had bought for her. Then she smoothed down her hair and gazed at her own reflection in the mirror. With the hard work at the pub and taking care of Peaches, any extra baby weight had fallen right off of her. She was wearing a dress Sean had bought for her, and even though it was shorter and brighter than her normal clothes, she loved knowing he'd picked it out with her in mind. She bundled them both into heavy jackets, and then with Peaches on one shoulder and the picnic basket on the other, she went to wait for the bus to Sean's village. It only ran every couple of hours, so she'd have to hang around for a bit before he got home, but that was okay. It would give her a chance to check everything out and get to know her new surroundings.

'Hey, sexy.' A car pulled up to the bus stop, and Sam blinked at the face peering out at her. She recognised the man inside, but at first she couldn't place him. Then her heart beat fast as it hit her: Alex. He'd grown a dark beard and his hair was much longer than when she'd last seen him, but it was definitely him. Instinctively, she clutched Peaches closer and stepped back. 'Where are you off to?' he asked. 'Hop in and I'll give you a lift. We can catch up.'

Sam stared in surprise. Did he actually expect her to get in the car? Had he forgotten that the last time they'd seen each other, he'd attacked her? She didn't have to be scared now, though, she told herself. So much had changed since that night. She had Sean, and she was about to be married. She wasn't alone any longer. 'That's all right,' she said, shaking her hair back. 'My fiancé is on his way to pick me up.' He wasn't, of course, but Alex didn't know that.

'Fiancé, huh?' Alex's eyes narrowed, his mouth twisting as he clocked Peaches in her arms. 'Hope it's not that bloke that knocked me out because he's got something coming to him. Thinking he can throw a punch and scare me off. Not likely.' He let out an angry puff. 'He cost me my job, you know. Couldn't work for a few days and they wouldn't take me back again. I had to do shit jobs for a goddamn *year* until I heard about a new project in High Wycombe that was desperate for labourers.' He grinned, but it looked more menacing than happy. 'Only a few miles away from you. Must be fate, right? A chance to see you again, and a chance to—'

'Oh, here's the bus,' Sam said, so relieved to see it she forgot she'd told Alex that Sean was coming to get her. She climbed on and dropped into the seat, trying to relax. Alex might be nearby working on a job, but he wouldn't bother her, and he wouldn't hurt Sean either. He wouldn't hurt *them* – they were as solid as a couple could be, and Alex was all hot air. No, she wasn't going to waste another second thinking about him. She was going to focus on Sean and their future together.

A few hours later, she was drooping. The bus journey had taken longer than expected, Peaches had needed her nappy changed twice, and the cute red outfit she'd been wearing had fallen victim to a huge poo. Thankfully, Sam had an extra Babygro on hand for instances like these, but now it looked like she'd dragged the baby from bed rather than making any special effort.

And she looked no better, Sam thought, grimacing at her reflection in a window. Her hair frizzed around her face, her mascara had run from the sweat of lugging a basket and baby, and her dress was wrinkled and riding up with each endless step she took.

It did seem endless, she thought, looking down the lane a villager had pointed her towards when she'd stopped to ask directions for the millionth time. Sean hadn't told her the house was on the edge of the village in practically the middle of nowhere! She'd thought she'd have time to rest and wander around, but it was taking her ages to find the bloody place.

Peaches let out a howl as a car blew by them on the road, and Sam patted her back and gritted her teeth. 'Not long now,' she said, praying it was true. 'You'll see your father soon. You'll see your home!' She started humming a tune, and before she knew it, her baby was smiling and nodding her little head along. Okay, maybe she wasn't – maybe it was just the up-and-down of Sam's steps – but she liked to believe her child had rhythm.

Her child. She dropped a kiss on Peaches's head, still unable sometimes to really believe that this was her baby. Peaches would be hers always; they would be everything to each other. Sam would never leave her. No matter what happened, she would always be this child's mother. No one could ever take that away.

'I think this is it!' She stopped at the end of a long drive, brows furrowing. 'Number 2, the sign says. But...' The house at the end of the lane wasn't a work in progress; far from. It was a two-storey stone house, with ivy climbing up one side and well-landscaped gardens spread out in front of it. Sam didn't know much about houses, but she did know that amount of ivy did not grow on new builds. And anyway, it was obvious that this house was anything but new.

'The secretary must have got the address wrong,' she said, heart sinking. 'Maybe it's the next one?' She started walking down the road again, but there was only one house and that wasn't a new build either. Sighing, she turned back around and stared at number 2. The lights were on inside, with Christmas lights twinkling from bushes in front. Maybe she could go there and see if they knew Sean. It wasn't a big village. Perhaps they could point her in the right direction.

She crunched down the long drive, admiring the view of rolling fields from either side. This place and all the land must have cost a fortune, she thought. Maybe one day, she and Sean could afford something like this. For now, she'd be happy with the sliding glass doors and downstairs loo. But none of that really mattered, she reminded herself. As long as she had her baby and Sean, she had everything she'd need for the rest of her life.

'Right,' she said to Peaches, and the baby turned her blue eyes and looked up at her. 'Let's ask and see where on earth your father might be.' She quickened her pace as she approached the house, peering through the large bay window at the front. The cosy scene warmed her heart: a woman was laying the table with a casserole dish, glistening crystal and cutlery, and candles. And... she turned slightly, and Sam could see the swell of her belly. She was pregnant.

Sam smiled as she watched the woman rub a hand over her bump, and she dropped another kiss on Peaches's cheek. Soon, she'd be the one serving up a meal in this idyllic setting. And maybe she would be pregnant again too?

She was so immersed in her vision that she wasn't even shocked when Sean walked into the room. For a second, she thought it wasn't real; that she was lost in the fantasy. But then he swept back his hair in a way that was so familiar and tucked in his shirt, and she blinked, jerking back. No, she thought, staring hard at the face in front of her. This wasn't her imagination; it wasn't her fantasy. This *was* Sean. It was Sean, and he was— Her mouth dropped open. He was putting his arm around that woman. He was drawing her close and kissing her.

Sam let out a little cry and moved back into the shadows, unable to process what she was seeing. She stared, as if it were a film playing out in front of her – a horror show, the likes of which she could never imagine. Not a fantasy now, but a nightmare. Sean sat down at the table with the woman, and they both tucked into the food, smiling and chatting. Sam squinted, taking a few steps closer. As Sean lifted his glass to his mouth, in the glint of the light, she saw something that was like a dagger straight to her heart.

He was wearing a wedding ring.

Her stomach twisted and her legs went weak, and she struggled to stay on her feet, to keep hold of Peaches, to keep her daughter wrapped in her arms. She drew in deep breaths, the fresh night air tearing at her lungs, the shards ripping at her throat with every mouthful.

Sean was married. He was *married*.

The knowledge filtered in like poison, blackening the edges of her bright vision of life ahead until everything was dark and rotten. Will had been right, all of those months ago when they'd met for dinner and Sean hadn't showed. He *had* been hiding something. And Jean had tried to tell her – tried to say she'd seen him with another woman – but Sam hadn't listened. She hadn't wanted to believe she was only his bit on the side.

That she wasn't enough – not even close.

But... Sam shook her head, trying to puzzle things out. Sean had been happy when she'd said she was pregnant. He'd asked her to marry him, for goodness' sake. Why would he do that if he didn't love her? Had he been planning to leave, and then his wife had got pregnant? And now he was going to stay?

Or maybe he was stringing her along; keeping her close so she didn't tell anyone until he could find a way to gently fob her off. Maybe that was why he didn't want to plan or even talk about the wedding: because it was never going to happen. And maybe that was why he'd been so secretive – not because of a traditional boss or out of worry people would disrespect her, but so no one would ever find out. For God's sake, he hadn't even registered his own daughter's birth.

A small cry escaped again and Sam clamped a hand over her mouth, watching as the wife put a hand on Sean's shoulder and he smiled up at her, leaning against her swollen belly. A pain clutched at Sam as she remembered he'd done that to her, too, and she turned from the window. The life she'd been dreaming of – her future in this house, with their family – would never be hers. It already belonged to someone; that place was already taken. And Sean wasn't going to be hers either.

He never had been.

Her stomach wrenched, and she turned to retch into the nearby bushes, but her stomach was empty – as if there was nothing left inside of her now, not even a *person*. Who had she ever been anyway? How stupid to think she could have a future... a proper family, in a beautiful house. That life wasn't for the likes of her, a woman whose own mother hadn't wanted her, who'd been dragged up through the care system and hadn't a qualification to her name. How dumb could she have been?

Tears stung her eyes. Peaches sagged heavy in her arms, and Sam hurried down the lane. Alex's leering face flashed through her mind, and she forced her legs faster. She was alone now... alone once more, with no one to protect her.

THIRTY-ONE

RACHEL

'There you go.' Rachel tucked the covers around her mother a few days later, her heart aching at how pale and thin her mum had become, even after the blood transfusions the hospital had given her. She should be fully recovered from the overdose, but it seemed like the medication still had a hold over her, making her drowsy and unresponsive. Dr Druckow visited almost every day now to check on her, telling Rachel and Victoria that although their mum should have weeks left, patients dealt with death in different ways. Some became almost manic, while others were more like their mother: sinking into sleep at every opportunity, as if it was a comfort blanket from reality. The best they could do was to keep her comfortable in the time that remained – to keep talking to her, to tell her they were there, exactly like they were now. She and Victoria sat for hours by their mother's bed, the three of them holding hands. And even though her mother barely spoke, finally Rachel had the family she'd longed for.

Rachel's gut twisted as she thought of her own family: of the distance that lay between her and Mo, both physical and emotional. He sent photos of their trip almost every day, and although she was glad to see them having fun, it hurt all over again that she wasn't there. Soon, she told herself. As soon as they were back, she'd tell them to come here.

Rachel glanced out the window, eyebrows rising when she spotted a police car coming down the lane. What now? The search for the missing child had ended a few days ago, and thankfully nothing had been found. The media had moved on to the next big story, and everything was quiet save for the landscapers Victoria had hired to try to repair the damage caused by the police search. Maybe the police were coming to say that after all of this, the baby had been found alive and well? Please God may that be true.

Rachel closed her mother's bedroom door quietly, then went down the stairs.

'Hi,' she said, beckoning Lucas inside. 'How are you?'

'I'm fine.' She could tell by his face that he was bursting with news. Was it about the child? 'You might want to sit down for this,' he said slowly, and apprehension shot through her. Surely, he wouldn't say that for good news, she thought, her heart sinking. Was the child dead? *No. Oh, no.*

Whatever it was, though, she reminded herself, they could get through it together.

'What is it?' She stayed standing.

'When we searched the grounds, we found some items in one of the outbuildings,' Lucas began. Rachel let out a breath, feeling a bit of tension leave her body. *Items in the outbuildings.* Maybe this wasn't about the missing baby, after all. Maybe he was here to tell her what she'd already suspected: that the items he'd removed had belonged to Samantha.

'What were they?' she asked.

'Baby clothes,' Lucas said. 'Lots and lots of baby clothes.'

Rachel tilted her head. Baby clothes? It made sense, she supposed. If those boxes contained Samantha's things, then there was bound to be some baby gear among them... clothes that would have belonged to the child they'd been searching for. But why did Lucas seem so serious? Why did he want her to sit down?

Trepidation stirred inside once more. Had they found that child?

Her heart picked up pace as she held Lucas's gaze. *Please may the child be all right. Please may he or she be walking around, happily living life, completely unaware of this horror.*

'And?' Her voice was even higher.

'We found the child. We found the child, and she's fine.'

'Oh, thank God.' Rachel let herself sink into a chair, relief whooshing through her. Her father hadn't killed the baby. She wouldn't have to tell her mother any more devastating news. A million questions swarmed through her mind: who the baby was, where she lived, what she knew. Rachel shuddered, sympathy going through her as she pictured finding out your father had killed your mother. It would be dreadful, and she had every sympathy, but she couldn't focus on that right now. All she wanted was to be with her mum in the time that remained.

'Well, thanks for coming,' she said, getting to her feet.

'Rachel.' Her heart dropped at his serious tone, and she met his eyes once more. What now? 'The missing baby... it's you.'

'*What?*' She jerked back. He couldn't have said what she'd thought. He couldn't have. He must be having a laugh, although God knows why he'd think to joke about something like that. 'Stop it, Lucas. That's not even funny.'

'I'm serious.' Lucas's touch on her arm and his intense gaze made her heart beat faster. *Was* he serious? 'You are the baby we've been looking for. Samantha Hughes was your mother.'

'No.' Rachel shook her head. He was serious, but he was wrong. 'No, I'm not.' She was adopted, yes, and her parents had hidden it from her. But it was a long way from hiding that to keeping secret that she was the child of the woman her father had killed. This was crazy. 'There must be a mistake.'

'There's no mistake,' Lucas said in such a definite tone it made her shiver. It might be crazy, but he certainly seemed to believe it. 'Have a seat and I'll explain.' He motioned her towards the table, and she sat down again, the familiar kitchen around her now feeling foreign and strange, as if she was in a world where nothing made sense.

'When we found the box of baby clothes, we didn't have high hopes,' he began. 'We thought they were family cast-offs. Still, we decided to take a punt and search through them for something, for anything that might give us a clue. One of our forensic team managed to find a small strand of hair, caught in the velvet nap of a little red dress. We tested it for DNA, and then compared the DNA to what we had from Samantha. The results showed that the samples were parent and child.'

Rachel nodded, unable to speak. His words swirled around her, merging with this strange landscape she now found herself in. The thought that he could be right was unfathomable, but deep down, a seed of dread was sprouting.

'And then we ran a search in the system to see if, on the off chance, it matched any other DNA samples we had on file. And it did.' His eyes burned through hers. 'Yours. It matched the sample you gave us after we discovered the body.' He shook his head. 'I can't believe you were right here all along. We had your DNA sample. But we never, not in a million years, thought to compare it with Samantha's.'

Rachel blinked, trying to take it in. Trying to make sense of something – of anything – he'd said. She ran the words through her head, repeating them inside her brain as if that could help her comprehend them. She was the child of the woman her father had murdered. The woman in the wall had been her mother.

'Your birth was never registered,' Lucas continued. 'I'm not sure why, but that's the reason we never knew Samantha had a child in the first place. We have a sample of your father's DNA taken from some items recovered during our search, and it's just as clear you are his daughter. They are – were – your parents.'

Rachel drew in a breath as a sharp pain hit. They *were* her parents – past tense. Her birth mother was dead. She was gone, forever, because of her father's actions. Her *father*. The word rang in her head like a hammer, landing blows each time. Her very own father had killed her mother, then buried her in the wall.

God.

'How are you doing?' Lucas met her eyes, and she turned towards him.

'I... I...' she said quietly, her voice barely emerging. She didn't even have the words to begin to express her emotions.

'Do you know...' Rachel swallowed. 'Do you have any idea how I ended up here?' How much had her mother – the woman upstairs – known? *Had* she realised her husband was having an affair? Had she known he'd murdered someone and that Rachel was his mistress's baby? God, Rachel couldn't even begin to imagine. How could you even start to form a bond with a child whose mother you'd resent so much, a child you might have taken in only to save your husband?

You couldn't. You *couldn't*.

Rachel closed her eyes, memories from her childhood flashing into her mind. Her mother putting her to bed, making her breakfast, taking her to school... Rachel had felt love in every single action. That was the reason she'd come back here now: to feel it again because she knew it was there. That was why she'd stayed. Her mother had shown through her silence about the adoption that she loved her still.

Could Rachel have been wrong? Could the reason her mother had remained silent about the adoption not been out of love, but out of fear? Was it possible her mother didn't want her here, after all?

'I'm afraid I'm not sure how your parents – Janet and Sean – came to claim you as their own.' Lucas drew out a birth certificate. 'They registered your birth late, a few months after the date they gave as your birthday. They're both listed as your birth parents here. No one suspected you weren't theirs.'

Rachel could only stare at the paper in front of her, the names she'd seen a million times. Her father, her mother, her. This was what she knew. This was who she was; who she had been for as long as she could remember. But it wasn't true. She wasn't this person. Maybe that wasn't even her birthday. And while that might be her father, her mother...

She focused in on the name. Her mother couldn't have known who she really was. She *couldn't* have, or Rachel never would have felt that love, then or now. Maybe the woman in the wall – Samantha – had given birth to her, and Rachel was sorry for what had happened to her, but the woman on the birth certificate *was* her mother. Rachel had no idea how her father could have produced this document or what he might have said to her mum to explain it, but whatever deception had happened, that was down to her father, and Rachel wasn't going to give him any more power to destroy things now. She breathed in, feeling something inside her steady again.

Lucas put a hand on her shoulder. 'I do have one piece of news I think you'll welcome. Now that the victim has been identified, her child – you – has been found, and we have evidence linking your father to the crime, the case is officially closed. My boss wants everything tied up now.' Lucas made a face. 'He says we spent too much time and money anyway, now that media interest has faded. The papers have moved on to something else, and there's no need to stir them up again with this latest bit of information.' He paused for her to say something, but she couldn't conjure up any words.

'Look, I'm going to leave you now.' He let out his breath. 'This case... well, I can't wrap my head around it. I'm not sure I'll ever be able to.' He squeezed her shoulder. 'Good luck, Rach. Call if you need anything.'

Rachel watched him leave, then slumped back into the chair, still trying to absorb what he'd said. She wasn't sure she would ever be able to wrap her head around it either. But as much as her world may have tilted, one thing stayed stable: her love for her mother, and her mother's love for her.

And as long as that remained, she could keep standing, no matter what else fell apart around her.

THIRTY-TWO

SAM

December 1986

'Sam?'

Sam lay in bed, the dark encasing her like a coffin. Through the gloom, she could barely make out the gentle rise and fall of her daughter's chest in the cot beside her. The voice came once more, but she didn't want to open the door. It was Jean yet again, coming to check on her for the millionth time.

'I'm fine,' she croaked when Jean kept banging. But she wasn't fine. Far from it. Ever since she'd seen Sean with his pregnant wife, it was like the darkness had closed in around her, keeping her captive. She'd crawled into bed after feeding Peaches, then told Jean she was ill and stayed in her room, getting up only to tend to her daughter. That had been five days ago, and Sam hadn't left her bed except for a few brief forays to the kitchen late at night to grab something – anything – to fill the hole deep inside of her.

What she'd had with Sean... that hadn't been special. It had only been a quick shag for him, nothing more – it had never been a real relationship. He'd asked her to marry him to keep her quiet, to delay her telling everyone about her pregnancy and to keep everything under wraps, not because he actually wanted to be with her. Not because he wanted a life with her. How could he when he already had a perfect life with someone else?

It was all so clear now. Like always, she'd been used and thrown away. Sean hadn't called or visited for days, even though she wouldn't have seen him anyway. She should be used to that by now, but it still hurt more than she could bear.

Peaches sighed in her sleep, and Sam turned towards her. How could she do this? How could she be a mother alone – be enough for her daughter – when she wasn't good enough for anyone else?

'I'm coming in.' Sam heard a key turn in the lock and she sat up in bed, blinking against the light Jean had snapped on.

'Now what is this all about?' Jean's no-nonsense tone filled the room. The bed creaked as she sat down beside Sam, reaching out to cup her chin. 'You don't look ill to me, although you could do with a good bath.' She glanced around the room, wrinkling her nose. 'And you two could do with some fresh air. Care to tell an old woman what on earth is going on? We miss you downstairs. Everyone keeps asking for you. Some bloke named Alex sends his best wishes too.' Her mouth twisted. 'How do you know him? Haven't seen him around here before. Doesn't look our usual type.'

Sam's heart thumped at the mention of Alex. As much as she hated to admit it, he was part of the reason she'd hardly left the room. She didn't want to face the fear inside whenever she pictured his face inches from hers; felt his grasp on her arm. She couldn't. Not when she had everything else to deal with.

She glanced up at Jean. 'I...' She swallowed. She hadn't said the words aloud, and speaking would make them even more real. But it *was* real, she reminded herself. As much as she wanted to believe all this was a nightmare, it was real. 'I went to Sean's house with Peaches last week,' she started. 'I wanted to have a picnic with him and see all the work he'd been doing to get the place ready for us.'

Jean stayed quiet, but Sam could see by her expression that she knew where this was going.

'But when I got there, it wasn't a new house. Not at all. And...' Jean squeezed her arm, and her eyes filled with tears. 'And Sean was there, having a meal with his wife. She was pregnant. And he...' A tear streaked down her cheek. 'He was wearing a wedding ring.'

'Oh, honey.' Jean's voice was soft, and she folded Sam into her arms. 'I'm so sorry.'

Sam fell into Jean's cushiony warmth, letting herself cry. Jean held her, patting her back, the same way Sam did with Peaches when she was upset.

After a few minutes, Sam pulled back. 'I know you tried to tell me,' she said, meeting Jean's sympathetic gaze. 'I know you tried, but I didn't want to hear it. I couldn't.' She swiped the tears away. 'It's always been my dream to be with someone like him – to be good enough for someone like him. A proper person, you know? With a house, a car, a family.'

'Good enough?' Jean shook her head, anger crossing her face. 'You're worth a million of him. He's a liar and a cheat and a million other names I could call him.' She paused, staring hard at Sam. 'It's not what we have or our qualifications that make us. It's who we are; how we treat other people, the love we can give them. And I can't think of a more caring, harder working or *loving* person than you, Sam. You came here a stranger and now you're like my daughter.' Sam's eyes welled up again, and she thought of how Jean had held her in her arms. 'Maybe you don't have a degree, and maybe your bank account isn't big. But you have the biggest heart of anyone I know. If someone doesn't appreciate that – doesn't give you that love back and more – they're not worthy of you.'

Sam stared, Jean's words going straight to her heart. Jean

was right. She'd been so focused on achieving the perfect life for her and her daughter – the husband and father, the house, security – that she'd forgotten what she'd wanted most: love. And despite telling herself he did, Sean had never given her that. He'd never even said it, but she'd been so distracted by the dream of that perfect life that she'd swept any doubts aside.

'And as for family, I'll tell you one thing I've learned over the years,' Jean was saying. 'Family can come in many shapes and sizes. Sometimes, it's a mum and dad. Sometimes, it's only a mum. And sometimes, like in my case, it's the people around you. People like you, my dear. People who have helped me these past few months get to all my doctors' appointments; who have taken on the brunt of the business when I'm too tired. It's the people who are there when you need them.' She smiled, light shining from her despite how pale she looked. 'Family means love, and you have plenty of that.'

A tear streaked down Sam's cheek, and she wiped it away. Maybe she'd been thinking of this all wrong. Maybe she'd been so busy seeking what she thought was perfection that she'd missed out on what was right in front of her: so many people who cared, surrounding her and lifting her up. She *wasn't* alone in the darkness, and she didn't have to face her fear by herself.

'And don't forget, you have your wonderful daughter,' Jean continued. 'She loves you so much, and I know you love her. I can see it every day in all you do for her.'

'I just...' Sam swallowed. 'I—'

'I know it's been hard, but you've been amazing,' Jean interrupted, before she could continue. 'And all children need is love. As long as you can give her that, that's all that matters.'

Peaches let out a squawk, and they both turned towards her, smiling.

'That's everything,' Jean continued, lifting Peaches out of the cot and holding her out to Sam. 'And I can promise you, it's more than enough.'

THIRTY-THREE

SAM

December 1986

Sam gazed at the mirror in her bedroom, then reached up to touch the necklace around her neck. She hadn't taken it off since Peaches was born, that wonderful moment her daughter had come into the world, the wonderful moment Sean had missed. She'd wanted to believe what he'd told her then – what he'd told her ever since they'd met. She'd been so desperate for the life she'd dreamed of that she'd missed seeing it lacked the one thing she really wanted: love. She'd thought the necklace meant that, but it didn't. None of Sean's actions did.

That was fine because Jean was right. Maybe Sean didn't love her, but she had plenty of love around her anyway; she had plenty of love inside. And most of all, she had Peaches, and no one would take her away. Sam picked up her daughter from the cot, her heart panging at the thought that she'd probably never know her father. She would have plenty of people around her who did care, though – people who wouldn't let her down. *Family.*

Sam bit her lip, thinking of Jean and praying she'd be okay.

She'd been taken into hospital for urgent tests yesterday, and although Jean still sounded certain it was nothing, Sam wasn't so sure. But she knew she'd do everything she could to help, the same way Jean had for her – the same way Jean had told Alex to 'sod off' when he'd asked Sam out one too many times recently, like Sam had known she would. Maybe Sam didn't have Sean to defend her any longer, but she did have Jean and the whole community around her. *They* were her family, not someone who lied and cheated.

She glanced in the mirror again, the chain heavy around her neck. She didn't need this necklace. She didn't *want* this necklace. It was time to give it back; time to face the man she thought she'd marry and tell him she knew that he'd lied. She wanted nothing from him: not now, not ever – nothing but the chance to face him and tell him she needed him no more. In fact, she never had.

'Come on, darling,' Sam said, smoothing her daughter's curls. 'Let's go take a bus ride.' There was enough time to get there and back before opening the pub. She shrugged on a coat against the chill, grimacing as she caught sight of the wedding dress still in the closet. When she came back, she'd return it to the shop.

As the bus bumped along the road and Peaches cooed in her lap, Sam couldn't help thinking of the last time she'd made this journey, full of hope with the picnic basket heavy on her shoulder and Peaches in her arms. She'd been wearing a dress and make-up, and now she was bare-faced in her pub uniform. Everything had seemed so bright, but it hadn't been real. Sadness filtered in, but she pushed it away. She wasn't going to let what had happened drag her down anymore. Things were still bright. Life – real life – was ahead.

She got off the bus and started making her way from the village down the long lane towards Sean's house. She looked at her watch: just gone 9 a.m. on a Saturday morning; he should still be at home. She swallowed, nerves rushing through her at the thought of encountering his wife. But she didn't know anything, Sam reassured herself. All Sam needed to do was ask for Sean. He could make up some tale or other to tell his wife. Goodness knows he was good at doing that.

God, she couldn't wait to take off this necklace now, she thought, her fingers touching it again. It felt more like a noose and less like jewellery with every passing second.

Finally, she and Peaches neared the house. The lights were on and Sean's car was in the drive. Sam quickened her pace now and unzipped the jacket to let in air, eager to talk to Sean, return the necklace, and go home again. She crunched across the gravel and up the few steps to ring the doorbell, praying Sean would answer. She could deal with his wife, of course, but she'd prefer if she didn't have to.

No one came, though, and so she rang again. Peaches let out a cry, and Sam jiggled the baby in her arms. God, she was getting so heavy now. *Please answer, please answer.* She wanted to get this over with.

'Can I help you?'

Sam gulped as the door swung open, revealing the woman she'd seen in the window: Sean's wife. Her dark hair was immaculately done, swept back in a low ponytail, and she was wearing a loose, draping grey jumper like Sam had seen in a shop window last week for an exorbitant price.

'Please may I speak with Sean?' She tried to match the woman's smooth tone, but her voice came out high and squeaky.

The woman tilted her head. 'Can I tell him who's here to see him?'

Sam swallowed. Maybe she should have thought this through beforehand. 'Er, well...'

The woman's eyes narrowed, and she stepped closer. 'Where did you get that?' she asked, jabbing a finger at Sam.

Sam moved back. 'Get what?' For a split second, she almost

thought the woman meant Peaches, and a panicky fear went through her. Did she know? Did she know Peaches was Sean's baby? But how?

Then she realised the woman was pointing at the necklace. Sam's fingers rose to touch it. 'Oh, this?' Her voice rose even higher. 'Um, well, someone gave it to me.' God, she wished she was one of those people who could lie easily. Her flatmates always said she was hopeless. Even now she could feel her cheeks flush and her eyes moving shiftily back and forth.

'Who?' The woman moved even closer, her face hardening. 'Who gave it to you?'

She knew. The thought darted through Sam's mind, and she clutched Peaches tightly. Somehow, she knew. 'A friend.'

'A friend.' The woman spat the words out through gritted teeth. 'I knew it. I knew he'd been seeing someone. I thought he'd stopped, though. I thought he'd stopped when I got—' Her face twisted, and she put a hand to her stomach. Sam noticed with shock that she was no longer pregnant. Had she had the baby? Sam tightened her grip on Peaches, noticing the woman looking at her with burning intensity. *Did* she know she was Sean's?

'Give me that necklace.' The woman stepped closer. 'It's mine. It's not yours to have. Give it back.'

The necklace was hers? Sean's *wife*? Anger shot through her that Sean could be low enough to take something of his wife's and give it to her – at such an important moment too; to celebrate the birth of their child, for God's sake. Sam had thought it was a symbol of their life ahead, but it had been his wife's all along, just like the life she'd envisaged with him.

Holding Peaches tightly with one hand, Sam tried to undo the clasp with the other, but it was practically impossible. She jiggled the chain, conscious of the woman watching her, fury darting out from her like flames. She shifted Peaches in her arms and fumbled again with the clasp, her heart beating fast.

All she wanted now was to get out of here and go back to the pub.

Back to the place that was really her home.

'Give me that necklace.' The woman moved closer, and Sam's fingers started trembling.

'I'm trying. I—'

Sam gasped in pain as the woman reached out and tried to yank it from her neck. The chain held, biting into her soft skin. The force of the movement tipped her off balance, and with Peaches heavy in her arms, she struggled to regain it. She staggered, one hand still on the chain, the woman's angry face swimming in front of her. And then she stepped backwards to feel air behind her, and she started to fall. She gripped her baby tightly, her one thought to cushion Peaches from the hard stones underfoot.

Then everything went black as the ground rushed up to meet her.

THIRTY-FOUR

RACHEL

Rachel opened her eyes a few days later, focusing in on her mother. She'd pretty much camped out in her mum's room after Lucas had left, as if by being so close, she could affirm that no matter what else had happened, this *was* her mother. And the more Rachel thought about it, the more she was certain that her mum couldn't have known the truth about who she really was and where she'd come from – her reactions to the news of the affair and the body in the wall proved that in itself. Rachel had no idea what story her father could have concocted, but she knew her mum had desperately longed for a child – and that she rarely questioned her husband.

'Why don't you take a break,' Victoria said, popping her head around the door. 'I'll sit with Mum for a while.' Rachel got to her feet, smiling at her sister. Victoria was here every day now, going home only at night. They'd take turns cooking meals, then sit together with their mother and try to encourage her to open her eyes and take a few bites. Despite all Rachel had learned, that sense of finally being a part of the family was increasing more every day, and in a strange way, knowing her birth mother had been here for so long too was comforting, as if she'd been watching over her daughter; as if they were all connected. The house no longer felt like a morgue they'd been trapped in. No matter the truth behind Rachel's birth, this was where she belonged. And tomorrow, when Mo and the kids were back, she'd ask them to join her here too.

'All right. Just for a second, thanks,' Rachel said, getting up and stretching. She was exhausted, but she couldn't sit still. Some fresh air would do her good, she thought, glancing out at the sun. Her gaze fell on the outbuilding where her birth mother's wedding dress was. Perhaps it was time now to get rid of it. She shook her head. No, not get rid of it – that felt wrong, as if somehow the garment was begging to be used. Maybe she could pass it on to a charity shop. After a bit of an airing, it would be in perfect condition. Such a beautiful wedding dress should be worn by someone, even if her birth mum never had a chance. It would give her a way to live on... to see the light again.

Rachel left the house and made her way across the fields to the outbuilding. She opened the door, that same musty scent meeting her nostrils, then went over to the stack of boxes in the corner and tipped down the top one. As she unfolded the drop cloth once more, questions scrolled through her mind. Her mum had been so young, working at a pub when she'd been killed. Could she work in a pub with a baby? Who had taken care of the child – of her? Had her mother been all on her own except for Rachel's father? Did she have family somewhere who could help?

Sadness curled through Rachel that she'd never know the answers; never know the woman who had given birth to her; the woman who had named her. But she was lucky, she told herself. She'd had a mother who cared and who wanted to be there, if only Rachel would have let her all these years. She was trying her best to make up for it now.

Her fingers touched smooth satin inside the box, and she drew out the wedding dress and held it up, running her eyes over the ivory fabric. It glistened in the light, and an image of her birth mother in this dress waved into her mind like a ripple on water. Her eyes were shining, her face glowing, and— Rachel squinted as the sun reflected off something on the hem. What was that? She bent closer, her eyes widening.

Wow. It was a beautiful necklace, multi-coloured jewels strung on a delicate gold chain. It must have cost an absolute fortune. How had it ended up here, caught on the delicate fabric of the dress? She tilted her head. Whoever had packed the dress must not have noticed it was there, or maybe it had been thrown in at the last minute.

Rachel carefully unpicked the chain from the material, then lifted it up, the jewels catching the sun, and for a split second, it felt like her birth mother was staring straight at her. Holding onto the chain, a wave of emotion, of connection, washed over her. As if her hands were acting on their own, she placed the necklace around her neck. The long chain looped under her jumper, and she paused as the chain hit her skin. She could feel her birth mother beside her now, reaching out to her, making sure that she was okay.

'I'm all right,' Rachel whispered, knowing her birth mum couldn't hear but feeling compelled to say the words. 'I'm sorry I couldn't be with you. I'm sorry for what happened. But I was in good hands, with someone who loved me.' She stopped, wondering what her birth mum would think about her lover's wife taking in her child. But as a mother, as long as her child was loved and cared for, wasn't that all that was important? Rachel grabbed the box with the dress, crossed the field, and eased her way back inside the house.

She closed the door quietly behind her and set the box on the table, hearing her sister in the kitchen getting another cup of tea their mum rarely drank but kept requesting. As silently as possible, she padded up the stairs and into the bedroom, sitting down on the chair in the corner. The chain of the necklace yanked on her hair, and she pulled at it to free it, watching it cast dots of light around the room as it shone in the sun, as if her birth mother was here now too. As if she wanted to see this woman who'd raised her daughter.

As if she was somehow thanking her for keeping her daughter safe.

'Where did you get that?' Her mother's eyes flew open as a dot of light hit her lids, and her gaze locked on the necklace. Rachel froze and dropped the chain. Oh, God. Did her mother recognise the necklace? Had she seen it before?

Seen it around her birth mother's neck?

Her mum's chest was rising quickly up and down. 'It's mine. Mine. Give it here.' She reached out for it, her hands slicing through air as Rachel fumbled with the clasp. Questions darted in and out of her mind. If it was her mother's, how had it ended up snagged on her birth mum's dress? How had it—

'I said, *give it!*' Her mother's fingers swiped at her neck, grabbing the chain and pulling with a strength Rachel didn't even know she still had. Rachel cried out as the chain bit into her skin, her head snapping forward with the force of the tugging. Just when she couldn't bear it any longer, the chain broke and she tumbled forward, banging her head on the windowsill. She lay there frozen, too stunned to move.

'Rachel!' Through the haze, Rachel could hear her mother's voice. 'Oh my God. Are you all right? Please be all right. Please.' She felt a hand on her back, lightly tapping her. 'This can't be happening. Not again. Not like this. Open your eyes. *Please.*'

'I'm okay.' Rachel slowly lifted her throbbing head. 'I'm all right.'

'You're okay,' her mother was murmuring. 'You're okay. Everything is fine. It's not like before. It *isn't.*' Rachel wasn't sure if she was talking to her daughter or herself, and her brow creased as she watched her mother slowly climb into bed and huddle under the covers, as if she could hide away there now.

'Mum, it's all right,' she said to her ashen-faced mother. 'I'm fine. I'll be fine, don't worry.' The words were an echo of her earlier ones to her birth mother, and somehow, they felt wrong now in her mouth. She stared down at the floor where the necklace lay, the chain broken with jewels scattered across the floor, and questions stung her mind.

Had her mother met the woman in the wall? Had she taken the necklace from her?

Had she known who Rachel's birth mother was? And if she did, then—

'What did you mean, it's not like before?' Rachel asked, cutting off the thought. She didn't want to finish it. She couldn't let it take hold; couldn't let the fear and doubt seep in again. Her mother loved her. She *did*. But with every breath Rachel took and each second that passed, those unanswered questions pricked holes in the certainty she'd held as a shield around herself. The silence seemed like forever as she waited for her mother to respond.

At last, her mum turned to meet her eyes. She held her gaze for what felt like years, everything fading away except for the two of them in this room, in this moment.

'That woman...' Her mum tried to sit up but couldn't, and she sank back against the pillows. 'She came here to speak to Sean about something. I don't know why she came. I wish she never had. And that necklace...' Her face contorted. 'She was wearing it then. She was wearing it, but it was mine.'

So she *had* known about the affair. Oh, God. Rachel had tried so hard to keep that from her, and she'd known already. Why hadn't she said anything? How much else had she been aware of? Rachel swallowed, trying to hold back that doubt and fear... trying to stay upright as the world began to tilt.

'I told her to give it back,' her mother continued. 'I was so angry; so hurt and in pain. I'd just lost a baby – a baby that was stillborn only weeks before the due date. I was home alone, and

I went into labour. He was already gone. That rose bush out front... I planted it for him. His ashes are there.'

Rachel's mind flashed back to the night Lucas's team had been searching the grounds, and her mother's anguish when they'd dug next to the rose bush. A baby boy, stillborn. That must have been awful.

'I'd been trying so hard to get pregnant, for years, and then *she* shows up with a baby in her arms – a baby that looked so much like Sean, I knew it had to be his.' Her mother stopped, staring straight at her. 'It was you,' she said, her voice raspy. 'That baby was you.'

Her mother's eyes bore through her, and Rachel sank down on the bed. Her mother had known. She'd known all along. Rachel clutched the duvet, but it didn't help steady her. She was sliding into darkness now, into the black hole about to swallow her. Because how could her mother love her when she was the child of a woman who'd had what her mother had wanted more than anything: her husband; a baby?

'His baby, and wearing my necklace...' Rachel's mother shook her head. 'I couldn't take it. I reached out to grab the necklace. I pulled hard to get it back – I didn't care if it broke.' She drew in a shaky breath. 'It jerked your mother forward, the same way it did with you, but it didn't break. And your mother... she had you in her arms, and she fell. She fell backwards off the step, and she hit her head on a rock. She didn't even try to break the fall. She was holding you so tightly. She wanted to keep you safe.'

Rachel stared, her mind flashing back to the scene a few minutes earlier. Her mother, lunging at her. Grabbing at the necklace, and the chain cutting into her skin. Falling forward, and the blow against her head. For a second, it was like the present was juxtaposed onto the past. She wrapped her arms around herself, like her birth mother had done to protect her; like she could protect herself now.

'Your father heard me scream, and he came out,' her mother continued. 'When he saw her there on the gravel, he handed you to me and knelt down beside her. I was about to go inside to call an ambulance, but he said it was too late. That she wasn't breathing any longer. She was gone.'

The room went silent. 'But...' Rachel's voice faded as she struggled to understand. 'But you weren't even here. You were in France.' How could she have killed Samantha if she'd been miles away?

'I wish I'd gone,' her mum said. 'I wish I had been in France.'

Rachel's eyebrows flew up. Her mother hadn't taken that trip? She *had* been here all along?

'Your father bought me the ticket as a surprise, a little while after I lost the baby. Looking back, I don't know now if he was trying to be kind or if he simply wanted me out of the way to be with her.' Her mum's face twisted, and she gazed down at the duvet. 'But I couldn't go. I'd buried my baby, and I couldn't face anyone, let alone my parents.' She met Rachel's eyes. 'I killed her. I killed your mother.'

Her voice was so low that it didn't seem to be coming from her, and for a second, Rachel wasn't even sure her mother had spoken. Her words had been wrenched from another place. A place of darkness and pain. And staring at the woman in front of her now, Rachel knew it *wasn't* her mother. It wasn't the woman she'd thought she'd loved and had loved her in return. How could it be? How could it be, when she'd *killed* Rachel's real mother?

'I didn't mean to,' she said, her eyes frantic. 'Please, believe me. I really didn't mean to.' She grasped the covers with her hand as if they were a life preserver, keeping her afloat in the sea of horrific memories. 'You were screaming and crying, and your father was bending over your mother with his head in his hands. And then he told me to take you inside, and said he would take care of it. He'd take care of everything, he told me. I wanted to call the police and tell them that I hadn't meant to; that it was an accident. But he said they would never believe me, that everything would come out, and it would ruin everything. It would ruin our *lives.*'

She breathed in shakily. 'And he was right. If his affair, the baby, the accident... if it all got out, then things would never be the same. My father would never let him back in the business. It was because of my dad that we were able to have this house, and the business was going to be Sean's when my father retired.' She was silent for a minute, as if gathering her thoughts.

'All that would be over if my father found out. And although I was furious about the affair and you, I couldn't lose Sean; couldn't lose our life. I was scared too. I was worried what the police would do to me. And I was grateful. Grateful that, even if he strayed, he *did* love me enough – loved our life enough – to do this. For me, and for us.' She shook her head.

'And so I took you inside. I...' She flinched. 'I went upstairs with you. I didn't know what he was doing. I didn't know he had put her in the wall in the basement. I never went down there.' She met Rachel's eyes, as if pleading with her to understand.

'After a few hours, he came upstairs. He told me he was going to get her things – he had a key, and it would be easy to get inside the pub without being noticed. He'd leave a note from her, he said, that she'd decided to leave and go back to London with her daughter. She didn't have any family, so it wouldn't be a problem. The only problem was you.'

The only problem was you. The words echoed in Rachel's mind as she stared at the stranger in front of her. She hadn't been wanted, not at all. She'd been a *problem.* She wrapped her arms even more tightly around herself, but nothing could protect her now.

'Even if we could say that your mum had abandoned you,

we could hardly explain why she'd left you here with us – that your father had an affair, and that you were his daughter. The only thing we could do was pretend that you were my child, my baby. You were only a few months old, and everyone knew I was pregnant – a difficult pregnancy, and I had barely been out. No one knew my son had died, though. We took him to High Wycombe and had him cremated, so I could keep him close. I didn't want anyone here to know; I couldn't bear the gossip and looks. Not even my own family knew.' She sighed.

'So we told everyone you were ours,' she continued. 'No one questioned us. Your father was right: your mother had no family, and everyone thought she'd taken you to London because of the note. We registered your birth, changing your age by a few weeks and saying you were a homebirth; apologising for leaving it so late. Your father called you Rachel after his grandmother, and that was that.

'I tried,' her mother said. 'I really did try to love you. I told myself that you were the baby I wanted. Your father had done all of this so we could have a life, and I needed to try my best to get on with it. To *enjoy* it.' She let out a breath. 'But I couldn't. You were more than a reminder of my husband's affair; that I hadn't given him the child he'd wanted, but another woman had. You were a reminder of what I'd done. A reminder that I killed someone.' Her voice went low again, and silence fell once more in the room. 'But I forced myself to pretend. To pretend that you were my child and that I loved you, as much for Sean as for me.'

Forced myself to pretend. Rachel stared, feeling her insides begin to blacken... blacken the place where she'd stashed away the memory of the love she'd felt.

'And then I did get pregnant, and I poured everything into that. Victoria was mine, ours. But you were still here. Still here to remind me. Here to remind *us*, and I can tell you, Sean never let me forget it. Never let me forget that he'd done this for me.

He might have done it out of love, but it became something to keep me quiet, something to stop me from talking about the other affairs he had later on. Something to give him power over me.' Her face twisted, and Rachel thought of all the times she'd believed her mother's world revolved around her husband. Maybe it had, but not because of love. It had been because of fear.

'I knew it wasn't your fault,' her mum was saying. 'I knew you thought I was your mother, and that you wanted me to love you. It broke my heart sometimes. But I couldn't give that to you. I couldn't.'

Rachel lifted her head, trying to breathe through the pain slicing into her. Even though she knew the woman in front of her wasn't her mother – even though she knew now she'd *killed* her mother, and that she'd never loved Rachel – her heart had yet to catch up. She'd loved this woman. She'd blamed herself for destroying her world and tried to do all she could to get back to her. To get back to the love she'd held at her very centre, clutching it close, even if it had been surrounded by guilt and blame.

And now... now the very core of her was false. It was false, and she was empty, the shell of the love she'd once had crumbling more and more with every breath. She had nothing except the darkness inside.

'When Sean died, I fell apart,' her mother was saying. 'I didn't know what to do. He'd been a shield between me and what had happened, and even though he'd held it over me, he'd protected me, in a sense. Without him, I had to face what had happened all over again. I had to face the fact that I could never leave here because your mother was buried somewhere on the grounds and I couldn't risk her being found. Sean may have left you the house – maybe it was his way of saying sorry for keeping so much from you – but it didn't matter. Owner or not, I was trapped here anyway. Trapped in this nightmare.'

Her voice shook, and Rachel's mind flashed back to her mother's emotional response when Rachel had given her the house – how she'd started trembling. That hadn't been because she'd wanted it, Rachel realised now. This place had never been a sanctuary for her like Rachel had believed. It had been a place of horror; of fear. She understood now why her mother hadn't signed the legal documents.

'I didn't tell you about the will because I couldn't let you have the house where I'd killed your mother – a place where your mother still lay. I couldn't hand you over the place where I'd taken away the person you loved most, even if you didn't know that.' She shifted in bed, wincing as she tried to turn over.

'And with Sean gone, all I saw when I looked at you was her. Not him any longer, but *her*. I couldn't bear it. Couldn't bear seeing her.' A tear dripped down her cheek, and she wiped it away.

Rachel held her gaze, anger mingling with the pain now as she thought of those years after her father's death when she'd blamed herself – when she'd thought her mother pulling back had been because she blamed Rachel too. It hadn't been blame, though. It hadn't been grief, either, like she'd later thought.

It had been because of *who* Rachel was.

'When all of this started – when you found her in the wall – I wanted to run away. I didn't want to face it again. It was easier to close my eyes and sleep; to try to block everything out.' Rachel raised her eyebrows in surprise. Had she known? Known Rachel discovered the body? After all her efforts to keep her mother oblivious about everything; all she'd given up? The anger grew bigger.

'And then when Lucas was searching for the child, well, how could I say that it was you? That you are the child, right here?' Her mother dropped her gaze. 'I could never do that. Never. I wanted to die. I tried to.'

She'd tried to die? Then Rachel remembered the pills – the

medication she'd blamed herself for counting out wrongly; the overdose that landed her mother in hospital. Had that been her mother's doing?

'But I'm going to die anyway, and I can't keep this in any longer. It's ruined my life, and maybe now I can have some peace.' Her mother's voice was so exhausted it was like the life was draining from her now. Rachel could see how much telling this story had cost her, but she didn't seem at peace. If anything, she looked even more tortured. 'So do what you need to. Tell the police, tell whoever you like. They can't keep me prisoner any more than I already have been.'

She turned to Rachel again. 'Now you know everything, and this house is yours. It's never been mine, and it never should be. So destroy it, sell it, make it something new. Do what you need to do to help you move forward, away from all of this. And please...' She gestured towards the necklace on the floor. 'Take it. It's the only thing I can do – the only thing I can give you. Please, *take* it.'

Rachel stared down at the broken necklace on the floor. She thought of when she'd first picked it up, stuck to the lining of her mother's wedding dress – thrown in with her belongings, as if it had been nothing. But it wasn't nothing. It was something her mother had received from the man she'd thought had loved her. But like everything else – like Rachel's entire world – it wasn't real. It was a lie, and it was because of those lies that her mother had died. Her heart twisted as she realised she'd lied to her own mother, back in that outbuilding, when she'd said she'd been loved. Like her mother, she hadn't been loved, not at all.

Her mum hadn't been able to free herself from the deception. She'd died from it. But Rachel could free herself, and she wouldn't take a lie with her.

She wanted nothing to do with any of this now.

'No,' she said, glancing over at her mother – at Janet. The name stuck in her throat and her heart lurched, but she knew that she couldn't call her Mum any longer. Real mothers loved you, like her own had. Rachel swallowed, thinking of how she'd died protecting her. She had loved her daughter, but Rachel didn't even remember her. She'd never know that love because of the woman in front of her. 'The necklace is yours. I'm sure if my mother had known it belonged to you, she never would have accepted it in the first place.'

Rachel turned and groped her way towards the door, eyes blind now and muscles numb, as if she was moving in a sea of black. Only one thought was clear in her mind: she had to get away from here. She paused for a second, thinking of all those times in the past when she'd run, believing she'd never be a part of this family. Pain jolted through her, and she shook her head. She'd been right. She would never be a part of this family. It had never been hers. She'd been as much a ghost here as her mother had been.

She left the bedroom and ran straight into her sister in the doorway. Victoria was white-faced, her eyes wide and filled with horror. She closed the door behind her and turned to Rachel. 'I heard,' she said in a halting voice, so unlike her usual efficient one. 'I heard everything. That Mum... that she killed your mother. That Dad hid her body, and they took you in. And that she tried to kill *herself*.' Victoria put a hand out to steady herself, and Rachel noticed her trembling. 'I can't believe it. I'm so sorry this happened to you. I...' Her voice trailed off, and Rachel touched her arm, sympathy and sadness mixing with the pain. This tragedy hadn't just happened to her: Victoria's world had been destroyed now too. Everything they'd both thought was real had been torn apart.

She drew her sister into her arms, and as they embraced, it struck Rachel that even though this had never been her family, Victoria *was* still her sister – half-sister anyway. They still shared the same blood, and over the past few weeks they'd become closer than ever, supporting each other like they were right now. No matter what horror existed in the past – maybe because of what horror existed in the past – they needed each other more than ever.

But Rachel couldn't stay, not any longer. She would support her sister as much as she could, trying to ease her pain like she had when they were little. But not here. Not in this place Janet said was Rachel's. She shuddered. It would never belong to her. She didn't want it. Its secrets might be uncovered, but the darkness would always linger.

'I need to go,' Rachel said simply, pulling back. 'I need to leave now.'

Victoria nodded. 'I understand. And I...' She swallowed. 'I need to stay.' She breathed in. 'I know she did terrible things, but she's my mother, and she's dying. I have to be here.'

'I know,' Rachel said gently, and she did. Despite what she'd done, Janet was still Victoria's mother. They loved each other and had a relationship Rachel had never experienced. Pain cut through her as she realised that no matter how close she and Victoria were, they would always be separated by the fact that Victoria's mother had taken away Rachel's. She loved her sister, but it would always be there. She squeezed Victoria's arm. 'I love you.'

'I love you too.' Victoria's eyes shone with tears, and the two sisters stared at each other for a second. Then Rachel turned to go pack her things.

To go back to where she really belonged.

THIRTY-FIVE

SAM

December 1986

A blinding pain shot through Sam's head. She groaned, the sound coming from what felt a million miles away. She struggled to open her eyes, feeling the cold seep into her body. Where was she? What was happening? She drew in a breath as the knowledge hit: she was at Sean's. She'd gone to return the necklace, and then... Then Sean's wife had reached out to grab the necklace, she'd fallen, and everything had gone black after that.

Peaches! Panic flashed through her. Where was her daughter? She'd had her in her arms when she'd fallen, but now she was gone. Her eyes flew open, and she gasped. Sean was looming over her.

'Sean!' She tried to sit up, but he pushed her back down.

'Don't move. Stay right there.' His face looked strange to her, and there was something in his tone she couldn't make out.

'Peaches?' She barely managed to croak the word. 'Where is she? Is she all right?' She tried to turn to see if her daughter was beside her, but Sean's heavy weight prevented her from moving.

In the silence, she could hear the faint sound of crying, and relief flooded into her. Peaches was okay. Thank goodness.

'You couldn't stay away,' Sean said, his face a mass of darkness, and Sam swallowed. What? 'You had to come here. You had to ruin everything.'

Sam shook her head, wincing at the pain. She wanted to tell him that she'd come to say that she didn't want to see him anymore; that she didn't need to see him anymore. That she and Peaches would make their own way, and that he never had to see them again. But she couldn't get the words out, and the dark shape loomed nearer. Peaches's crying grew louder, and every inch of her strained to go to her daughter.

'What did you say to my wife?' Sean was saying, as she struggled to move. 'Did you tell her about Peaches? If you told Janet everything, then you've ruined me. You've ruined everything I've tried to build. Her father will dump me from the business faster than she will.' His face twisted, and Sam's eyes widened. Sean's boss, the man he was so keen to hide her pregnancy from, was Janet's father? She drew in a breath as the pieces fell into place.

'And I can't let that happen. I won't let that happen. Not for some rubbish shag at a pub in the middle of nowhere. God, wasn't it enough that I gave you something?' He gestured towards the necklace. 'I even said I'd marry you, but you still weren't happy, were you?'

Sam listened, fear building inside as Peaches's cries got louder. She had to move. She had to get away. But even if she could get her body to respond, Sean's hands were heavy on her.

'I won't say anything,' she managed to say. 'I promise. Peaches and I will go, and—'

But Sean put a hand over her mouth. 'It's too late. Don't you see? Maybe you won't say anything, but Janet knows now. She knows, and she'll go to her father. Unless...' His face darkened again, and that same fear swept through Sam – the same instinct that told her she had to get away.

'I'm sorry,' he said in a soft voice that chilled her to the bone. 'I don't want to do this, but I have to. I wouldn't have needed to if you'd left it all alone.'

And then his hands closed around her throat, and he squeezed. She struggled against him, but his grip was too strong, and the last thing she heard before the darkness closed in was her daughter crying.

I love you, she thought, frantically telegraphing the words towards Peaches. *I love you so much. Please know that. Please never forget.*

Please never let anyone take that away.

THIRTY-SIX

RACHEL

'Mum! Tilly kicked me!'

Rachel sighed and got to her feet, trying to rouse the energy to referee yet another skirmish between the kids. They'd been playing up ever since she got home a week ago, as if they were trying to cram everything she'd missed into a few short days. Rachel didn't mind, though. Since returning, she'd thrown herself back into her world, telling herself *this* was her family and where she belonged, desperate to shake off the darkness that had followed her here. The darkness that beat a deathly drum roll of terrible truths into her head with every breath.

You did everything for Janet's love, but she never loved you. She wasn't even your mother. She killed *your mother – the one person who did love you. You'll never feel that love now.* And whispering underneath it all was the insidious voice that even if she did know how her real mother had died and how Rachel had ended up with Janet, she still knew nothing about herself. Her name, her birthday, who she was to the person who loved her most. Her mother had been found, but Rachel was still a ghost, trying to navigate her way in a world where everything felt real but her.

Rachel would attempt to shove aside those thoughts and force herself to concentrate on work or whatever YouTube video Tabitha was showing her. She made an extra effort with Mo, too, cooking his favourite meals and even organising a night out for them both to show how much she wanted to be with him. He'd been delighted that she'd come home, thinking she was going to let him be there for her; going to let him help. And she'd tried to lean on his strength, telling him everything. He'd been horrified, the truth sweeping away any remaining distance as he held her close. She'd put her head on his shoulder, trying to drink in the love between them, trying to let it fill her up. But no matter how tightly she held him, and no matter how hard she hugged the kids, she still couldn't find anything to banish the terrible emptiness inside.

Rachel was about to tell Tilly and Ryan to knock it off when her mobile rang.

Her eyebrows rose in surprise when she spotted the name: Lucas. She hadn't spoken to him since he'd told her the case was closed. Why would he call her now?

'Hi, Lucas,' she said, cradling the phone in her neck and shoulder while trying to close the bedroom door, away from the noise of her battling children. 'How are you?'

'I'm all right. How are you doing?'

She hesitated, wondering how to answer that. Should she tell him she was going crazy? That no matter what she did, nothing made her feel better? That she was starting to wonder if anything ever would?

'Look, I wanted to let you know that we finished the autopsy, and we can now release your mother's body,' Lucas said before she could respond. 'Your birth mother,' he added hastily. 'Sorry, I still can't believe it's your mother we found. In case you wanted to plan a burial or something?'

'Oh. Right.' That feeling of being lost in the dark intensified, and she drew in a breath. She was burying her mother, but she'd never have a chance to know her; to feel her love. She'd never know who *she* really was. 'What did the autopsy say?' She knew what it said, of course: that her mother had died from a blow to the head. She wanted to hear him say it, though, as if speaking the words aloud could somehow help put all this behind her and close the door on the pain inside.

'The report shows your mother died as a result of compression to the neck,' Lucas said. 'One of the bones in her neck was fractured, which indicates strangulation.'

What? Rachel drew back. Strangulation? 'It wasn't because of her head?' she asked, confusion swirling inside.

'No.' Lucas's tone was puzzled. 'There was nothing that showed anyway.'

'Okay.' The word left her mouth automatically as her brain spun. Janet hadn't said anything about touching her mother's neck – only that her mum had fallen after pulling at the necklace. And surely... surely a delicate chain wouldn't be enough to damage the bones. It wouldn't have suffocated her either.

So, how?

Rachel swallowed as she remembered Janet saying that Sean had come out and taken care of it; that she'd seen him bending over her mother. She jerked as a thought jolted through her. What if her mother hadn't been dead from hitting the ground, after all? What if she'd been unconscious, and then she'd come round when Sean was there?

And what if, like Janet had said, he'd been so worried that either Janet or her mother would say something that he'd thought of a way to keep them both quiet? By killing Rachel's mother, and then letting Janet believe she'd caused the death and he'd helped cover it up? That was a great way to gain power over her, like Janet had said.

Rachel let out a breath. She'd never know for sure that was what happened. But it made sense given what she'd learned from Lucas, and it felt right, as if her mother was beside her now, nodding her approval. And for a split second, she felt like that truth had let a crack of light into the darkness inside her.

She shook her head, thinking of the woman she'd believed to be her mother. Janet had suffered in the shadow of the knowledge that she'd killed someone. She'd believed her husband had helped her, and she'd done everything in her power to repay him – out of a misplaced fear, maybe; out of a misplaced love. Because he hadn't loved her, like he hadn't loved Rachel's mother. They'd both been objects he'd used for his own gratification, whether it was sex or wealth. Janet wasn't blameless, not by a long way, but she was a victim too. She was someone who, like Rachel, had lived with a lie all of these years.

A lie that had blighted her life.

Rachel said goodbye to Lucas and hung up the phone, staring out the window as her brain spun. Finding out Janet had killed her mother had plunged her even further into pain – plunged them *both* into pain, because she'd seen how tortured Janet had been after facing the truth.

But that wasn't the truth at all.

Now Rachel knew what had really happened. She wasn't sure she could ever forgive Janet, but clearing away the debris of the past – telling Janet everything – felt right, as if somehow, with every bit that was unburied, she was bringing light not only to her, but also to the memory of her mother.

'Okay, Mum,' she whispered. 'I'll go. One last time. One last time to say the truth, and then you can rest.'

And maybe, just maybe, she could too.

THIRTY-SEVEN

RACHEL

One hour later, Rachel pulled into the lane that led to the house. Memories flashed through her head of when she'd first come here almost a month ago with one thing on her mind: to get through to her mother and have that relationship she'd always longed for. She shook her head as she neared the building, breathing in to stop the pain overwhelming her. She'd found her mother – her real mother – in a way she never could have dreamed, and she'd never have that relationship.

She parked next to Victoria's Mini and got out, crossing the gravelled drive. She stopped for a moment on the step, picturing her mother falling backwards; picturing her father squeezing the life from her, and anger swirled inside for all the lives that had been ruined. She forced herself forward, then opened the door. The familiar scent of the place washed over her, and she tried to hold back the tidal wave of loneliness and longing that accompanied it. That loneliness and longing wasn't for the woman inside, she reminded herself. It was for a woman she would never know. The grief was like a sharp poker in her heart.

'Hi!' Victoria was coming down the stairs. 'What are you

doing here? I mean, it's good to see you, of course. But I wasn't really expecting you to come back again.'

'I wasn't expecting to be here,' Rachel said. 'But I need to talk to Janet.' She paused, thinking again how strange it felt to say that name. 'How is she?' Rachel had messaged her sister a few times since she'd left, and while Victoria had always responded, she'd kept news of Janet to herself... likely unsure if Rachel wanted to know. She sighed now, thinking of that distance between them.

'The nurse says she has only a few days left, if that.' Victoria rubbed her eyes, and Rachel thought how she'd never seen her sister so *real*. Without her usual immaculate make-up and hair, she looked much more vulnerable; softer, and Rachel put an arm around her. 'She's sleeping pretty much all the time – the nurse is keeping her on a high dosage of morphine – but she opens her eyes sometimes for a minute or two.' She bit her lip. 'You're... you're not going to upset her, are you? Sometimes, she can get very agitated, even though I'm not really sure if she's awake or not.'

'No,' Rachel said, staring at her sister with sympathy. 'I'm not going to upset her. I'm hoping what I say might bring her a bit of peace.' Anger twisted through her again at the thought that her own mother's death had been anything but peaceful, but that hadn't been Janet's fault. She'd kept many secrets, but she hadn't taken Rachel's mother from her. Rachel put a hand on Victoria's arm. 'And it might help you too.' She winced, remembering Victoria's devastated expression that day in the corridor. Learning her mother hadn't killed Rachel's mum would hopefully help ease some of that pain. Maybe it would help bring the sisters together once more too.

Victoria raised her eyebrows. 'What is it?'

'I'll tell you later, okay?'

'Okay.' Victoria nodded. 'Do you want to go up or have a cup of tea first?'

'I'll go up now.' Rachel didn't want to wait. She squeezed Victoria's hand. 'I'll be back down soon.'

She climbed the stairs to Janet's bedroom, then went inside. She caught her breath at the sight of Janet on the bed: her skin stretched over sharp cheekbones, her eyes sunken in like two dark cavities. For an instant, Janet's face replaced the body in the wall, and Rachel shuddered. They were two very different women, but they'd both suffered at the hands of the same man. Maybe it was too late for one, but she could do something for the other.

Rachel sat down on the bed. 'I've come to tell you something, and then I'll go.' She stopped for a second, even though she knew there'd be no answer. 'You didn't kill my mother,' she said softly. 'It was Dad. She died of strangulation, not because of falling and hitting her head. He must have killed her when you were upstairs.' She still couldn't believe he'd done that – not just to her mother, but also to his wife, to his *family*. 'I wanted you to know. I wanted you to be free of that before... before you go.'

She swallowed, listening to the ticking of the clock. It was a reminder that Janet's life was leaving her with every second – that soon, she would be gone. Had Janet even heard her, or was it too late? Rachel sighed. At least she'd tried. At least, if nothing else, the truth was out at last, floating in the air around them. Maybe that was enough. Maybe that would have to be enough.

But as Rachel got to her feet, Janet's eyes opened. She gazed up at Rachel, and her features softened as if she'd shed years in an instant; as if she'd shrugged off a weight. She didn't say a word, but Rachel knew she'd heard. She'd breathed it in, and it had changed her. No longer would anyone else hold her captive. Now, she only had herself to make peace with.

As Rachel stared at the woman before her, she felt something shift inside of her too, as if her mother was beside her also, gazing on with love and approval... the love Rachel had longed to feel. She sensed the presence so strongly that she almost turned to see if her mother *was* here, and even though she knew it wasn't possible, it felt tangible. All three of them had been bound together in a terrible tragedy, starting from the day her mother had been killed, each of their lives buried under an avalanche of secrets and betrayal. Evil had dragged them all down, the darkness snuffing out life and light alike.

But now the very last piece of rubble had been cleared away, letting the light burst through. And as Rachel sat here, the warmth from her mother streaming into her, she realised that the light – the love – had never stopped shining. She'd thought the love she'd treasured inside had never been real, but it was. It was, and it had been there all along. It was there when her mother had cradled her in her arms, protecting her from pain when she'd fallen, and it had lived on inside of her, every day she was alive. It might have been buried in darkness, but it hadn't gone out, patiently waiting for Rachel to find her way back to it, the same way the woman in the wall had been waiting there all of these years to be uncovered.

And finally, *finally*, she had.

Rachel might never know her own name. She might never know her birthday, or what her mother's voice sounded like. But this... this was everything. This was enough to make her feel whole. Make her feel *real*.

She whispered goodbye to the woman in the bed, then turned and left the room.

THIRTY-EIGHT

RACHEL

Rachel stared at the ground as her mother's coffin was lowered into the grave. The wind whipped her hair across her face like a veil, and she blinked to clear the tears from her eyes. Her mother was at peace. She had a proper resting place where she could be remembered by everyone who had loved her. She wasn't missing. She wasn't lost any longer. Her daughter wasn't either. Rachel was here, and at last she was able to use every single piece of herself to embrace those she loved.

She turned to look at Will, so happy she'd been able to track him down through Lucas. Thanks to him, she was learning more about her mother. And the more she learned, the stronger her mother's presence felt – the stronger this fragile new wholeness was becoming. She loved his stories about life in the pub; about her mum's determination to make the best life she could. Through his stories, she could feel her mother's love even more.

Rachel sighed, thinking of the woman she'd believed was her mother. She was gone now – she'd died a few days after Rachel had told her the truth. She'd never regained consciousness after Rachel's visit that day. Rachel hoped that she had found peace, and that after all of this time, she really was free.

Rachel had sat down with her sister and told her the truth, too, and the two of them had gripped hands. Nothing was between them now. Their mothers were both gone; both lives ruined by their father. But even though they were united in such terrible tragedy, Rachel was determined not to let the darkness drag them down again. Their father had done enough damage.

Victoria put a hand on her back, and Rachel touched her arm in thanks. She hadn't been sure whether Victoria would come today, and she'd said she didn't have to. But Victoria was adamant that she wanted to be there for her sister, and even though she'd just buried her own mother, here she was.

The vicar began a closing prayer and the small group bowed their heads, but a figure in the distance moving slowly towards them caught Rachel's eye. She squinted. Who was that?

Will moved towards the person Rachel could now see was an older woman, her face lined and her hair white. She watched as Will put his arms around the woman and held her close, then took her arm and supported her as they made their way towards Rachel. As they drew level with her, Rachel met the older woman's eyes. A tear streaked down the woman's cheek, and even though Rachel had never met this woman before, as they held each other's gaze, she could feel a connection between them, like they somehow knew each other.

'This is Jean,' Will said. 'She owned the pub your mother worked in. She was there the day you were born.'

Rachel's mouth dropped open. She'd been there the day she was born?

Will shook his finger at the older woman. 'If you knew the trouble I've taken to try to find you! Thank God my old-school network of pub contacts pulled through. I'm glad you could make it,' he said, his face going serious again. 'Sam would have wanted you here.'

'I'm glad I could make it too,' Jean said, giving him a hug before turning to Rachel. She touched Rachel's cheek. 'You're so like her, so like Sam. Looking at you is like turning back time. I wish I could.' She shook her head. 'I'm sorry I didn't reach out sooner. I had no idea what was happening. The world could end, and I'd only hear about it days later. Thank goodness the local pub owner knew me from visiting his mum in my care home.'

'How did you end up there anyway?' Will asked. 'If I'd have known what happened, I'd at least have come visit.'

'When I went into hospital, I had an emergency operation on my brain. It affected everything. It took months to recover, and they shunted me to some home in the middle of nowhere. I didn't even know that Sam had left until much later – didn't know she'd left a note. I couldn't feed myself, let alone worrying about the pub. I always wondered where she and her daughter had gone, but I never...' Her face contorted. 'Never in a million years would I have imagined this could have happened to her. To *you*.' She reached out to Rachel again. 'I've thought of you every day on your birthday. The fifteenth of September. I'll never forget.'

Rachel nodded, the date wending its way into her heart. *The fifteenth of September*. That was when she was born. That was her real birthday – a concrete date linking her with her mum, a date that solidified who she really was.

'You were a beautiful baby, and your mother was absolutely smitten. She called you Peaches because your cheeks looked like ripe fruit.' Jean smiled, and tears filled Rachel's eyes. 'She was waiting to give you a proper name until she and your father married. Then she was going to register your birth. I urged her to do it sooner, but she insisted on waiting.' Jean sighed. 'When she found out he was already married, she was devastated. She wanted a life for you – with a family. She'd never had a family herself, and she'd always dreamed of it. But then she realised that she was enough. She could give all the love you needed –

the life you needed, with people who did care – and that was enough for her too. She loved you so much.'

Jean folded Rachel into her arms, and Rachel leaned into her embrace. It was as if her mother was reaching out from the past, like her love was pouring through this woman who'd known her so well, who'd given Rachel what she'd needed to strengthen the sense of her mum around her. To strengthen *her,* like a piece of clay exposed to the sun.

'Thank you for coming,' Rachel said, when they drew apart. 'I'm so glad you found us.'

Jean smiled. 'Somehow, I feel like she found us.'

Rachel squeezed Jean's arm, thinking that was exactly right. Rachel may have uncovered her mother's body, but her mum had been the one to show her the way: the way back to love; back to life.

She smiled at Mo, then gazed over to the field by the side of the cemetery, where her three kids were racing in circles across the grass. Their laughter floated in the summer air, and for a split second, she could see her mother smiling back at her.

'Let's go,' she said, turning from the grave. She wasn't leaving her mum here in the ground. Her mother would always be inside her, a part of who she was – the missing part that she had finally found. 'Let's go home.'

And even though they hadn't moved, she already felt like she was there.

A LETTER FROM LEAH

Dear reader,

I want to say a huge thank you for choosing to read *A Secret in the Family*. If you did enjoy it, and you want to keep up to date with all my latest releases, just sign up at the following link. Your email address will never be shared and you can unsubscribe at any time.

www.bookouture.com/leah-mercer

I hope you loved *A Secret in the Family*. If you did, I would be very grateful if you could write a review. I'd love to hear what you think. It makes such a difference helping new readers to discover one of my books for the first time.

I really enjoy hearing from my readers – you can get in touch on my Facebook page, through Twitter, Goodreads or my website.

Thanks,

Leah

www.leahmercer.com

facebook.com/AuthorLeahMercer
twitter.com/leahmercerbooks

ACKNOWLEDGEMENTS

A massive thanks to everyone who has read and continues to read my books over the past ten years. Writing really is my dream job, and I feel so fortunate to be able to share my words. A big thank you to Mel Sherratt, who's been by my side since the beginning, as well as Madeleine Milburn and Hannah Todd for making it all happen behind the scenes. Thanks, too, to Laura Deacon and the formidable Bookouture team for their valuable input and hard work to get my books out there! And finally, thank you to my husband for his support, and to my son, who is never at a loss for great ideas when I need help.

CPSIA information can be obtained
at www.ICGtesting.com
Printed in the USA
LVHW021800310822
727260LV00003B/575

9 781803 147130